T0300603

ALSO BY HELENA GREER

Season of Love
For Never & Always

Praise for Helena Greer

FOR NEVER & ALWAYS

"A moving lifelong love story complete with a satisfying dose of personal growth for both protagonists...Readers, like the charming supporting characters surrounding Hannah and Levi, will be rooting for this well-matched pair."

—*Publishers Weekly*, Starred Review

"A wonderful example of what readers love about second-chance romances: a couple that is now ready for happily ever after in a way that they weren't before."   —*BookPage*

"Once again, Greer has written a gem of a book. FOR NEVER & ALWAYS is equal parts romantic and heart-breaking, perfectly capturing the experience of growing up and growing together, and of true love finally finding a right place and a right time. Could not be happier to be back at Carrigan's."

—Rachael Lippincott, *New York Times* bestselling co-author of *She Gets the Girl* and *Five Feet Apart*

"FOR NEVER & ALWAYS is a story about a love that doesn't let go, doesn't ask questions, and doesn't listen. Which means Helena Greer does a masterful job, penning characters you believe will do all three as they fight for themselves and the happy ending to their story they deserve."

—Stacey Agdern, author of *B'Nai Mitzvah Mistake*

"An absolute dream of a second-chance romance! The pining and the tension leap off the page and will grab you right in the feels. Helena Greer has crafted a gorgeous sophomore novel with the most relatable characters and the most charming setting. Once I started reading, I couldn't put it down!"

—Falon Ballard, author of *Right on Cue*

"Take the history and angst of both a marriage-in-trouble and second-chance romance, wrap it in the warmth and complications of found family, and you'll have just a little taste of Hannah and Levi Blue's epic love story...It always feels like a special privilege to read a book like this one that clearly lives so deeply in its author's heart. Visiting Carrigan's feels like getting wrapped in a huge, queer, Jewish hug, and I cannot wait to return."

—Anita Kelly, author of *How You Get the Girl*

"Helena Greer's second book packs a major emotional punch. It's got a lovestruck, pining hero and a heroine who takes no crap but still can't help falling hard. The book is delightfully queer and with small-town charm—and complications—aplenty, there's a lot to sink your teeth into. Every page is a revelation of emotions and readers will find themselves completely lost in Hannah and Levi's swoony love story."

—Jodie Slaughter, author of *Play to Win*

"FOR NEVER & ALWAYS captures the vibrancy of a 1940s black-and-white screwball film and displays it in bright, dazzling, inclusive color. Hannah and Levi's love story is a jubilant reunion romance that deftly balances heartfelt angst and aching sweetness. A second trip to the enclave of Carrigan's was just what my queer heart wanted!"

—Timothy Janovsky, author of
You Had Me at Happy Hour

"This book made me so happy. It was an absolute fire hose of angst and drama, but in the sparkliest way—I love that our prickly asshole chef Levi is also pining so openly, and our clinically anxious hotel manager Hannah is a font of strength when the chips are down. I love how complicated and messy people are in this book: they make mistakes and they misinterpret and it's all part of the roller coaster. I love the food and the side characters and the emotionally resonant haircut. Can we get a Carrigan's book for every major holiday?"

—Olivia Waite, author of *The Hellion's Waltz*

SEASON OF LOVE

"[This] love story is by turns heartbreaking and delightful."

—*Library School Journal*

"There's plenty of fun to be had...like frothy eggnog amid the holiday bustle."

—*Publishers Weekly*

"A warm, queer romance with holiday cheer and emotional depth."

—*Kirkus*

"SEASON OF LOVE is holiday romance perfection. Warm and cozy, emotional and swoony, Greer has expertly crafted a delightful queer, Jewish holiday story that will easily steal your heart and leave you longing for a weekend away at Carrigan's."

—Rachael Lippincott, *New York Times* bestselling co-author of *She Gets the Girl* and *Five Feet Apart*

"If you are like me and completely obsessed with Hallmark and holiday movies, then you don't want to miss Helena Greer's debut novel, SEASON OF LOVE. This book hits on all your favorite Hallmark tropes as it weaves a beautiful journey from hate to love for Miriam and Noelle. A cozy, queer, heartfelt holiday romance that will have you grabbing a blanket, a cup of hot chocolate, and snuggling down to read this charming book."

—Rachel Van Dyken, #1 *New York Times* bestselling author of *The Godparent Trap*

"A heartwarming and inspiring story about letting go of the past to find your joy and being open to love."

—Abby Jimenez, *New York Times* bestselling author of *Part of Your World*

"If you need the cozy feel of a Hallmark holiday movie in book form, visit Carrigan's! SEASON OF LOVE has all of the warm, queer, Jewish holiday vibes you could possibly want. It's a cup of cocoa with the perfect amount of marshmallows, it's a sweet kiss under the mistletoe. Helena Greer creates characters and settings that I never want to leave behind."

—Jen DeLuca, *USA Today* bestselling author of *Well Matched*

"SEASON OF LOVE is a warm and witty romance with characters that leap straight off the page...Greer's writing is vibrant and she handles grief and complicated family dynamics with tenderness..."

—Alexandria Bellefleur, bestselling author of
Count Your Lucky Stars

"SEASON OF LOVE uses the magic of the holidays to do what romance novels do best: convince its main characters (and its readers) that the healing power of love is something every single person deserves. This heartwarming debut has everything you want in a holiday romance—and I can't wait to recommend it to my friends."

—Therese Beharrie, author of *And They Lived Happily Ever After*

"A warm, cozy holiday romance, SEASON OF LOVE is a vibrant exploration of embracing that which is most unexpected in life...and in love. Best read under the glow of rainbow twinkle lights and a cup of cocoa."

—Ashley Herring Blake, author of *Delilah Green Doesn't Care*

"Stepping into this book is like stepping into an eccentric winter wonderland—exactly the kind of holiday escapism I crave. Come to Carrigan's for the loveable cast of kooky characters, but stay for the meaningful reflections on grief, family relationships, and identity. At turns a holiday confection and a deep character study, SEASON OF LOVE filled my heart. I can't wait to visit Carrigan's again and again!"

—Alison Cochrun, author of *The Charm Offensive*

"Greer has crafted an idyllic setting I want to whisk away to for Christmas (but then stay all year) and a charming cast of characters I want to befriend. Readers are going to lament that Carrigan's isn't a real destination they can jet off to."

—Sarah Hogle, author of *Just Like Magic*

"Satire and romantic holiday magic in equal measure, SEASON OF LOVE is a sly, bighearted book that will have you laughing even as it makes your heart grow three sizes."

—Jenny Holiday, *USA Today* bestselling author of *Duke, Actually*

"One of the most unique and uniquely queer things I've ever read, SEASON OF LOVE is more a place than a book: Carrigan's Christmasland's heart beats just as strongly in these pages as all of its loving, messy, large cast of characters, all of whom are looking for home in their own ways, even if they're already there. By the last page, readers will feel as if they're part of this special family, too."

—Anita Kelly, author of *Love & Other Disasters*

"Greer's debut simply sparkles. It's so easy to get lost in the magic of Carrigan's with Miriam and Noelle, and a stellar secondary cast that includes a fat cat named Kringle. This delightful Christmas Chanukah mash-up will have you braiding challah by a Christmas tree."

—Roselle Lim, author of *Sophie Go's Lonely Hearts Club*

HELENA GREER

FOREVER

New York   Boston

This book is a work of fiction. Names, characters, places, and incidents are the product of the author's imagination or are used fictitiously. Any resemblance to actual events, locales, or persons, living or dead, is coincidental.

Copyright © 2024 by Helena Greer

Cover illustration and design by Leni Kauffman. Cover copyright © 2024 by Hachette Book Group, Inc.

Hachette Book Group supports the right to free expression and the value of copyright. The purpose of copyright is to encourage writers and artists to produce the creative works that enrich our culture.

The scanning, uploading, and distribution of this book without permission is a theft of the author's intellectual property. If you would like permission to use material from the book (other than for review purposes), please contact permissions@hbgusa .com. Thank you for your support of the author's rights.

Forever
Hachette Book Group
1290 Avenue of the Americas, New York, NY 10104
read-forever.com
@readforeverpub

First Edition: August 2024

Forever is an imprint of Grand Central Publishing. The Forever name and logo are registered trademarks of Hachette Book Group, Inc.

The publisher is not responsible for websites (or their content) that are not owned by the publisher.

Forever books may be purchased in bulk for business, educational, or promotional use. For information, please contact your local bookseller or the Hachette Book Group Special Markets Department at special.markets@hbgusa.com.

Library of Congress Cataloging-in-Publication Data

Names: Greer, Helena, author.
Title: Hers for the weekend / Helena Greer.
Description: First edition. | New York ; Boston : Forever, 2024.
Identifiers: LCCN 2024003235 | ISBN 9781538768686 (trade paperback) |
    ISBN 9781538768693 (ebook)
Subjects: LCGFT: Romance fiction. | Novels.
Classification: LCC PS3607.R4726 H47 2024 | DDC 813/.6—dc23/eng/20240125
LC record available at https://lccn.loc.gov/2024003235

ISBNs: 9781538768686 (trade paperback), 9781538768693 (ebook)

Printed in the United States of America

LSC-C

Printing 1, 2024

This one is for my mom, a badass blond lawyer who never walks away from the fight for justice.

Content Guidance

This book contains descriptions of off-page emotional abuse by parents, past trauma, on-page familial homophobia, and a building fire. Please take care of yourself if any of these topics are painful.

THE BAD IDEA

December 3-19

Chapter 1

Tara

The day Tara Chadwick received wedding invitations from three different ex-girlfriends, she had her first ever twinge of regret at being a lesbian.

The first invitation, for a destination wedding in Cabo from her college girlfriend, she turned down with real regret because she was set to be at trial. She made a note to send them some Le Creuset and mourned the opportunity for a beach vacation. The second, for a lavish affair at an old plantation from the second-to-last girl she'd dated, she shredded without responding. Getting married at a plantation automatically disqualified them from either gifts or attendance.

The third had a New York postmark and a return address for Carrigan's Christmasland. She would have scowled at it, except that her mother had invited her to a Botox party last week, and as a newly minted partner in her law firm who couldn't afford to make waves, she was expected to attend

certain events. And because the wife of an influential judge
had been there, she hadn't been able to decline. So, forehead
frozen, Tara just thought hard about scowling, threw the card
on the table, and called Hannah Rosenstein.

"You're coming," Hannah said instead of hello when she
answered. "It's not optional."

The invitation wasn't for Hannah's wedding (which Tara
had missed because it was a surprise, something she was still
annoyed about); it was for Miriam's.

Miriam Blum, Hannah's cousin and Tara's ex-fiancée.

The problem was, Tara was still friends with Miriam—
they'd been more friends than lovers to begin with—and she
was even closer with Hannah. She wanted to go to Miriam's
wedding.

Or maybe she wanted to want to go.

She wasn't angry about their breakup, and she'd long since
gotten over being hurt, but she couldn't seem to get over feeling embarrassed. Miriam had disappeared to the Adirondacks,
fallen for a tree farmer, and not bothered to break up with
Tara until she had shown up in person. She was doing a pretty
good job of not dwelling on what a fool she felt like, but revis-
iting the scene of the crime was sure to bring up more feelings
than she wanted to have.

She didn't say, "I don't want to be there as the loser single
ex everyone feels they have to include as an amends." Instead,
she said, "It's only three weeks from now. You can't ask me to
upend all my Christmas plans."

Hannah made a scoffing noise. "You've known they were
engaged since August. You probably blocked out the date in
your calendar as soon as you got the text."

She had, even though she hadn't been sure she would get an invite.

She'd been prepared to go, had in fact already told her family that she wouldn't be available for Christmas dinner. But now that the date was looming nearer, attending felt impossible. She would almost rather spend the holiday with her awful family than be a not-quite-insider observer to the Carrigan's circus.

Carrigan's Christmasland was a Jewish-owned, Christmas-themed tourist extravaganza opened by Miriam's eccentric great-aunt in the 1960s. Both Carrigan's the place and the Carrigans' found family were a nonstop roller coaster of A Lot. It made Tara, who had been raised in a menacing Southern gentility, very stressed out.

Tara sighed into the phone. She had to come up with an excuse Hannah would never agree to. "I will come on one condition."

She texted Hannah a link to the re-creation vintage wallpaper she'd found. It looked exactly like the hideous parrot wallpaper in the Christmasland Inn at Carrigan's, and it cost a fortune.

"I'm not setting foot in that inn again while that moldy, disgusting wallpaper is still up. Let me pay to replace it, and I'll come." This was perfect. Hannah was weirdly attached to the mold and would never, ever let her spend that much money (although why come from absurd amounts of ill-gotten wealth if you couldn't spend it on your friends?). Besides, how could they change all the wallpaper in three weeks, as this was their busiest time of year?

"You know we can't accept that kind of gift from you—"

Hannah started. There was a shuffling noise, and then Hannah's husband, Levi, came on the phone.

"We absolutely *can* accept it. The wallpaper is a hazard, and it's a miracle we haven't gotten a health code violation yet. If Hannah would let us replace it with something attractive, instead of forcing us to find a reproduction of the original wallpaper, the cost would be reasonable."

He paused, and she could hear him add, in a muffled voice, "Besides, babe, you have to think about—"

Hannah shushed him, and Tara's spidey sense lit up.

She squeaked in glee. "Hannah Naomi Rosenstein! You're pregnant!"

Hannah shushed them, even louder. "I haven't told my in-laws yet and I do *not* want them to find out by overhearing us."

"Levi, tell that stubborn wife of yours to count the cost against Cole's grocery bill," Tara said. "I'm buying you the wallpaper whether I come or not. It's a baby present."

Cole Fraser was Tara and Miriam's best friend—he'd been the one to introduce them, back when Tara was in law school and Miriam was hiding out from her shitty family. Through Miriam and Tara's relationship, Cole had been the glue that held them all together. Currently, they were sharing custody of him, bouncing him between their houses, because he'd been disowned by *his* shitty family. He'd been at Carrigan's for the past few months, moping and eating and pining for Sawyer, the hot bartender at the nearby dive bar. At 6'5", he could put away a breakfast spread. While the inn was doing well, an unexpected guest who wasn't paying or doing any work must be straining their budget.

"SOLD!" Levi declared. "I'll get my dad to install it."

Damn. Tara had forgotten that Mr. Matthews, Levi's dad and the inn's handyman, probably *could* change an entire hotel's wallpaper in three weeks.

Hannah's voice came back. "Should I put you down for one, then? You can call me about your meal choice later?"

"There are no meal choices," Levi argued from somewhere farther away. "I'm not a short-order cook. There's one meal. It's vegetarian. People can eat it."

"Maybe Tara has a gluten intolerance, honey."

Levi was a famous TV chef, but he was also often an actual short-order cook because he covered shifts at the Christmasland Inn, where he oversaw the culinary part of their events business. Tara wasn't paying attention to their argument, though. It was better to tune out Levi and Hannah when they argued, which was most of the time. They treated it as foreplay.

Instead, her brain was stuck on the idea of RSVPing for one.

A movie played out in her mind, of her showing up at Carrigan's with all its melodramatic gauche festive cheer, trying to keep her cool while surrounded by live reindeer and sticky gingerbread frosting and the world's creepiest animatronic cherubs. It was a nightmare scenario at best, but to also have to watch Miriam and her fiancée Noelle *and* Hannah and Levi *and* Cole and the hot bartender be adorably in love, while she sat at the singles table?

She would be alone with the parrot-covered walls closing in on her, raining tinsel in her hair. Her friends would pity her and feel obligated to worry about her and maybe even, God forbid, try to matchmake. Pretty much every person whose opinion actually mattered to her was going to that wedding, and she refused to be a bother, a burden, or pathetic.

She might have to go to her ex-fiancée's wedding, but no way in hell was she going solo.

"No," she interrupted, "I don't have a gluten allergy. I am allergic to avocados, but I eat them anyway. Life's short. I'm also not coming alone."

"You're not what?" Hannah asked, obviously giving Tara her full attention again, as Levi's voice faded in the background.

"I'm bringing someone." Tara managed to sound certain, a by-product of her time in front of juries.

"And who might that be?"

"My . . . girlfriend," Tara replied brusquely. "Who I'm not ready to talk about yet." Because she didn't exist.

"You're Carrigan's crew, Tara. Everything's our business," Hannah argued.

She was warmed by this statement against her better judgment. She should not want to be adopted into their little island of misfit toys, since Carrigan's was the Hotel California of Upstate New York, but it was nice to be wanted. "I am certainly not Carrigan's crew!"

"I'll ask Cole," Hannah said. "Love you, byeeeee!"

She hung up.

Shit. Cole.

Tara would definitely have to call Cole as soon as she fortified herself. First she needed a cup of coffee and a slice of cake. Besides, what the hell was she going to tell him? She'd never been able to lie to him.

She decided to walk down to Emma's. The cafe wasn't

clean and minimalist or overpriced in the way her social set preferred; it just had good coffee and great pastries and wait-staff who knew her by name. It was comfortable and faded, unfashionable in the best way.

She and Miriam had come here together a thousand times over the course of their relationship, hashing things out over cups of coffee, and the last time they'd seen each other, it was where they'd put their relationship to rest. Those memories hadn't ruined the cafe. Instead, they'd seasoned it, like a good cast-iron skillet.

Tara needed that right now—and she was a little bit (or a lot?) hoping to see Holly. Truly, having a raging, unrequited crush on your regular waitress was almost as pathetic as going to your ex's wedding alone, but it couldn't be helped. Today was Holly's day off (and why did Tara even have her schedule memorized?) but sometimes she was there, anyway, baking.

Emma's was decorated for Christmas with a pink plastic tree hung with silver garland and would have delighted Miriam. The cook shouted at her through the passthrough to sit wherever she wanted, and the cashier waved at her like an old friend.

Did she spend too much time in this cafe? It was more comfortable than her pristine, carefully curated Single House. Her house had been called cold and silent, but until recently, she'd always thought of it as calm. Everything was beautiful, and nothing was loud.

Only lately had it seemed…like a set piece she'd built for a one-woman show. Like she was method acting her personality.

Which she was, kind of, because her real personality wasn't good for anyone.

Chapter 2

Holly

Shirley Manson was screaming in Holly Delaney's earbuds, the lattice crust on her apple pie had turned out impeccably, and she was getting overtime for coming in on her day off to deal with pastry. She bopped on the balls of her feet as she tightened the handkerchief knotted on top of her head, then pulled the pie out of the oven and bumped the door closed with her hip.

Garbage was right in the middle of beseeching the listener to pour their misery down when they were rudely interrupted by a text notification. She ignored the noise, focusing on trying to get a tray of croissants into the oven before the lunch rush. Her phone immediately started buzzing again. It was probably a scam bot texting about her car's extended warranty, as if her beater had seen a warranty in...ever.

Just in case, she slid the oven door shut, brushed the flour off her hands, and fished it out.

Through the spiderweb cracks of her screen, her brother's name flashed, and Holly groaned.

> **Dustin:** Mom needs to talk to you.

> **Holly:** Has she lost the ability to text? Are you the Mom whisperer now?

> **Dustin:** She says you never take her calls.

> **Holly:** Correct. She only calls when I'm in the middle of work and cannot answer. But she can, and should, text! I know she knows how. She texted me a chain letter last week with some pretty wild claims about essential oils!

No one could conveniently forget your work schedule like a Midwestern mom.

> **Dustin:** She thinks you're ignoring her, and she's heartbroken about it.

This was, unequivocally, a falsehood.

Her baby brother had moved back home recently and appointed himself their mother's knight in shining armor, a position for which she'd never advertised and didn't need filled. In theory, Holly supported anyone moving in with their parents. Considering late-stage capitalism, it made perfect sense, and it was a uniquely American idea that the nuclear family only involve a single generation in a home.

In practice, she would have an easier time supporting Dustin's life choices if he weren't such a little shit about everything.

> **Dustin:** You can't be that busy if you have time to text me. I'm telling her you'll call her in 5 minutes.

That manipulative little punk-ass bitch.

> **Holly:** I should have left you up that tree when you were four.

Since she had five minutes before she had to call her mom or risk her mother reporting her as a missing person, she texted her sister.

> **Holly:** What the hell does Mom want?

> **Caitlin:** What do you think? She wants you to come home for Christmas.

> **Holly:** Fucckkkk

Her phone rang. So much for waiting five minutes. Or for letting Holly call.

"Mom, I'm at work," she answered, tucking the phone into her handkerchief headband so she could have her hands free.

"Your own mother doesn't get a hello? Anyway, your brother says you're not busy."

Holly bit her nails into her palms, reminding herself that she loved her mom, exactly as she was.

"Hi, Mom," Holly said, rolling her neck to relieve the beginning of the stress headache often brought on by conversations with her family. "I'm at work."

This time, her mom didn't even address the issue, simply bulldozing past it.

"You will never guess who I ran into at Rosenstein's when I was picking up some chocolate babka for Leigh's daughter's baby shower."

"Hadlee's having another baby? Didn't she just have one?" Holly knew she shouldn't engage. Any morsel of interest she showed in the gossip from her hometown would feed her mother's (wildly unfounded) hopes that Holly would, eventually, return to take part in said gossip.

Her mom tsked. "No, no, Mykylee! Won't that be wonderful? The cousins will only be six months apart."

Holly managed to bite her tongue before pointing out that Mykylee was seventeen and it was maybe *not* that great. Who knew, maybe it would be. Wonderful. And not a disaster.

Her mom didn't notice her lack of response. "You still haven't guessed who I ran into at the store!"

Holly was not going to get out of this, and she hated guessing games. "Why don't you tell me, Mom?"

Taking a deep breath, like an internal drumroll, her mom announced, "Ivy!"

Oof. A gut punch.

"Yay?" Holly managed with the air left in her lungs.

"She looked so great. She's finally letting her hair go back to its natural blond. You know, I always thought you two were meant to be, and you'd get back together once you got a little older."

It was, no question, absolutely wonderful that her Irish Midwest mom was so very supportive of her lesbian daughter, and always had been. Unfortunately, that meant Holly wasn't exempt from her mom's extreme matchmaking.

"Ivy's with someone else, Mom," she pointed out patiently. "Remember Wren?"

She did not say, "Remember how things ended with Ivy? Remember how I was so mean to her, and she blocked my calls, and I spent years avoiding getting involved with anyone else because I didn't want to treat them the way I treated her?" Her mom wasn't great at hearing things she didn't want to.

"Oh, sure, but how serious can they be?" Her mom brushed this off. "They've been together for years, and they're still not married?"

The stress headache was unavoidable at this point. "Maybe Ivy doesn't want to jump into marriage." The "again" was silent, but they both heard it loud and clear. "People don't get back together after almost a decade, Mom. You've been reading too many romance novels."

There was a *hmmm* noise that Holly knew well. It meant her mom was ignoring her. "Well, all I know is, she said she'd love to stop in for coffee for the holidays, and if you happened to be there..."

"Ope! I hear Matt calling from the front. He needs me to take a table!" Holly said. She should have just hung up, but if she hung up on her mother, she would still be hearing about it in the afterlife.

"You haven't been home for Christmas in five years, Holly Siobhan." Ah, the guilt trip was right on time.

Holly needed a distraction. "Is Dustin bringing a girlfriend to Christmas? I thought he told me he was seeing someone. You should ask him."

This lure proved too much for her mother to ignore, and Holly finally got off the phone.

Christ on a cracker. What was her mom thinking? Trying to get her and Ivy back together? She was going to need a good excuse for not going home, immediately. "Matt, if my mom calls the cafe phone, I'm swamped with tables, okay?"

"She must have riled you up." The manager gave a half-smile. "You sound like you just got off the bus from Fargo all of a sudden."

This earned the middle finger it deserved. As if Iowa and North Dakota accents sounded anything alike.

"If you feel compelled to actually do some work," Matt said, chuckling, "Tara's out there."

"For what it's worth, I *was* working. I was saving your ass by getting all the baking done. I'm not even supposed to be here today," Holly grumbled. "You could, I don't know, make me a full-time baker, and then you wouldn't have to call me in on my day off when your baker no call no shows again."

Matt laughed at her, which was what he always did when they had this conversation. It was unbelievably frustrating. "You're too good a waitress, Holly. No matter how delicious your coconut cake is."

That was always the answer. "Can't pay you to do what you love, Holly. You're too skilled at something else that happens to pay less—oh, but we can still have you *do* the thing you love, at your lower salary, once in a while."

She liked this place, but not enough to stay if she was going to be taken advantage of. Charleston was hot, and sticky, and full of rich assholes, and maybe it was about time she moved on. The only thing keeping her from picking up her last check and using it to fill up the tank in her held-together-with-zip-ties 1979 Subaru Brat was the beautiful woman currently in the dining area, waiting for a cup of coffee.

Tara was her favorite (and hottest) customer, a perfect blond Southern ice queen. When they'd first met, Tara had been engaged. Holly liked Tara's ex, Miriam, a great deal, and missed her now that she'd left to go live out a Hallmark movie plot. Since Tara wasn't engaged anymore, Holly had been flirting hard. She hadn't had any luck so far, but hope sprang eternal. And every time she thought about leaving Charleston without tasting those lips, something stopped her.

She peeked out the round port window in the swinging kitchen door, to where Tara was sitting in her normal spot. Somehow, her perfectly flat-ironed hair looked droopy, her shoulders hunched up several degrees past power pose. Most worryingly, she seemed to be in her house clothes with no eyeliner on, which meant she'd gone out in public without her full armor. It appeared they were both having difficult days.

Holly didn't know how she would thaw Tara's ice long enough to get her in bed, when no amount of flirting had worked, but as for how to fix a Southern girl's terrible day?

She had that covered.

Chapter 3

Tara

O h, Lord," Holly said, setting down a carafe of coffee. "You look like you've seen a ghost. I'm bringing cake."

Tara was, temporarily, distracted from her panic about the whole "I made up a girlfriend" thing by how hot Holly looked in ripped up jeans and a skeleton tank, her long red hair in a messy bun, a green shamrock bandanna tied at the top in a bow like an emo Rosie the Riveter. When she was working, Holly dressed in fit-and-flare dresses and rockabilly hair, but Tara had noticed that on her days off, she was more punk than pinup.

"That obvious, huh?" It shouldn't matter that Holly was seeing her at full freak-out. Holly had seen her at her worst. Holly was one of the only people on earth Tara didn't need to act for, and all of the rest of them were currently up in the Adirondacks in a godforsaken moldy hotel in the middle of the woods. And while she might be Tara's favorite waitress and secret crush, she might be tall and willowy with waves of red hair and green eyes and legs for days, she was not for Tara.

So Tara didn't need to impress her. Even if she wanted to.

There was a clunk, and a plate landed in front of her with the biggest slice of coconut cake she'd ever seen. She almost cried. God bless Holly for knowing just by looking at her that this was not only a cake emergency, but a coconut cake emergency. For a girl born and raised in South Carolina, some occasions could not be gotten through without it.

"Girl, if you're going to cry into the cake, I'm going to put you in a corner booth where no one can see your mascara run," Holly said, sliding in across from her. This was new. Holly never sat down, was always on the move serving tables.

Tara looked around, to find that the place was mostly empty.

"I have some time to sit," Holly said, like she knew what Tara was thinking. She probably did—apparently, she could read Tara's face. After a decade in front of juries, Tara wasn't used to anyone being able to read her unless she let them. "You wanna talk about it?"

Tara almost dropped her head on the table, but her training was too strong.

"I got an invitation to Miriam's wedding," she began, and everything came pouring out. Her panic at having to show her face, single, at the wedding of her ex and the girl her ex left her for. Her sudden unwillingness to be the odd one out in a group of her coupled friends. (If Cole wasn't secretly making out with the hot bartender, she would eat her best Sunday hat.)

Holly listened, the dimple in her cheek telling Tara that she was trying not to laugh. That was fine, Tara would be laughing at herself, too, if she hadn't just told all her friends that she was bringing a date to a wedding that she categorically didn't have a date for.

"How am I going to find a girlfriend by Christmas? It's already December third."

"This is easy," Holly said, taking a bite of Tara's cake. "I'll go. I'd love to see Carrigan's, I love Miriam, it'll be great."

"But I told them I was dating someone," Tara reiterated.

Holly shrugged. "You can pretend to be dating me for the week. I'd be a good fake girlfriend: I look fantastic dolled up for a wedding, I smile at strangers for my job, and I have good stories."

Tara couldn't tell if she was serious. "Wait, what? Why would you spend your Christmas pretending to be my girlfriend?" Somehow, even though Tara had gotten herself into this, Holly actually offering to pretend to be her date made her fully process what a wild idea it was.

Truly, it was top-tier terrible.

Even leaving aside the basic premise of "maybe don't lie to your best friends," Miriam knew Holly and knew the two of them could never date. On the other hand, Miriam knew that Tara wanted Holly and had been pining after her for most of a year. Miri would be so excited that Tara was dating seriously, and so distracted by the wedding, that she might not ask too many questions. There was a slim possibility that Tara could go to this wedding with a beautiful woman, who would be a buffer from the overwhelming energy at Carrigan's, and keep her friends from worrying about her.

Except for Cole.

She looked down at her vibrating phone. Cole was another story that she needed to figure out how to deal with, right now.

Tara grimaced. "Want to say hi to Cole?"

"Cole!" Holly cried happily as Tara answered and put him on speaker. "My favorite Yacht Bro Felon!"

"I've never been convicted of a felony," Cole said breezily. "Hi, Holly. WAIT. Holly?!" His voice was getting louder and screechier. "What is Holly doing with you? Is Holly the person you're secretly dating? That you're bringing to the wedding?!"

Holly raised an eyebrow at Tara across the booth, silently asking what Tara wanted to do. She didn't want to do anything. She wanted to go back in time and tell Hannah that she was coming as Cole's plus-one, assuming he wasn't bringing Hot Bartender, or that she was going to be out of the country that week so she had to send her regrets, or . . . anything other than what she'd said.

The silence stretched as their eyes caught, the phone between them.

"Tara Sloane Chadwick, tell me the truth," Cole demanded, his voice dropping into a serious register.

This was the quintessential problem with Nicholas Jedediah Fraser III. He could command she tell him the truth, and she would. Because once you'd committed felony arson with someone—whether you were charged or not—they had certain privileges.

"I am bringing Holly to the wedding. Maybe," she said, and waited for him to stop yelling on the other end of the phone. It was a good thing the cafe was mostly empty and that all the staff knew Cole. "But we're not actually dating. I just didn't want to come alone. And I haven't even decided if she's coming. You cannot tell Miri, though. Or anyone."

Tara waited, her leg bouncing under the table despite

her ordering it to stop. She waited for Cole's judgment, or for Holly to rescind her offer, or for her brain to stop whirring long enough to be able to make a sound decision. Holly reached over to squeeze her hand, and the touch of their fingers was electric. Maybe she didn't want to make a sound decision, her brain whispered. Maybe she wanted to make an absolutely ridiculous one.

All Cole said was, "I can't keep secrets from Miriam! It goes against my character!"

Of course he wouldn't be the voice of reason on this—Cole was basically five to seven bad ideas in a pair of lobster-embroidered shorts. He wasn't worried that she was planning to keep secrets, only about his ability to be a useful accomplice.

"What do you do for a living, Nicholas?" Tara asked in her best criminal defense lawyer voice. Because whatever it was, he was absolutely keeping it a secret from Miriam.

"So, *if* Holly comes, are you…pretending she's your girlfriend?" Cole asked, sounding both skeptical and thrilled. The man did love a hijink.

That was the question, wasn't it? Were they actually going to go through with an absurd deception so Tara didn't have to feel embarrassed? "I don't know yet, but it's not off the table, so try not to confirm or deny anything."

His sigh could have powered wind turbines. "I hate you very much and I will keep your secret and I will see you up here for the wedding, but you will owe me for this. Also, you should probably date Holly for real."

"She's out of my league," Tara deadpanned, although she wasn't kidding. She would be terrible for Holly. Holly would probably be great for her, emotionally, but terrible for her life plan.

The justice system of South Carolina was deeply corrupt, and she came from a family deeply embedded in, and benefiting unfairly from, said system. She couldn't dismantle the system—no single person could. A robust, well-organized movement was working on that. So she gave them a lot of money, showed up and did the work they needed done, and tried to not take up too much space.

Miriam had once quoted the Talmud to her: "it is not up to you to complete the work, but neither are you free to desist from it." That quote had embedded itself in her heart, and led her steps in her career. Had led her, specifically, to leave divorce law and use her privilege by offering representation, pro bono, to clients in need of a good defense attorney.

It wasn't world-changing work, but she loved it, and until the system was toppled, it helped even the playing field in the courts just a fraction.

However, because she was a lesbian with a, well, colorful past, she had to walk a careful line in order to maintain proximity to the Old Boys network she was currently exploiting. If she got involved with someone who was not just a Yankee, but also a waitress, she would lose access—or Holly would pretend to be someone she wasn't and the Old Boys would still be horrifying to her. There was no way Tara would get entangled with anyone who wasn't trained to be a society wife. It wouldn't be fair to them.

She liked Holly far too much to ask her to put on that cursed mask.

Chapter 4

Holly

Cole was right, which, in Holly's limited experience with him, was usually true. He might be a giant blond whirlwind of jokes, but he was surprisingly insightful.

She and Tara should, actually, date. In fact, she'd been trying to get Tara to ask her out for months, as soon as she realized that Tara wasn't devastated by her breakup with Miriam. Normally, Holly would have made the first move, but Tara was skittish and used to being in charge. If she could make dating seem like it had been Tara's idea all along, they were more likely to get somewhere.

It was not, on the surface, a great idea.

Tara was settled in Charleston and Holly was on her way out, sooner rather than later given the job situation. She'd already been here for three years, which was longer than she'd intended to stay. After she left home, she'd never stayed anywhere for long. There was a lot of world to see, and she was still in the middle of seeing it.

Not to mention Tara's crowd was stuffy, and they kind of sucked. Holly had no interest in playing the society girl-friend, brunching with drunk plantation owners while they complained about woke cancel culture or chatted about polo. But something about Tara was so incredibly sexy, so fascinating to Holly. The perfect hair, the Lilly Pulitzer wardrobe, the way she always smelled like magnolias—she projected this aura of impeccable Southern sweetness, but right under the surface was a prickly, ice-cold bitch who would take any prosecutor to the mat and who made Holly want to beg to be stepped on.

So yes, it would be a bad idea to get involved long-term, but dating didn't mean they were getting married, after all. Holly didn't do serious relationships. They tended to make her feel trapped, and then she got shitty and lashed out, hurting the other person to cut their ties. What she did do, though, was fun. She and Tara could have a hell of a lot of fun.

Tara hung up with Cole, and Holly pushed up from the booth. "I have to go back to work, but we should get dinner, somewhere that's not here, and talk about whether or not we want to do this, and if we do, plot logistics. Want to go for pizza?"

Tara sniffed. "I have a very good pizza oven at my house. Why don't you come over."

Holly noticed this was an order, not a request, and shivered a little. She smiled, making sure the dimple in her cheek popped, and let the waterfall of her red waves cascade over her shoulder, for added effect.

"Text me when," she said, and handed Tara the bill, with her number on the bottom.

This would be perfect. They'd get out of town, away from all the ties that bound Tara and creeped out Holly, and have an adventure. Tara would use her to avoid feeling left out and lonely with her friends. Holly would use Tara to avoid going home for the holidays so her mother could try to set her up with her ex. She didn't see why an expiration date should keep them from getting naked together. Actually, it was in the plus column. Everyone got orgasms, no one got hurt. Tied up but not tied down, as it were.

Which made her envision Tara tying her up, an excellent distraction from the rest of her shift.

When Tara texted her about dinner two days later, she was about ready to climb out of her skin. She was convinced that Tara was going to change her mind and that that's why she hadn't been into the cafe. This would be fine, Holly told herself. She didn't *need* to embark on fake-dating hijinks, either to avoid going home for the holidays or to get into Tara's pants, although she'd gotten her hopes up about both. Especially since her little brother had texted her several more times to try to guilt trip her about how sad their mom was.

She spent more time than she would have liked to admit picking out a bottle of wine to take over. She knew Tara had wine, probably much better wine than Holly could ever afford, but she'd been in the South long enough to know that you didn't show up to someone's house without a hostess gift.

Flowers seemed like they would send the wrong message, since she was trying to convince Tara that hooking up was her idea—Holly didn't want to seem like she was coming wooing. She could have baked something, she knew exactly what Tara liked, but that made it seem like they were still waitress and customer, instead of...friends? Partners in crime? Acquaintances who accidentally knew everything about each other?

Except that, while she knew a hell of a lot about Tara, Tara knew almost nothing about her. The inevitable power dynamic between server and regular.

Finally, wine in hand, hair looking amazing, heels a little too high, and nerves stuffed down, she rang the doorbell to Tara's Single House. Charleston had a booming business renovating these old colonial houses, built long and narrow so the air could go straight through from front to back, in the days before air-conditioning. Of course Tara lived in one. The perfect home for a daughter of Charleston's Old Money. It was painted the softest pale coral, with a wash of haint blue under the porch roof. The blue was meant to ward off evil spirits in the Gullah tradition, and Holly wondered if it kept Tara's parents from entering, like vampires who'd had their invitations revoked.

Her fencepost had the traditional pineapple embellishment. It was the perfect symbol of the mask Tara was always wearing—the emblem of Charleston's white settler-colonial roots guarding the entrance to the home of a woman who gave every impression of hating the whole system built on those roots. She wondered, not for the first time, how Tara balanced that juxtaposition without breaking. Holly itched to help her let off some of the tension she must be constantly under.

The door swung open, and Tara stood there in a cotton tunic, barefoot. Her toes were painted a gray-blue that matched the Atlantic on a cloudy morning, and Holly almost swallowed her tongue. It wasn't that she'd never seen Tara casual, or in sandals. They lived in a swamp, and sometimes the only way to leave the house in the summer was in as little clothing as possible. But she'd never seen her this comfortably undone.

"I brought wine," she managed. "It's probably not very good."

Tara's smile blossomed. "And here I thought you were a mannerless Yank." She moved forward to hug Holly, but hesitated. Her smell, magnolias and star jasmine, like a steamy garden party, drifted forward and pulled Holly in, until she completed the hug.

She kicked off her shoes in the foyer, unwilling to risk Tara's perfect heart pine floors with her heels. Tara led her back, through a showcase of a living room, toward the kitchen. Like most homes of the type (or at least, so Holly had gleaned from reading back issues of *Southern Living*), there was ornate crown molding and hand-painted wallpaper, but unlike many people who layered intense patterns and dark colors, Tara had opted for washes of pale yellow against white, washed out greens in the plush carpets, varieties of cream in the china she displayed in the antique cabinet, white embroidery on white pillows piled up on her chaise. It should look sterile, compared to the careful clutter of many of her peers' homes, but Holly loved it immediately. Although she was very worried she was going to spill something on a throw pillow.

"I hope you don't mind that I ordered in," Tara drawled, her voice sounding even more South Carolinian in this quintessential Charleston setting. "I have to admit that I can't cook at all, fancy pizza oven or not. My mother despairs of me, but I never learned."

Her ears got red when she said this, and Holly stored away the knowledge that ice queen Tara could blush. And also that Tara deflected criticism by preemptively acknowledging any perceived faults, with a breezy self-deprecating shrug that made it seem as if being imperfect didn't bother her.

"Please, there's no shame in a woman not being able to cook, even a perfect Southern belle. You're highly accomplished enough."

Tara's hands twitched where they were folded on the marble countertop, and Holly could tell she was digging her nails into her skin. Apparently there was some shame in it, if you were a Chadwick. Maybe it made Tara uncomfortable to be told she didn't have to be good at everything.

Food arrived, a selection from Hank's because of course, when Tara ordered, she ordered the best seafood in the city. Tara arranged it impeccably on plates that probably cost more than Holly had ever made in a month. It was the most beautifully displayed platter of shrimp she'd ever seen. She immediately bit one of the little sea bug's heads off. You didn't waste good shrimp where she came from—hell, you never even got good shrimp where she came from.

"I think we should drive," Holly said, and watched Tara freeze.

"To New York?" she said, her voice appalled.

"It's only a couple of days," Holly pointed out, dunking another shrimp in sauce. "It will give us an opportunity to go over our story, make sure we know what we're telling people.

Memorize important details. Miriam will notice if I don't know anything about your family except what I can Google, even if she is distracted by the wedding. Besides, there's some beautiful country up there. We could drive up the whole coast!" *And make out the whole time.*

Tara's shoulders were up by her ears. Oh, sweet Jesus, Holly wanted to make this woman come apart at the seams. Preferably all over Holly's face. She should probably get her thirstiness under control.

Tara bit her lip, and Holly imagined biting it for her.

She would definitely get her thirstiness under control...at some point.

"I'm already expected to be up there for days, missing work to do a bunch of random pre-wedding crap," Tara said, lining up objects on her granite counters in a gesture Holly suspected was nervous, though Tara kept her face completely calm. "I don't think I can add any more days away to that. I have too much work. We should fly. We have a couple of weeks before we have to leave—we can get our stories straight then."

"You want to fly into JFK that close to Christmas, get on a train for five hours, then take a shuttle to Carrigan's?" Holly made a gagging face. She'd researched how to get to Carrigan's so that she would have ammunition for this argument. "We'll lose an entire day each way, it will be miserably stuffed with holiday travelers, and you won't be able to get any work done. Driving, it will be two comfortable days in a car. You can sit in the passenger seat with your laptop. Billable hours, Chadwick. I'm afraid I'm going to have to insist. If we do this, we do it as a road trip."

"We haven't even agreed for sure that we're going to

pretend to be dating," Tara hedged, dragging her shrimp slowly through a puddle of butter on her plate, like she was painting with it instead of eating it.

Holly piled fried seafood high on her plate. Could she get a to-go box? she wondered. "You keep talking about dating and a girlfriend, but couldn't we just be, like, sleeping together and keeping each other company on a long weekend in the mountains? We could even really sleep together. You know. For veracity." She winked.

Tara didn't respond to this offer. Instead she said, "We need to be seriously dating because I only date seriously. I would never sleep with someone I wasn't considering marrying, much less bring them to a wedding at Carrigan's."

There had to be *quite* a story there.

"Anyway," Tara continued, "what would be in it for you? I feel like I'm taking advantage of your goodwill."

Holly laughed. "Hey, you're really not. You're taking me along on an adventure, something I desperately need, you're paying for a vacation, and I'm going to have a great time. Besides, my mom is putting on the pressure hard for me to come home for the holidays, because she's decided to set me up with my ex. Having a wedding to go to, and a fake girl-friend to go with, would solve several problems for me. If it makes you feel better, you can upgrade my hotel rooms to the best suites on the road."

Tara studied her, and Holly thought she was going to call the whole thing off, but instead she poured them both a little more of her much-better wine and motioned Holly over to the couch, where they settled on opposite ends, looking at each other.

"If we're going to consider doing this, believably, I need to know as much about you as you do about me. Maybe more." Tara managed to gesture with a glass of red wine over a pale pink velvet pillow without ever threatening to spill it.

It was very impressive, but Holly set her own glass down on a coaster on the coffee table, out of the way of her arms in case she gesticulated. She tucked her legs beneath her.

"I'm an open book," she said, spreading her arms wide. "What do you want to know?"

"Where are you from? Do you have any siblings? What did you study in college? Anything! I don't know anything about you." Tara's diction got more monied and her posture got more stiff the more uncomfortable she was. Holly knew other people thought she was an insufferable snob, but Holly personally thought she was a very charming, socially awkward snob.

"I'm from Iowa, the Quad Cities area. I'm a middle child between an older sister and a much younger brother, my sister and I are close, while my brother...he's still figuring out being human. I didn't go to university. I went to welding school because I thought it sounded like good money, but I kind of hated it. Lotta dudes not thrilled to share professional space with me."

"Oh!" Tara exclaimed, somehow managing to sit up even straighter. "I shouldn't have assumed about college."

As much fun as it was to ruffle Tara's feathers, Holly realized she was supposed to be putting Tara at ease about this whole situation, so Tara would agree to take her. How do you put a generations-deep Southern belle at ease about a girl who grew up in the Midwest on food stamps?

"You're so smart, though. Is there anything you'd want to go back to school for? There are lots of scholarships for returning students, opportunities to finish at your own pace..."

Now Holly's back was up. No matter how nonchalantly she mentioned not having gone to college, or how totally unfazed she appeared to be about waitressing, eventually people tried to save her from herself.

She smiled, a little brittlely. This, at least, had thrown ice water over her lust. "I don't have any interest in college. I've discovered, as I get older, that I'm pretty content to be a career waitress. I love that I can get a job in any city, that I can pack up and move on to the next thing. You can't take that for granted, growing up poor. Ironically, our mobile home wasn't mobile. I love that I get to give people food all day, that the worst work disaster I ever have is an angry patron, and I only ever work at places where the owners have my back. When I'm off the clock, I'm done. I never take any bullshit home with me to stress over. And I get free meals, which means I never go hungry and I never have to eat government cheese again, unless I want to because it makes great nachos."

She watched Tara shift her weight on the couch, obviously trying to process the words *career waitress*, *mobile home*, and *government cheese*. This was a well-rehearsed speech, one Holly could give in her sleep, but this time it meant more for some reason. She wanted Tara to believe her, to understand that she wasn't miserable—she was fulfilled and living the life she'd chosen.

Chapter 5

Tara

This was the best possible news, Tara told herself firmly, because there was no way she would be tempted to get involved with Holly now.

Not that there was a problem with not going to college or being a career waitress—or being poor, obviously. All of those things were unrelated to a person's value, worth, and character. They just made Holly off-limits because now she knew, for sure, that she could never marry her, and Tara only dated women she could marry. She needed a society wife who could fit into her social circle. They'd tolerated Miriam because of her fame but what Tara really needed was a socialite. Someone raised to the role, who would make Tara "respectable" even if she insisted on being a lesbian. Holly was amazing, free-spirited and snarky and fun, which by default meant she wasn't society wife material in the way Tara needed. Tara wasn't in the market for a fling, so they simply wouldn't get involved.

And if there was no danger of them getting involved, there was no reason *not* to go through with this scheme. Other than the fact that it was a terrible idea, obviously.

"Okay. I guess...Yeah, maybe we should do this?" she said, and Holly pumped a fist holding a fried oyster. "We'll have two long days of driving with a night somewhere in the middle," Tara said. "Maybe Baltimore?"

"I love Baltimore!" Holly smiled mischievously, wrapping her thick waves of red hair around her hand. "I know an incredibly posh little B and B you'll be obsessed with. No one knows about it—you have to get referred by a friend. It's the opposite of Carrigan's."

"I already love it," Tara mumbled.

She didn't *hate* Carrigan's Christmasland, exactly. Hating Carrigan's would make her a Scrooge who hated joy and fun. She simply didn't *get* Carrigan's. It didn't feel magical to her, just old and decrepit, and full of allergens. She didn't have an innate appreciation for kitsch. Antiques, yes, tasteful ones, but anything that was over-the-top on purpose gave her anxiety.

She'd been over-the-top, arguably, most of her life until she was seventeen. A rebellious, angry whirlwind doing everything she could to piss off her parents—drinking, stealing, paying her way out of trouble. If it was a cliché for a spoiled rich Southern kid, she'd done it, and dragged Cole along with her. Unlike most spoiled Southern kids, though, she hadn't been rebelling because she could, but because she hated everything her family stood for.

Then she'd nearly burned her whole life to the ground, literally, and she hadn't gone over the top since. She was very, very good at...well, not blending into the background, she definitely never did that, but standing out for being precisely what she was supposed to be. Carrigan's Christmasland was too loud, and it put her hackles up. Carrigan's rebelled against every social norm, and Tara never did, not anymore.

"Are you...okay?" Holly asked, interrupting her thoughts. "Your eyelid started twitching."

Tara shook herself. "You call the friend of a friend, or whoever it is you know, and see if they have a couple of rooms the night we need to be there, and I'll get an oil change. I guess we're taking a road trip."

"We should start posting about each other on social media. It will look weird if we're serious enough for you to be taking me to a wedding, but not serious enough to have ever mentioned each other on Instagram," Holly pointed out.

Tara took a sip of her wine, trying to figure out what about that statement freaked her out the most. "I've been taking a rather long hiatus from Instagram, personally, since that whole...business." She waved, assuming Holly knew that she meant "the business of being very publicly dumped for someone else by an influencer and having it play out all over the gay internet."

Miriam had garnered her huge online following, complete with its own fandom that was rabidly interested in her love life, by making weird upcycled antique art. Their breakup had been covered in Autostraddle.

"Also, I would rather not have to explain any of this to my parents, if I can avoid it, since that would defeat the purpose of making my life easier," Tara continued. "A lot of my life's work would be undone if certain people found out I was involved with a diner waitress. No offense."

"Oh," Holly said, "anyone who would think that is definitely the party who should be offended, by their total ethical bankruptcy. I'm thrilled to be the kind of person of whom they'd disapprove."

"As you should be. But how are we going to get Carrigan's to believe we're dating, without anyone else believing it?"

Holly tapped her chin. "Maybe I post about it, sort of coyly, like I'm seeing someone but I won't tag her because she values her privacy? I can take some pictures of our shoes together and cute shit like that."

Tara nodded. This was smart. She could do this. "Two iced coffees leaning against each other on a table."

"Ah, yes, the classic lesbian relationship soft launch." Holly nodded, mock seriously. "I'll get started on that project. It's already the fifth, and you need to be at Carrigan's, what, the twenty-second? For pre-wedding stuff?"

Tara rolled her eyes. "You underestimate the number of pre-wedding activities my beloved Hannah has planned. I plan out of anxiety, but Hannah plans out of passion." She paused. "Well, and anxiety. I shouldn't be there later than the night of the twentieth, if I want to escape her wrath."

Hannah and Tara had bonded after her breakup with Miriam because they were very similar people—intense, type A, a little bitchy—and Hannah had, at the time, been healing from a breakup of her own. Their friendship had, unexpectedly, become an important part of Tara's life. Which was why she was showing up to all of Hannah's (ridiculous) planned activities.

"Okay, so we're leaving the nineteenth. Two weeks from today. You let me know when and where you're picking me up, and I'll be there, with bells on. Maybe not literal bells, although they would probably be appreciated at Carrigan's." Holly suddenly looked panicked. "Wait, what *should* I wear to this wedding? Something glittery?"

"Oh God, I need to buy a dress." Tara rubbed her collarbone, trying to calm her suddenly accelerating heartbeat.

"I'm pretty sure you already own something you can wear," Holly said skeptically. "Do you want me to help you go through your closet? We can do a fashion show."

Tara shook her head, her hair swishing around her ears with the movement. She shivered. Was it cold in here? "I don't have anything appropriate for a Jewish wedding in the woods in December, and I need the, I don't know, the distraction and ceremony of a shopping quest for the exact right thing. It will be good. A new dress will be good armor." Her breath started to come back into her lungs.

"To the most lesbian road trip of all time: heading to your ex's wedding," Holly declared, holding her glass up for a toast.

Tara chinked her glass and argued, "It would be even gayer if they were both my exes."

Holly threw her head back and cackled, and the sound reverberated through the house. How did she do that? How did she just…laugh, out loud? It wasn't that Tara never laughed, but not like that, without caring how she looked or who heard her. She watched the line of Holly's neck, freckles leading down it like a trail, and felt her body heat.

How could she handle four days trapped in a car with this woman?

But no, she was perfectly capable of keeping her lust under control, no matter how good Holly's hair smelled. She was

Tara Sloane Chadwick, the phoenix of Charleston. She had remade herself in an image of her choosing using only her willpower (and her family's vast resources and connections, she reminded herself). She could get through one road trip and one uncomfortable wedding without cracking her composure. She wouldn't even have to deal with moldy wallpaper!

This self-pep talk completed, she packed Holly off with a distant cheek kiss and a takeaway plate. She should make a list of everything that needed doing before they left, should go shopping, should create a document for Holly of everything she needed to know to be a convincing fake girlfriend.

She didn't do any of those things.

Instead, she put on her rattiest, most comfortable pajamas that no one ever saw, not even Cole, climbed under every blanket she owned, and put on a carefully curated playlist of *X-Files* episodes. Somehow this was going to be okay, but only if she could figure out how to keep cool.

In the two weeks between agreeing to pretend to be dating in front of literally all her real friends in the world and the day they actually left, Tara spent eighteen-hour days at the office trying to get ahead on work before her vacation, and rethought the plan thousands of times. If Holly were not already posting about them on her social media, Tara would absolutely have called it off at least once a day. But they were already lying, and if the truth came out, she would be even more humiliated. There was no reason now not to go through with all of it.

And, after all, she still couldn't imagine showing up to this damn wedding single.

The morning they were set to leave for the wedding, Tara pulled up to Holly's apartment complex and texted to say she was there.

HOLLY: I'm not quite ready, come up. 367, back corner apartment on the left.

Tara bristled. They had agreed, December 19, seven a.m., because they wanted to get an early start. She was prepared for a long day of driving. She wasn't prepared to see Holly's home, didn't want to see that vulnerable side of Holly.

It would only make Tara like her more, and Tara didn't have any room for that. She gritted her teeth. This was the sort of thing she liked to know beforehand, so she could have a script and an exit plan. Although, she was Holly's ride out of town, so she couldn't have an exit plan. Which was the other problem—she had a very specific schedule, and this delay was going to throw it off.

She practiced breathing techniques all the way to Holly's door, where she spent several moments trying to decide if she should knock, and, if so, should she do a standard knock or a jaunty sort of rhythm, or should she ring the doorbell. Her hairline started to sweat, which was going to ruin her blow-out, so she decided on the bell.

A muffled voice yelled for her to come in. *Shit.*

She ordered her sweat glands to get their shit together. Just because it wasn't Done to walk into someone's home for the first time without having been met at the door didn't mean she was physically incapable of doing it. She had done, in her life, many things that Simply Weren't Done, up to and including sleeping with women, and she was still here to tell the tale. She would survive this.

God, she hated surprises. Why did this trip that she was already so freaked out about have to start with a surprise?

She stared down at her shoes, rather than around at Holly's apartment. She was intensely curious about Holly's space, but she refused to snoop. She didn't want to have any fodder for her imagination when it came to Holly's couch, or bed, or other soft horizontal surfaces.

"I'm almost ready, I swear!" Holly's voice broke through her concentration.

She glanced up to assure Holly that it was fine, although it wasn't really, and stopped mid-thought.

Holly was standing in the hallway in front of Tara, wearing a neon-pink towel with giant green flowers on it. It was not a lot of towel for a tall woman. A large expanse of Holly's muscular legs, and a significant portion of her perfect breasts, were exposed. Her hair was dripping rivulets of water down the valley of her cleavage, and when she reached up to wring it out, Tara was convinced the towel was going to hit the floor. A small, evil part of her prayed that it would.

Tara slow blinked, trying to clear her lust fog.

"Oh my God, you look so panicked!" Holly giggled. "Are you okay? Did you suddenly realize you left your Jag alone in my shitty apartment parking lot? You're welcome to wait in the car."

"I don't own a Jag," Tara said, then processed the rest of

Holly's words. "And I'm not worried about my car. I expected you to be..."

"Ready?" Holly guessed.

"Dressed," Tara corrected.

Holly waved this off with one hand, and for a moment, Tara really did think the towel would slip. "I'm completely packed and ready. I literally just need to pull on some clothes. Give me five minutes!"

When they settled into the car (only ten minutes later), Holly cocked her head, her wet hair now braided down her back. How did she leave the house with wet hair? Tara's scalp itched.

"You don't drive a Jag but this is, in fact, a Benz."

"It's electric," Tara said defensively.

"Yeah, they definitely don't make midrange economy electric cars or anything. You couldn't have bought a LEAF, say," Holly teased. When Tara started to protest, Holly waved her off. "I know, I know, you can't roll up to court in a Nissan. I get it."

It was a sore spot, because she liked the LEAF better, but she'd "compromised" when her mother was horrified by the idea. Why her mother was involved in any way in the purchase of her vehicle, when she'd paid for it herself, drove it herself, and avoided driving it to her parents' home on the island if she could avoid it, was a thought that kept her up at night.

She didn't want to tell Holly any of that, because her mother was an insidious poison and made her feel like a spineless child, so she said, "It's very reliable."

Holly raised an eyebrow at her prim tone. "Are we allowed to eat in this very reliable Mercedes?"

Tara balked. "Obviously. We're going to be on the road for nine hours today. I would never tell you that you couldn't eat."

Holly grinned. "Perfect." She opened the backpack at her feet far enough to show that it was stuffed with snacks. "What's your snack profile?" she asked. "Sweet? Tart? You're a Sour Patch Kids girl, aren't you? Or maybe licorice?"

Tara felt the corner of her lip twitch into an almost-smile. "Do you have any hot lime Cheetos in there?"

"Please, I'm not a monster. Of course I do." Holly tossed her the bag.

"I'm picking the music, and when we switch, you can put on whatever you want," Tara told Holly. "I can't do highway driving without a soundtrack."

"Fine by me. Let's roll."

Tara put the car in reverse and then swung out onto the street as Mary Chapin Carpenter's voice filled the car.

"Let's roll."

THE ROAD TRIP

December 19–21

Chapter 6

Holly

"Hey, before we leave, can we send my mom a selfie?" Holly said. "She thinks I'm lying about spending Christmas with a girlfriend."

Tara looked at her, amused. "You *are* lying about spending Christmas with a girlfriend."

"Obviously. Help me make the lie more convincing?" Holly batted her eyelashes, and Tara shrugged. "Come closer so I can get us both in the picture."

When Tara leaned toward her, Holly held up her phone to get a good angle, kissed Tara on the cheek, and snapped the picture. She sent it to the family group chat.

Holly: Getting on the road with this hottie! Happy holi-gays!

Mom: She's real!

Caitlin: And she's CUTE!!!

Dad: You should bring her here instead!

Dustin: I still think you're lying.

She looked up from her phone, breathing through her life-long instinct to strangle her brother (especially when he saw through her dissembling). "We need to talk about what the Carrigan's crew would expect me to know about you," she said, popping open a diet Red Bull.

The secret to a long-haul driving day was the most caffeine possible in the least amount of liquid so you didn't have to stop to pee. She'd perfected her road trip essentials over many years crisscrossing the country.

Tara made an interesting noise in the back of her throat, something between resignation and misery. The woman did *not* like talking about herself.

"Would you like to start with the basics, or should I dive right into the deep end?" Tara's posture had somehow gotten even straighter as she talked. Who drove with their seat at a ninety-degree angle?

Holly was a jump-in-feetfirst kind of girl, and she was tempted to tell Tara they should get into the good stuff right away, but she decided to take pity. "Let's do a rapid-fire of the easy stuff, and then once you're fortified with snacks and lulled by the comfort of nineties country, we can tackle the more difficult topics."

Tara nodded, the corner of her mouth twitching in what might be the start of a smile. "Okay. Uh...you know about my parents. They're the kind of people who give interviews to *Garden & Gun* about how their families go back to before the war of Northern aggression."

"My family is annoying, but their worst crimes are varieties of Tater Tot casserole and trying to interfere in my life." Holly laughed. If she and Tara had a fling, she'd have to ensure it was long over before she ever had to meet Tara's parents, because she would tear them apart.

"That sounds lovely, honestly," Tara said. "Should I ask what's in a Tater Tot casserole?"

"You should not. What about siblings? Did your parents make an army of evil blond minions?"

"I have an older sister who has always done everything my parents have ever wanted. Went to the right school. Pledged the right sorority. Got her MRS degree."

Holly gasped. "Tara Chadwick, are you the black sheep of your family?!"

"More like the rainbow sheep, but yes. You have no idea. I've never been good enough at being..." Tara's fingers tensed on the steering wheel, and she bit her lip.

"A manifestation of demonic energy in an overpriced dress?" Holly supplied.

Now Tara did smile. "Something like that. I went to Bryn Mawr, and then Duke Law—to the horror of my father, who is on the board at University of South Carolina School of Law. And of course, I not only failed to get my MRS but my fiancée broke up with me for a lumberjack."

"Noelle is a tree farmer." Holly laughed. "Which I know you know, because I can see you liking the Carrigan's Instagram stories."

Tara grumbled. "Yeah, yeah, she has a master's in forestry. From Yale. It hasn't stopped my family from judging me as less desirable than a woman with a collection of dungarees."

"Doesn't Miriam also have a collection of dungarees?" Holly asked. "Wait, why are we calling them dungarees? And Noelle went to Yale? That's impressive. Go Miri."

Tara glared at her, and Holly giggled.

"What else? Hobbies?" she said, since the topic of Noelle's eligibility as a spouse was obviously a little sensitive.

"I play tennis and golf well, but I hate them. I sail with Cole when he's here. I keep up with the WNBA."

"The very model of a modern rich white Southern lesbian," Holly said. She'd meant it to be teasing, but she saw Tara flinch. Maybe they didn't know each other well enough for that kind of teasing yet. Maybe Tara hated *The Pirates of Penzance*.

Everything about Tara's perfect exterior made Holly itch to mess her up, but she had to go slowly or Tara would bolt.

"I wasn't, always. The model of decorum. Arguably I was a very good model of the sort of harmful, reckless privilege that is so common among the children of South Carolina's old money. A lot of our set, Cole's and mine, got away with more than we ever got caught for. We never killed anyone—but we did enough."

Holly watched her as she spoke, hands clenched so tight on the steering wheel that they might have to be pried off with a crowbar. "Were they really your set, though? I don't know you that well, but even if you've changed a lot since you were a teenager, I have trouble imagining you putting up with those people."

"That's a very kind assumption," Tara chuckled sadly. "Given the kind of people I put up with now."

She wasn't kind, but she liked Tara seeing her that way, so she didn't contradict her.

Holly decided to change the subject. Their fake relationship didn't require unpacking Tara's deep-seated feelings of guilt about her teenage years.

"What about Carrigan's? What do I need to know?"

"No one has ever been as weird about where they live as the people at Carrigan's Christmasland, to begin with. It's like they've been brainwashed into wanting to spend their lives in the freezing wilderness. They're all obsessed with the place, and I say this as a person from Charleston."

Tara's voice had dropped into her lawyer cadence, like she was arguing her case in front of a jury. Holly stuffed a chip in her mouth to stop herself from laughing.

"Also, they all have nicknames. Like Cole calls Miriam 'Mimi.' Miriam calls Hannah 'Nan.' Hannah calls Levi 'Blue.' No one can just go by their name."

Holly waited a second to see if Tara was done. "Isn't Cole a nickname? Don't Southerners call grown men things like Buster? Also, I feel like it's a pretty core tenet of queer liberation that sometimes people don't go by the names their parents gave them."

Holly had never seen someone's shoulders touch their ears before.

"What about it annoys you so much?" she asked, more gently.

Tara pursed her lips. "It's so embarrassing, but I always wanted people to call me by my middle name, Sloane, and I could never make it stick."

Holly didn't mean to make a noise in her throat, but she must have, because Tara looked over quickly.

"What?" she asked.

Holly hmmed. "Did you...tell...people? That you wanted to be called Sloane?"

"Yes!" Tara said. "I mean, I didn't push. You can't push nicknames, or it's not organic!"

Holly just watched her, until Tara started to squirm.

"I obviously support anyone's right to change their name to anything that fits them best and feels good but I...resent that easy collegiality and how none of them seem to have to work at it. They all make friends like it's simple. I have Cole, and I'm not sure I can call Cole a friend. He's mostly my brother, and I don't even know if he likes me."

Tara's phone, connected to the car's Bluetooth, heard "Call Cole."

The car announced, "Calling Cole."

Tara looked at Holly with an Oh Shit face, and Holly mouthed, *Oops!*

"Tara Sloane Chadwick, as I live and breathe," Cole drawled over the speaker. "I was fixing to call you to make sure you got on the road okay."

"She was extremely punctual," Holly told him.

"Of course she was." His voice was thick with both amusement and affection. While his accent was the same as Tara's— they'd grown up attached at the hip, after all—somehow his invoked long, slow summer days on the water with a bourbon and a cigar, whereas hers brought to mind sweet tea so cold it crackled. "And how are you? Ready to experience the magic and splendor of a Jewish-owned Christmas tourist extravaganza?"

Even when she couldn't see him, she could see his spirit fingers.

"Surely we'll be focusing on wedding prep and will not be subjected to the full onslaught of a Carrigan's Christmas?" Tara protested, alarm in her voice.

Cole's laugh filled the car, bubbling like the tide coming in. "Oh, honey, there's no escaping Christmas at Carrigan's. The season started November first. People have been coming here for their winter vacations for generations. We couldn't tell them to go somewhere else! Miriam and Noelle invited them all to the wedding!"

Tara's eyes became huge. "Where are they sleeping?!" she demanded. "Where are *we* sleeping?"

"You are sleeping in the Christmasland Inn," Cole said, and Holly thought she detected a hint of smugness in his voice. What was he up to? "I booked you myself. Everyone else, you let us worry about."

"Us? Since when do you work at Carrigan's?" Holly teased.

"Once you're here, you're on the team!" he singsonged back.

"See, I told you they were in a cult," Tara grumbled.

"A very glittery cult," Cole agreed. Part of Miriam's artistic vision was to cover everything around her in glitter glue. If she were going to start a cult, it would be shiny. "It's good to hear your voice, darlin', but what did you call for?"

Holly expected Tara to seem panicked, since she hadn't meant to call him at all, but she'd obviously used the beginning of the conversation to come up with a reason.

It was weirdly hot, how smooth she was at dissembling. Holly would unpack why that was, later.

Chapter 7

Tara

Tara had not come up with a reason for calling Cole that he would believe, but she didn't want to tell him that she'd essentially butt-dialed him.

Despite her suspicion that he didn't actually like her so much as put up with her, he was sensitive, and his feelings would be hurt. He needed to know that people thought about him, that he was taking up space in other people's heads.

She couldn't ask him what he wanted for Christmas. It was mid-December and he knew she always finished her Christmas shopping by Labor Day. She'd bought him a bottle of his outrageously expensive custom Italian cologne, because he was currently low on funds since his parents had disowned him for being gay and he was not, technically, supposed to get his trust fund until he was forty. She'd also bought him a wool fisherman's sweater embroidered with crabs in sunglasses riding surfboards. (He notoriously collected clothes covered in lobsters, dressed in beach clothes even in the dead of winter, and sailed instead of surfed. He was going to hate it so much that he'd love it.)

He'd already told them he had their rooms booked, so that was out as a conversational gambit. She could tease him about Sawyer, the hot bartender he was definitely fooling around with, but he would turn around and tease her about Holly.

While on speakerphone. With Holly in the car.

"Does Miriam need anything?" she finally settled on. "We're driving through a whole bunch of country, and I can pick something up or have something shipped. I know y'all have limited options in that backwater."

There. That was good. It made her look like she was totally over Miriam leaving her for a lumberjack and was eager to help make the wedding a success.

Out of the corner of her eye, she saw Holly give her a thumbs-up.

"Nah, Ziva is going full Mother of the Bride and making sure every tiny detail is taken care of. Which is making Hannah, the actual wedding planner, blow a fuse."

"What an interesting choice, considering that Ziva was barely a mother to the bride," Tara said icily.

Like Tara, Miriam had terrible parents, something that had always connected them. However, now that Miriam's mom was divorcing her shitweasel of a dad, she'd decided to try to be a good parent. Tara assumed that pigs would fly out of Satan's asshole before her own mother ever considered altering her parenting style.

"I thought that, too!" Cole agreed. "Anyway, if you have anything to distract overbearing mothers trying to make up for a lifetime of neglect by micromanaging their child's wedding, please bring it! Otherwise, just bring your beautiful selves. Drive safe, babycakes! I love you!"

He hung up.

"Why do you think that man doesn't like you?" Holly teased. "Is it the part where he sounds genuinely thrilled to hear from you? Makes sure to tell you to be safe? Tells you he loves you?"

Tara sighed. "I don't doubt that he loves me. I'm like a...branch on the tree of his life that he's always had and wouldn't know how to keep growing without." She could feel Holly's disbelieving eyes on her, but damn it, she was right about this. "I said I wasn't sure he *likes* me. Cole is basically a golden retriever, if golden retrievers hacked world governments for fun, so he's always thrilled to see everyone. But he's never had to decide if he would choose to have me around."

Holly made a huffing noise that Tara couldn't interpret.

"Do you like him?" she asked.

"He's my favorite person I've ever met," Tara groaned. "Never tell him I said that; it would make him insufferable."

She didn't like to think about the fact that she loved Cole best, while Cole loved Miriam best. Cole was her best friend, and she was Cole's...obligation. It would be unconscionable to admit that she was jealous of his having other friends.

So she pretended she was barely putting up with him, most of the time.

It was complicated.

Since knowing the depths of Tara's insecurity wouldn't help make Holly a better fake girlfriend, and they had limited time, she skated over that chasm. "What about you?" she asked. "Any dark secrets I should know?"

Holly gave her a sidelong glance. "I don't think it's dark secret time. I think it's lunchtime! There's a truck stop up here. You can buy me a burger."

This wasn't where Tara had planned to stop for lunch.

She didn't like to go anywhere she hadn't vetted. She could pass for straight—in fact, she usually did, whether she wanted to or not—but she could feel her stomach drop when she walked into the kind of roadside place that sold bumper stickers with the Punisher logo overlaid with the Blue Lives Matter flag, the oppressive, coiled violence waiting to erupt. It wasn't just that she didn't like to give money to places where many queer people would never feel safe stepping foot.

It was that she knew, if the owners could see inside her heart, they would want her dead, and only her mask was keeping her alive.

Still, if they stopped to use the bathroom and it wasn't okay, she would simply tell Holly they needed to go. Holly would obviously understand. She didn't seem like the kind of girl to happily spend her hard-earned money on assholes. Although she might call Tara a hypocrite, considering how many genteel bigots Tara put up with in her daily life. That didn't mean she had to deal with them on vacation, or when she wasn't using them.

They wandered the aisles of the truck stop, and Holly cajoled her into trying on bedazzled cowboy hats. Tara took a selfie in one and texted it to Miriam, who immediately asked her to buy it. There were no Confederate flags in sight, and Tara slowly relaxed.

Holly turned to her, wearing a pair of giant sunglasses. "You thought this place was going to be real homophobic, huh?"

"It crossed my mind," Tara admitted grudgingly.

Twirling, Holly replaced the sunglasses and picked up a purse embroidered with a saguaro cactus in neon green. Tara tried not to ogle her ass. This place might not be homophobic, but they were still in public.

She was only marginally successful. Her hormones didn't care that they were in a truck stop; they hadn't cared about anything since seeing Holly in a towel this morning.

"I would never bring you to a place like that," Holly was assuring her while Tara was trying to shake the mental image of the towel out of her head. "Also, they have, genuinely, the best fries I've ever eaten in my life."

"Well," Tara said, taking the glasses Holly had set down and placing them on her own face, "what are we waiting for?" Taking Holly's hand, she tugged her toward the cafe tables in the back. Holly laced their fingers together, and Tara didn't pull away.

"I recommend anything but the salad," Holly said as they read the menu. "They make everything fresh in-house, but the produce tends to be, uh, a little wilted."

"How do you know so much about this place?" Tara asked, distracted, because she'd been planning on the salad and now she had to scramble for a second choice. She always ordered a chicken Caesar. While she read, she arranged the Sweet'N Low packets into a perfect line and tried not to touch the sticky yellow floral tablecloth.

Holly sipped her water through a bendy straw. It was cute, and made Tara think about her lips. *Nope! We're at a diner,*

Sloane. "I worked here for a couple of weeks once when I was out of gas money. That's how I knew they were good people."

The waitress arrived with a plate of fries they hadn't ordered and fawned over Holly. Tara gave her order of eggs over easy—with absolutely no goopy white, but with the yolk still runny—bacon, and hash browns extra crispy (this was why she always got the salad, because she hated being Meg Ryan in *When Harry Met Sally*), then peered at Holly over her sunglasses.

"She sounds like she hasn't heard from you since you drove away," Tara observed.

Holly stared down at her plate, pushing fries around with her fork. "Yeah, I'm not great at maintaining friendships once I leave for somewhere else. I like her, and a lot of people I've known over the years, but once I start to feel obligated...I don't know, it's like a part of my brain gets resentful, and I start picking at them until they go away and don't expect anything from me. If I ghost them, they can remember me more kindly."

Tara couldn't imagine not having obligations to anyone. Sometimes it felt like all she had were obligations. Maybe that's why she was always kind of a bitch.

Instead of digging more deeply into what Holly had said or how it made her feel, Tara steered the conversation back to the things they needed to know to lie to her friends. "So. Secrets. Spill."

"Well, as I said, I'm an open book," Holly repeated, but Tara was trained to know when people were lying to her, and it was as plain as the nose on her face that Holly was in fact the opposite of an open book. "So what do you want to know? I told you about jobs, family, school."

"Any significant exes? Best friends?" Tara asked, because she'd finally figured out what Holly had been actively avoiding bringing up. "You know all about mine."

Holly flicked her bendy straw, staring at it as if it held the secrets of the universe. "I think we can save that story for a later chapter."

Open book, my ass.

Tipping her head and stealing a french fry (She should have ordered fries. How were they this good?), Tara decided not to argue. Instead she said, "We should get back on the road if we're going to make good time to the bed-and-breakfast."

Tara needed to be back in the car, where she could focus on the road, because sitting across from Holly, watching her close her eyes in ecstasy every time she dangled a dripping, ranch-covered fry into her mouth, was the sort of pornographic dream Tara would have said she definitely didn't have.

She didn't even like ranch.

They arrived at the B&B that Holly's friend's aunt's college roommate, or whoever it was, owned just before dark. (Honestly the connection was very vague, but Tara was Southern, and having connections based on a tenuous someone-knew-someone link was baked into her DNA.) It was not understated, posh, or "the opposite of Carrigan's," as Holly had promised. Instead, it was like Carrigan's had been taken over by a hostile Laura Ashley regime.

The B&B was just as full of vintage kitsch, but instead of parrots, everything was pastels and lace and dolls.

Tara had developed a very high tolerance for creepy antique dolls while living with Miriam, who tended to collect them for her art, but the sheer number of them watching her from every corner now was unnerving.

"I almost miss the parrots," she muttered. Holly looked confused. Tara shook her head to say it was nothing. "This is not what I was led to expect."

Holly winced. "Yeah, so, I haven't been here for a few years and it seems the owner has, uh, had a pretty drastic change of heart vis-à-vis home decor."

They were booked for a two-bedroom suite with a shared living room. As soon as the door closed, Holly began stripping off layers. She kicked off her shoes at the door and began hopping on one foot so she could pull off the sock on the other.

"I'm going to shower and take a nap before dinner!" she said, and headed toward the bathroom, leaving a trail of socks, a sweatshirt, and a ponytail holder behind her.

Tara watched her go, blinking against a combination of confusion and lust. She had to physically stop herself from picking up and neatly folding each piece of clothing. "I'm going to, uh, turn some of the dolls to face the wall, I think."

"They would make a great wedding present for Miriam," Holly called from the bathroom, the door still open. Before she could look away, Tara saw she was now down to a bra and underwear. "You could smuggle several out in a suitcase for her to glitter glue, and the owner would never notice."

It wasn't only that Miri loved haunted dolls and anything macabre that she could bedazzle—though she did; it was that she thrived on maximalism and whimsy and creativity, which were all things Tara had tried to exorcise from her life. In fact, when Miri had lived with her, Tara had never let her keep her art in the Single House.

Maybe they would have stayed together if Tara had let some of Miriam's whimsy in, instead of trying to separate the artist from the artistic temperament, but she'd been too focused on her mission, and how Miriam could aid it. She wasn't sorry they'd split up, but she regretted trying to clip Miriam's wings.

Improbably, Tara's ex-fiancée, and Tara's failures in that relationship, seemed like an emotionally safer subject than the beautiful half-naked woman in her hotel room. *You have got to reexamine your life choices, Sloane.*

Finally, she retreated to her room, making an excuse about having to change out of her sweaty travel clothes for dinner. She sent up a prayer of forgiveness to her poor grandmother, who must be yelling at her from heaven that a debutante never admitted she could sweat. She could if she spent several hours next to a smoking hot woman in a car with the heater turned up!

Could a debutante pass out from lust? She might be about to find out.

Dinner, they'd been informed, was a mandatory social affair for all guests. Tara felt firmly that this was not how bed-and-breakfasts operated, being a place to enjoy a bed, and then a breakfast, but she also didn't want to go out for a nice dinner alone with Holly. How many lustful thoughts, after all, could she have while drowning in dust and lace and dining on (she checked the laminated menu they'd been given, which had certainly been printed on a dot matrix) duchess potatoes and roast goose, in honor of the holiday season?

Amazingly, she could have a *lot* of lustful thoughts, even

while three children—the offspring of, apparently, the only other guests—screamed at the top of their lungs.

Tara cleared her throat and tried to avoid Holly's eye so she wouldn't laugh. "Do you, uh, want kids?" she asked before stuffing a whole duchess potato into her mouth. It was as golden and frilly as any of the B&B's decorations and melted sensuously in her mouth. Debutantes definitely didn't eat whatever this concoction was. It was probably a sin.

Yes today, Satan.

"Oh my God, no!" Holly exclaimed, sounding horrified. Tara had to think back to remember that she was talking about wanting children. "Why would I?!"

Then she peeked furtively at the adjacent parents, who were too caught up in trying to wrangle their children to hear her. "That sounds terrible. I like children in concept but I don't ever want to live with any."

"It doesn't sound terrible to me. I also don't want any, and while I'm aware that other people do, I have trouble understanding why. Eccentric auntie is fine with me."

Holly laughed. "You're the eccentric auntie?! What are the other aunties like?"

"Haha," Tara drawled. "My sister thinks I'm basically a Riot grrrl, and if Cole ever has kids, they'll be used to all the oddballs at Carrigan's and I'll be the unusual one."

"Thanks for not thinking I'm an unfeeling monster for not wanting to be a mother," Holly said wryly.

"It's actually perfect that you don't want kids. Miriam would never believe I was headed toward marriage with someone who did."

Perfect for their charade, but less perfect for Tara's resolve to remember that Holly was un-dateable. These moments of synchronicity were bad news for her daydreams.

"Right, because you never date anyone you wouldn't marry." Holly looked like she wanted to comment on this general life philosophy, but she bit her lip instead. "Well, if we're supposed to be in love, should we practice?"

She reached over and placed her hand on Tara's, stroking one finger down the back of her hand. All of the hair on Tara's arms stood up. Holly ran a foot up the inside of Tara's leg, along her tights. Tara sucked in a breath.

"I didn't say we needed to be in love," Tara corrected in a strained voice, "just that we needed to be seriously considering marriage."

Holly trilled out a laugh, and this time the entirety of the other party looked over at her. She didn't even notice, and Tara was once again captivated by Holly's ability to let herself laugh out loud. "What's the difference?" she asked.

Tara tried to shrug nonchalantly, although she was intensely self-conscious about being judged for this. The truth was, she and Miriam had been in an engagement of convenience, and she had no regrets about that. Miriam had realized she wanted to be in a love story, and eventually she and Tara would have been unhappy because of it. (If she hadn't already been unhappy, because of the whole wings-clipping thing.)

Tara's best-case scenario would be to find someone else who actually *was* interested in a business marriage. Preferably someone without an artistic temperament. But people tended to respond to that proposal with horror.

"I don't enjoy being in love. It's messy, and I need to be

married, for my social standing," she explained. "Hence, I would actually rather not be in love, if I'm getting married."

"That's wild," Holly said, but her voice wasn't censorious, and she hadn't taken her hand off Tara's. "I think I'll play it like I'm desperately in love and trying to hide it from you. I'll make moon eyes at you behind your back and sigh as you walk by."

"I'm sure everyone will absolutely buy that and won't at all wonder what a woman like you would be doing sighing after me," Tara joked. Even if Holly wanted her, the idea that she might fall for a woman like Tara was hilarious. No one ever fell for her. There wasn't anything to fall for, just ice walls to slip down.

"Hmm," Holly said, watching her. "Why wouldn't a woman like me sigh over you? Because I'm too low class to breathe your rarified air?"

She sounded like she was joking, but Tara sensed a sharpness underneath the words.

"Not at all. Because you're vibrant and stunning and kind, and I'm an uptight bitchy lawyer with social anxiety?"

Holly's body relaxed, but she cocked her head.

"How can you be both the rainbow sheep of your family and too boring for a girl to have a crush on you?" She laughed, shaking her head. It was sort of gratifying that she didn't take it as a given that no one would ever have a crush on Tara. She probably hadn't known Tara long enough.

"I can be too much for my family while also being not enough for everyone else," Tara explained. "My family's expectations of decorum are very high—I could be too much by being beige instead of ecru."

Wow, that was way too much information. She pushed her wineglass away. "Sorry. You didn't ask for me to dump that on you."

"I literally did ask, Tara," Holly said, squeezing her hand. "You don't have to apologize."

She had to change the subject. Or eat more potatoes. She could not keep talking about herself. "I think it's time I asked you some questions. You know about me, but I still need to be able to convincingly fake that we're serious."

"I told you I'm an open book," Holly said, spreading her hands. "Shoot."

There was that open book line again. It was a good tactic, saying a lie so many times that people started to believe it. It had worked wonders for George W. Bush. Holly had a sly way of deflecting attention away from deeper interrogation. To get answers, Tara would have to ask something that would catch Holly off-guard. "What are you afraid of?"

"Like, existentially?" Holly asked.

Tara laughed. "No, like, spiders, heights, talking animal animatronics…"

"That's a very specific one."

"They're terrifying. Have you ever been in a Chuck E. Cheese?" Tara demanded. "And you're not getting out of answering this question."

Holly groaned, running her hands through her hair. "I don't like eels."

"Like, existentially?" Tara teased.

"Moray eels grow to ten feet long and attack people." Holly shuddered. "Also, their mouths do not open in a natural way."

Tara stared at her.

"I think I might have watched *The Princess Bride* too many times as a child."

"That's wild, you know that, right?" Tara turned Holly's words around on her again.

Holly grinned. "I do know that."

"When you were little, what did you want to be when you grew up?"

"Rich," Holly said easily. "But I also wanted to work for Rosenstein's because we lived near the home office, where the flagship store started, and it was a point of hometown pride. I thought if I worked there, I would get to eat all the hamantaschen I wanted."

Tara nodded. "Sure. Some people dream of being rich in love, others of being rich in hat-shaped cookies."

"Oh no, let me be very clear," Holly said, pointing a fork full of goose at Tara, "I wanted to be rich in cash money. Because then I could buy hat-shaped cookies, and also, like, health insurance."

There was a time in Tara's life when she would have told Holly that being rich was overrated. When she was young, and desperate to be anything her parents weren't. When she was at boarding school her senior year with a bunch of senators' daughters. When, her first year out of law school, she'd been a divorce attorney for her parents' friends, watching them tear each other to shreds over who got which vacation home.

Having spent years in the criminal justice system and working closely with prison reform activists, she would never, ever say that now.

The B&B owner, Barb, bustled over to make sure they

were enjoying their meal. She was round and glowing, a mother from a Renoir painting come to life. Her radiant smile when Tara praised the goose made Tara feel guilty about how harshly she'd been judging the decor. Perhaps this floral fantasia brought her great peace.

"I'm so glad you girls called me to stay. I don't know why you asked for two bedrooms, though. You look at each other the way my Dotty used to watch me when we were courting."

"You never know," Holly said gently, before Tara could object, "when you'll need to keep up appearances. For safety."

Barb nodded gravely. "Back when we were meeting with the Daughters of Bilitis, we thought by now the young girls would be able to woo each other in public, but for all the rainbows in the Targets, it's dangerous as hell out there. Still, as long as you're here, you don't have to hide. You know that, Holly. You were here when Dotty was still alive."

"I was so sorry to hear of her passing," Holly said softly, reaching out to squeeze Barb's arm. "She was a force."

Barb nodded. "I miss her every day. Although, you'll notice now that she's gone, I'm able to decorate this place the way I always wanted to."

Holly grinned. "I like it. And I'm glad to hear we can indulge in a little PDA while we're here." She leaned over and kissed Tara. It was a peck, the most fleeting glance of lips against lips, but the touch electrified Tara down to her toes. Barb smiled at them indulgently.

"I'm so interested in your time with the Daughters of Bilitis," Tara choked out, trying to seem cool even while her whole body was on fire. "Will you tell me a little about it?"

The Daughters of Bilitis was a lesbian organization founded

in the fifties that had played a huge role in the early gay rights movement.

"Well, you know, Phyllis and Del…" Barb started, and Tara settled in, because she actually was deeply fascinated by that time in queer history, when the movement had been split between people who wanted to appear respectable to get access to rights and revolutionaries who wanted queer liberation.

Tara often felt that she, herself, was torn in two by those opposing instincts.

After dinner, they had intended to take a walk, but the temperature plummeted fast, keeping them inside. It was going to begin snowing tomorrow, so they'd have to get out of Maryland early if they wanted to stay ahead of the storm. Otherwise, they would be spending Christmas here with Barb instead of at Carrigan's.

As Tara carefully applied her series of serums, Holly stood in the bathroom door, watching her.

"You know"—she smirked—"if you're going to blush up to your roots when I kiss you, everyone's going to know we aren't accustomed to it. We might need to practice some before we get to the Christmasland."

Holly bit her lip and batted her eyelashes, just a little. Tara gave her a glance that she hoped was more withering than panicked. "Holly, I think I can manage to kiss a pretty girl convincingly."

"Can you?" Holly asked, a dare in her voice.

Carefully, Tara replaced the lid on her La Mer eye cream

and set the jar down. She pivoted to face Holly, who was wearing an oversized T-shirt and, it appeared, nothing else. Tara felt overdressed in her satin and lace cami and short set, but she'd learned from the cradle that you never slept in clothes you wouldn't want the firefighters to see.

She moved the two steps to the doorway and bracketed Holly with her arms. Holly was taller, her legs as long as a July day, but Tara almost made up the difference in height with impeccable posture and a lawyer stare that made everyone else shrink several inches.

Holly's back slid down the door frame until their heads were even. Tara leaned over slowly, their eyes locked together. Carefully, deliberately, she placed her lips over Holly's.

Holly brought one hand behind Tara's neck to pull her in tighter, and Tara murmured, "Uh-uh," against her mouth. She stopped the kiss from becoming more frantic, letting their mouths slowly get to know one another, holding her body slightly away from Holly's and resisting Holly's attempts to press into her.

When Tara finally pulled away with a last nip of Holly's lower lip, she said, "I don't need to practice. The bathroom's all yours."

She walked away, refusing to show that her knees were weak.

Chapter 8

Holly

olly closed the bathroom door and slipped down its length to the floor.

Holy Kissing, Batman.

She'd never been kissed like that, ever, in her entire life. Her brain wasn't entirely functioning, but she wondered in a distracted way if it would look strange for her to shower again, since she'd done so a couple of hours ago.

But that was before. Actually, everything in her life was now Before. Before the ice queen of Charleston had kissed her so slowly and thoroughly that she'd melted into a literal puddle on the floor.

How had Tara walked away from that kiss? Holly couldn't even stand up!

She'd known that she wanted to get Tara in bed, had been fantasizing for months about thawing that ice, but now she was wondering if sleeping with Tara might actually kill her.

Putting a hand on the sink, she hauled herself up and splashed water on her face. If sex with Tara did kill her, she would gladly face God and walk backwards into hell.

She had to talk Tara into a fling.

Tara didn't date anyone she wouldn't marry, and Holly would never marry again, and the two of them were as romantically compatible as orange juice and toothpaste, but a fling was not dating. A fling was sex with a prearranged end date.

Just when she thought she'd gotten herself together, she remembered those little ice-blue satin and white lace pajamas. Oof. She almost ended up back on the floor.

"We're going to need a plan," she told her reflection. She couldn't think of one right now; she was too full of Christmas dinner and stories about lesbian resistance movements of the 1960s, too tired from a long day of driving, and also, too horny.

"We're going to masturbate, and sleep, and then think of a plan," she amended.

The next morning, Tara shook her awake before the sun rose. "I'm so sorry, but we have to get on the road. The storm is coming in earlier than forecast."

Holly groaned and rubbed her gritty eyes. It had taken her a long, long time to fall asleep last night. Now Tara was leaning over her, and she was sorely tempted to reach up and pull her down into bed. Except Holly was fairly certain she had horrifying morning breath.

"If you acquire coffee, I'll acquire pants," she told Tara groggily.

Tara nodded, turning on her heel and exiting the room before Holly could kick off her covers. Holly needed to remember that Tara had a weakness for her legs. She wondered if she could get away with wandering around the Adirondacks in late December in denim cutoffs.

She checked her phone, which had three texts from Matt complaining that the baker hadn't shown, again, and was she sure she needed those vacation days?

Suck it, Matt. When all this was over, she was definitely getting another job. Preferably as a baker.

There were also, of course, a barrage of messages from her family.

Caitlin: I'm so mad that you're leaving me alone with these people. Mom baked a head of cauliflower in mayo, Hol.

Mom: When can we facetime with you and the new lady?! I need to know her sizes so I can knit her something.

Dad: You said Tara is a lawyer, right? You know we have lawyers in Iowa! I know how your people like to move in together. Maybe consider moving in close to me and your mom?

Dustin: It's not very responsible of you to be so far away, wandering around doing whatever you want, when Mom

and Dad are getting older. They need you here to take care
of them.

Ah, Dustin was obviously starting to feel the tightening bonds
of family and hoping his older sister would come take over. It
was cute that he made it sound like she never came home at all,
when the truth was that she just didn't come home at the holidays, when her mom was at peak sentimentality, and she didn't
stay indefinitely. Or for longer than a long weekend. She fell
back against the pillows and closed her eyes in annoyance, until
the idea of Tara living and working in small-town Iowa made
her laugh so hard her stomach hurt.

No one in the whole Quad Cities could make a decent mint
julep or glass of sweet tea.

When Tara returned with coffee in to-go cups and cinnamon rolls from Barb wrapped in napkins, Holly had clothes on
and her hair semi-tamed into double Dutch braids.

Everything in the suite had been perfectly packed or put
back in its place, including the dolls. She wondered if Tara
had, in fact, smuggled one into her suitcase. Knowing Tara,
she would probably write Barb a check for it. Holly had never
met anyone with a more meticulous sense of fairness.

"I know you're tired," Tara said, shaking Holly out of her
thoughts, "but do you have any experience driving in snow?
It's not my most practiced skill."

"Tara Sloane Chadwick, there's a thing you're not good at?"
Holly teased.

"I'm from Charleston," Tara said flatly. "It doesn't snow
much."

Oh, Holly remembered, Tara did not like admitting when

there was something she was bad at. Unlike cooking, driving in snow wasn't even a traditional Southern belle accomplishment. It was almost like Tara was worried any flaw would be used to justify returning the whole woman for a refund.

"Well, luckily, I'm a Midwestern girl, and I could drive us safely through a snowstorm, blindfolded, in my sleep."

"I don't think that will be required," Tara said, handing Holly the keys. "Just get us out of the DMV metro area in one piece."

Holly flashed Tara a smile that she knew showed her dimples. "As you wish."

"I hate that movie," Tara grumbled.

Holly gasped. "Never mind, deal's off. I cannot even pretend to date someone who hates *The Princess Bride*."

"Give me twenty minutes to tell you why, and you'll hate it, too," Tara told her. "I'm a very persuasive debater."

"Don't you dare," Holly warned her. She slipped into the driver's seat, adjusting the position and mirrors, since Tara had driven the last stretch the day before. She leaned the seat *waaaaay* back to get it to a normal driving angle (Was it years of posture lessons? Why did Tara drive like she was wearing a boned corset? Holly quickly stopped thinking about Tara in a corset), buckled, and reached over for one of Barb's cinnamon buns, which Tara was holding primly in her lap, trying to avoid getting frosting on her dress, some sort of vintage floral skirt suit.

The dress wasn't warm enough for the weather today, much less the weather she expected they would find in Upstate New York, and she idly wondered if Tara actually hated Carrigan's, because she didn't own any warm clothes and she hated feeling like she'd dressed incorrectly for an occasion. As Holly was thinking this, Tara reached over and turned up the heat.

"These are not as good as your cinnamon rolls," Tara observed, "but they're not bad."

Holly bit into one and confirmed Tara's opinion. "The orange zest in the frosting is genius, but she's overproved her dough. I'll email her my recipe."

Pulling out onto the road, through snow that was beginning to swirl menacingly, she glanced over. "Not to blaspheme, but do you mind if we take a break from Legendary Women of Country?"

Tara startled. "Oh, of course. The driver chooses the music. I didn't mean to trap you with eight hours of country yesterday."

"Please. Linda Ronstadt's voice is a national treasure. I just think it might be time to mix it up."

Tara scrolled through her phone. "Um, I have…Beth Ditto, Hayley Kiyoko, Lil Nas X, King Princess, Janelle Monáe, Tegan and Sara, Megan Thee Stallion, Melissa Etheridge, k.d. lang…"

"I'm sensing a trend." Holly laughed.

Tara shrugged primly. "I am who I am."

"Give me your best lesbian shuffle mix, bartender."

The sultry voice of k.d. lang crooning about a constant craving washed over Holly. She smiled. She remembered watching YouTube videos of k.d. singing this song, as a teenager. She slid her eyes over to Tara. "'You Can Sleep While I Drive' might be more apt."

"Oh, don't worry, it's on here. The duet, obviously."

They were supposed to be using this time to get to know each other, but Holly found herself unwilling to break the cozy quiet of listening to gay music together, warm in a car on the highway, surrounded by snow. It was like they were in their own little lesbian snow globe music box.

Being comfortable alone was something Holly had long since gotten used to, but it was rare that she ever spent enough time with someone else to experience this kind of peace with them.

Outside of Philadelphia, the snow, which had been stalking them like a jungle cat for the past two hours, started to become too intense for even Holly's comfort.

"I hate to say this," she told Tara, "but I think we may need to hunker down for a while. Find somewhere for second breakfast, and maybe elevenses."

Tara giggled, which was incongruously cute for her, and Holly wanted to make her do it again.

"I don't know why," Tara said with a smile, "but I wouldn't have pegged you as a fan of hobbits."

"I'm a fan of Liv Tyler. I was at a very impressionable age when *Fellowship of the Ring* came out."

"Hmm." Tara looked like she was doing the math. "You were, what, seven?"

"Some of us have deep roots, Tara. Deep, gay roots."

"You don't have to defend your Liv love to me. I saw *Empire Records* young," Tara assured her. "And I have an aunt in Philly who would probably be thrilled to host us for brunch. I'll call her."

The phone rang, and a raspy Southern drawl that made Tara sound like a Canadian crackled through the car speakers. "Hello, sugar," the woman said. "It's so good of you to call."

She and Tara exchanged pleasantries, each inquiring after the health of the other's relations and offering prayers and condolences when the answers were unhappy, for a full five minutes. Holly was beginning to think they'd be through Philly by the time Tara got around to asking if they could stop.

It wasn't that Holly didn't understand Southern manners, exactly. She was Midwestern, so she was well versed in saying anything but the thing you meant and expecting the other person to understand what you were actually asking. Still, something about the way genteel Southerners circled each other made her skin itch a little.

Finally, Tara said, "Aunt Cricket, I'm driving to New York with a friend, and we happen to be about to drive through your little old town, and I thought, we can't drive right by without stopping to inquire with my favorite aunt."

Cricket snorted. "I'm sure this call has nothing to do with the storm outside and y'all needing a place to stop until it blows over."

"Aunt Cricket!" Tara exclaimed, feigning indignation. "You know I adore you. I would never dream of imposing on your hospitality on account of some snow!"

"Well, I sure wouldn't want you driving in it. Your sainted mother would never let me hear the end of it, if something happened to you. Y'all better come by."

Tara blew out a breath as she hung up and reset the GPS with her aunt Cricket's address.

"Your sainted mother?" Holly asked, amused. "Isn't your mother…"

"Awful?" Tara finished for her. "Yes. Genuinely insufferable.

So is Aunt Cricket, for that matter. I hate that old woman with the fire of a thousand suns."

"Why are we going to her house, then?!" Holly asked, aghast. "We could have stopped in a Waffle House."

Tara groaned. "I wish. I would kill for some cheese eggs. But if my mother found out I stopped in Philadelphia and didn't go to Cricket's, there would be hell to pay."

"What kind of hell, Tara? You're thirty-six years old. You're independently wealthy. You don't have to listen to an old woman yell at you for the way you live your life. You could just, I don't know, not talk to your mother."

Sometimes, listening to Tara talk about her family was like watching *Invasion of the Body Snatchers*. One minute, she was the smartest, wittiest, most interesting woman Holly had ever met, and the next, a switch flipped and she was robotically spouting total nonsense.

Tara turned her body in the passenger seat to look at Holly, although Holly was keeping her eyes on the road due to the limited visibility. In her peripheral vision, she saw Tara's face tighten.

"The kind of hell where I stop being invited to parties, or golf, or polo weekends, and lose the opportunity to chat up the people in those spaces, to make under-the-table deals before we go before the judge so that my client has the best shot possible at trial. The kind of hell where my law firm suddenly realizes that they don't need a lesbian firecracker junior partner who defends clients they see as disposable."

Holly raised an eyebrow. "All for not stopping to see your aunt? What, did she give your mom a kidney? Save her childhood dog from a burning building?"

"It's not about my aunt," Tara told her. "She's not actually my aunt, by the way. She's my grandmother's sorority sister's daughter."

"Oh, of course, the traditional definition of an aunt. Do they make a Hallmark card for that relationship?" Holly joked, and she snuck a fast glance to see a corner of Tara's mouth quirk up. "So is it about control, then? Live your life the way we say, or it's over?"

Tara made a skeptical sound. "They hold access hostage if I don't do things the Right Way. Besides, if I'm doing things the Right Way, things are less likely to light on fire."

Holly sort of thought Tara's relationship with her family could use some lighting on fire.

"Is the access you get worth the hoops you need to jump through?" Holly would cut her own mother off for good if those kinds of machinations were normal.

Tara hugged her knees to herself. "The work needs to be done, and I love it."

Holly digested that.

"The other thing," Tara said quietly, after a long silence, although Holly wasn't sure what the first thing was, "is that we can't pretend to be dating with my aunt Cricket. Actually, we can't pretend to be anything. And there's a non-zero possibility she'll go on a homophobic rant about Cole. Don't stab her with a salad fork, no matter how much you want to."

Holly cleared her throat. *Stay patient.* "Does your aunt Cricket not...know? I thought you were out to your family."

"Oh, I am, and she does. She just enjoys pretending I'm not, to get under my skin."

Here were the body snatchers again—why was Tara putting

up with family (or barely-counted-as-acquaintances that her parents called family) who were this toxic? She ground her teeth in exasperation.

"I can hear you judging me," Tara said. "You're not wrong, but it's not that simple."

It seemed pretty damned simple to Holly.

"You don't have to go in with me." Tara sighed. "In fact, your life will probably be immeasurably improved if you don't. You don't need to be subjected to that."

No way was Holly letting Tara go into that lion's den alone.

"And stay out in the snow?" Holly scoffed. "I'd much rather watch the storm with you."

When they arrived at Cricket's row house, an actual butler was waiting for them on the sidewalk, holding an ineffectual umbrella. He offered to take the car and park it, and Holly looked to Tara for confirmation. Tara nodded, so Holly handed him the key fob.

As their coats were taken by a maid and they were seated in a glass-ceilinged atrium to await Cricket, Holly peered around cautiously.

"Have you ever seen *Suddenly, Last Summer*?" she asked Tara quietly.

"I'm gay and Southern, Holly," Tara whispered, sounding amused. "I am intimately acquainted with all the works of Tennessee Williams."

"This looks like the kind of garden where a woman would find out her son had been eaten alive as penance for his sins,"

Holly hissed, pulling at the neck of her sweater. In the humid heat of the atrium, she suddenly felt suffocated.

"The Venus flytrap, a devouring organism, aptly named for the Goddess of Love," drawled a voice behind her, quoting the play.

Tara stood, running her hands down her impeccably neat skirt to smooth an invisible wrinkle.

"Aunt Cricket, I'm so pleased you were available to host us. It's so gracious of you, especially on such short notice." She was putting on a brand-new voice, one Holly had never heard before.

There was the icy deep Southern politeness she used when she was uncomfortable, and a terse brevity when she liked you enough to not waste your time (ironically, this was her more relaxed voice). This, though, was syrup sweet and full of poison, designed to tell the listener exactly what you thought of them without ever crossing a single social boundary.

It was the Charleston version of Midwestern Nice, and it made Holly glad she wasn't on the wrong end of it.

Tara gestured to her, and she also rose. "Cricket Bailey, this is my friend Holly Delaney."

Aunt Cricket stared at her so long and witheringly, Holly expected her to pull out a monocle. "Delaney. Irish, are you? Explains that whorish shade of hair."

Ah, outdated ideas about redheads on top of everything else. How tired.

The question seemed rhetorical, so Holly didn't bother to respond, though she considered mentioning that we called them *sex workers* now. She didn't think Cricket would appreciate it.

Eventually, Cricket turned to Tara without acknowledging

Holly's outstretched hand. Holly had been in the South long enough to know that whoever annoyed another person into breaking with hospitality rules automatically won a standoff. *Score one for Tara.*

"Your mother tells me you're skipping Christmas with the family to attend the sinful nuptials of that *woman.*" Something about the way Cricket said *woman* led Holly to believe that she really meant a slur of some kind. Whether one about bisexuals, Jews, or women Cricket viewed as loose, Holly didn't know.

Perhaps all three.

"God will never acknowledge their union, you know," Cricket went on.

"Bless your heart," Tara said, the cruelest thing one Southern woman could say to another, "it's *so* kind of you to worry about her eternal soul, but I think I'll leave her relationship with God between her and her rabbi."

She smiled up at the servant who was bringing in finger sandwiches, nodding politely in response to the silent offer of shrimp salad. It would have been seasonally inappropriate except that Cricket seemed to keep her house in a state of perpetual South Carolina summer. Like the Snow Queen in Narnia, but with more carnivorous plant life.

Holly didn't understand how Tara could be so totally unbothered by Cricket's hatred. Holly herself was half tempted to turn the table over and dump her sweet tea on Cricket's helmet of hair, throwing Tara over her shoulder as she ran out the door, snow be damned.

Under the table, Tara dug the nails of her free hand into Holly's thigh, and Holly realized Tara didn't need a white knight—she needed backup.

"How did you end up in Pennsylvania, Miss Bailey? Surely they must miss you below the Mason-Dixon," she asked instead of throwing anything. She may have emphasized the *Miss* in Miss Bailey extra hard, since women like this often had sore spots about being spinsters (instead of all the other things they ought to have sore spots about, since spinsters were amazing, but bigots less so).

Holly was also certain no one had ever missed Cricket Bailey a day in her life.

Cricket turned to Holly. The corners of her mouth turned up in something that she certainly thought resembled a smile, although the fact that no other part of her face moved ruined the effect. It was a little uncanny valley, like someone had programmed an android to smile but had forgotten to code for the muscles above the nose.

"Well, Holly, was it? That's a very interesting story."

She went on to tell them a very long story that was not, in fact, even the tiniest bit interesting and somehow made Holly hate her even more. She paused only for dramatic effect when she wanted her audience to react, and to chide Tara for eating so much, reminding her that she was going to get fat.

At this, Holly shoved her mouth completely full of petit fours.

By the time the butler arrived to inform them that the snow had abated, Holly had moved from wanting to stab Cricket to wanting to stab herself, so that she could be rushed to the hospital and escape this greenhouse of genteel horrors.

Back in the car, Tara shook silently, grasping her hands together to presumably stop her reaction from being noticeable—but Holly noticed.

She wanted to hold Tara, or kidnap her and take her somewhere she would never have to talk to her family again, but most of all, she never ever wanted to get involved with her romantically.

Not that she ever wanted to get involved with anyone romantically, long-term, but if she did, hypothetically, it would be someone who didn't constantly subject themselves to the worst people in the world. Even if Tara hated these people, she'd chosen to stay close to them.

Holly couldn't imagine a life where she had to make nice with any of them, ever again.

She heard They Might Be Giants in her head, singing "Your Racist Friend." Sure, these people would never accept her, and even if she did get involved with Tara, they would make it their sworn duty to tear her to pieces like they'd obviously tried to do to Miriam, but that wasn't the problem.

The problem was, Holly would never accept being in a room with disgusting bigots for any reason, even for Tara.

Chapter 9

Tara

Tara needed to drive off the rage, but she had to wait until she could see through the haze in front of her eyes, so she let Holly start the next leg while she put her forehead on the dashboard and breathed deeply.

When would the point come when she'd stand up to her mother and say she wasn't going to enter a classist, homophobic old snake's house, no matter who she was? When would she admit that the ends didn't always justify the means, if they made her a hypocrite?

She looked up to find Holly chugging Red Bull, driving like a bat out of hell, to the degree that was possible on the snow-covered roads. As pissed as Tara was, at herself and at Cricket, she couldn't deal with Holly's sizzling anger.

She had to somehow explain.

"There's a piece to this puzzle you don't have," Tara said, wringing her hands. "I don't think it will change your mind about the choices I've made but…it might help you understand why."

"Let's hear it," Holly said. "I would love any context for why the fuck you put up with that. Because nothing you've said so far makes that bitch worth talking to."

She didn't know where to start this story, because she'd never told it before, but she gave it a shot.

"I always hated my family, but when I was a teenager, I didn't know how to deal with that, so I ran wild and called it rebellion. Stealing cars and boats, running amok. And, in the end, arson."

Holly spit diet Red Bull out of her nose. "ARSON?"

"There are napkins inside the center console if you need one," Tara said primly. "We didn't intend to commit arson. Well. We did, but slightly less impactful arson."

"I'm going to need some more details."

"When we were seventeen, Cole and I decided it would be a great idea to write 'Eat the Rich,' in fire, in the grass on the front lawn of our parents' country club."

"Oh *no*." Holly let out a horrified little giggle. "I'm guessing it didn't go as planned?"

Tara shook her head. "The whole place burned to the ground. Thank God it was two a.m. and there was no one inside. The flames were…a nightmare. It was so fucking irresponsible and childish. It's a miracle we didn't hurt anyone. It haunts me every day. How close we came to killing people."

"Holy shit, Tara," Holly breathed. "But you didn't go to prison. Did you not get caught?"

Tara shifted in her seat, keeping her face tight and eyes glued on the road ahead of her. "Oh, we did. But my daddy is very good friends with the circuit solicitor and Cole's daddy is Nicholas Jedediah Fraser II. It didn't matter if we were caught, we were never going to do a lick of time. Cole had access to his trust fund blocked; I was sent to boarding school for my senior year. Cole reacted by becoming a criminal and I…"

"Started following every rule there is?" Holly guessed.

Tara shook her head. "No. Well, a little. Mostly I got mad. I saw that if we had been anyone else, our lives would have been over, and maybe rightly so. Not that I believe we should have gone to prison. I don't believe anyone should go to prison—prisons should be abolished—but we should have faced the same consequences as any other South Carolinian. Hell, any consequence."

Holly went silent, either digesting the fact that Tara Sloane Chadwick believed in prison abolition or had once committed arson. "How does what you do now help even the scales?" she asked finally. "Aren't you just part of the system now?"

Tara nodded. "The system needs to be dismantled, and I support the national network of activists working on that any way I can, but mostly I'm just making sure that a few people who get caught in the system get the kind of defense I would have gotten if we'd gone to trial. And, a little bit undoing the work my father's done as a prosecutor for so many years."

"That's admirable," Holly said slowly, obviously carefully choosing her words, "and doable in many ways. Why do you need to stay connected to your family to do it?"

"It would be irresponsible of me to give up my access when it can help people," Tara tried to explain. "I was handed this privilege, and it's the only way I have to use it that might do any good. Honestly, my career is the best thing I've ever done. The most joyful thing I've ever done."

Holly made a grumbling noise Tara couldn't interpret. "Are you sure you're not using them to punish yourself for the fire or something? Seeking absolution through misery?"

Tara snapped. "I don't require absolution from those people." She felt like her skin was on fire.

"Does your family hold it over your head? Have they convinced you that you don't deserve to be happ—"

Tara cut her off. "Holly, with all due respect, this is the life I've chosen. I hear that you don't agree with it. You don't need to."

Just a few minutes ago, Tara had been questioning if she, herself, agreed, but Holly's interrogation made her slam up all her defenses.

No, she didn't think she deserved better. Not because her family had told her so. Actually, once they'd paid to make all the legal trouble go away, they'd only cared that she'd been messy and gauche in her troublemaking. She wasn't using them for absolution, because she didn't think she could be absolved of the kind of reckless endangerment she'd taken part in. Punishment, though—maybe she was staying miserable as punishment. Because misery was what she deserved.

Holly cleared her throat. "This was all the big stuff, right? There's not, like, even bigger stuff you have to tell me about yourself?"

Her tone was lighter, and Tara could tell that an olive branch was being offered. She decided to take it.

"Well," Tara sighed, "I'm also a lesbian."

"What a wild coincidence! I, too, am a lesbian!" Holly joked.

After a long moment, Holly said more seriously, "Okay, you told me your big secret. It only seems fair to tell you mine. You asked me if I had any best friends or ex-girlfriends. I do have both, the same person. My ex-wife. I mean, we're not best friends anymore. We *were* best friends, we got married, we split up, and now we're friendly strangers."

"I didn't realize you're divorced," Tara said evenly. It was another reminder that she and Holly were, truly, mere acquaintances. It might be safer if they stayed that way, but Tara couldn't help being wildly curious about this woman and her past. She didn't ask a question, though, because she'd found that people who wanted to avoid talking about things often balked at questions but spilled all sorts of info when left with an opening.

"We met in middle school, in the comments of a Paramore LiveJournal account. We were best friends in high school, then fell in love. We got 'married' as soon as we graduated, although not legally, obviously. When *Obergefell* came down, we talked about getting legally married and realized that we should probably break up instead. Divorced by twenty-two!" She made a self-deprecating face and a peace sign.

"You seem stunned," Holly said. "Is it the divorced thing, or the Paramore LiveJournal thing? Because if you speak ill of Hayley, I will end this charade right now."

Tara shook her head. "I was trying to do the math. You're a little over thirty now, right? So you've been divorced for almost ten years? Have you..." She wasn't sure how to end that sentence in a way that didn't sound judgmental, which wasn't her intention.

"Been single that whole time? I definitely wasn't celibate,

but I didn't get into any relationships. Not because I wasn't over Ivy, but...we broke up mostly because she wanted to play house and I had grown up poor and didn't want to ever feel stuck, in the same way I had as a kid, in the same little Midwestern town I'd always lived in. So, I didn't want to get involved with yet another girl I would let down in the same way. I still don't want to settle down, have a white picket fence and a dog."

There was something in Holly's voice, and Tara wondered if she was still hung up on her ex. "I was actually going to ask if you've been without a best friend this whole time. Single, I can understand, but I've never been able to live without a best friend."

"Trust me, it's better this way," Holly told her. That wasn't the first time she'd referenced being a bad friend, and Tara was itching to dig deeper. What had convinced Holly that she needed to be a lone wolf?

She was going to figure it out, but she had to be subtle or Holly's walls would go up.

So instead, Tara asked, "I need to know about the fact that your name is Holly and you married a girl named Ivy. Holly and Ivy?!"

Holly laughed. "Well, Ivy never called me Holly, she called me my middle name, Siobhan, which I always wanted to go by but no one could ever pronounce."

"See?" Tara said. "You wanted to go by your middle name, too! It's not weird."

"It's not." Holly shook her head. "Although in the end, I kind of liked that only Ivy called me that. There's something about having someone call you by a name no one else in the world does that feels precious. But yeah, we did think our names were fate when we were kids. Like it was a sign that we were destined to be together. Our little dollar-store wedding with our Goodwill dresses and fake ivy leaves and my grandma's old Christmas lights. We thought it looked so sophisticated. Silly babies."

Smiling, Tara said genuinely, "It sounds beautiful."

All Tara had gotten for her high school graduation was Cole dragging her back from boarding school, since no one from her family had bothered to show up to take her home. A dollar-store wedding lit by little twinkling lights sounded, honestly, really lovely, even if they had been silly babies.

"So, there you go. I didn't go to college because I'd just gotten married and we couldn't afford it, and by the time we split up, I didn't want to. I wanted to live, as much as I could, as free as I could, for as long as I could."

"It sounds like you're living the dream," Tara said, although she couldn't imagine much of a dream life without a community, without friendships. Tara's real friends might all live in the Arctic tundra, but she needed them.

"Yes and no. I mean, it came with some sacrifices, but doesn't every life?"

Holly stopped, like she was trying to figure out how to explain. "I always said, once I was an adult, I would go by Siobhan and I wouldn't care if people didn't know how to spell it, but then..."

"You did care?" Tara guessed. "Or it was too tied up in your ex-wife?"

"Both? It was easier to have a common name waitressing, because anything that invites people to stare intently at the name tag over your boobs and comment on some personal part of you is not ideal."

"Although they do that anyway, I'm guessing," Tara said.

Holly nodded. "Oh, of course. No force in the galaxy could stop cis straight men from deciding that waitresses exist for their personal entertainment. But Siobhan? Somehow I was too tired for the fight."

Tara didn't mean to snort in disbelief, but she did.

"Yes, okay, yes, I've always been the sort of person who leads with my chin and spoils for a fight," Holly rushed on. "I rush in and ask questions later, I do things because so what and fuck people who don't like it. I had blue hair and self-done tattoos and snakebite piercings in Davenport, Iowa. But I...I don't know, I put myself out there all the way in my marriage, and when we broke up, I kind of created another version of myself so no one could see the real me. I hid Siobhan away to keep her safe."

"I wasn't going to judge you," Tara said. "Not for spoiling for a fight, or for leading with your chin. I haven't rushed in or asked questions later or done a single damn thing because so what, for a couple of decades."

It intrigued Tara, Holly's ability to, well, to do anything. To not be constantly frozen in fear and indecision. It made Tara want to know her so much more.

"So, this whole sunshine rockabilly girl thing is just a character?" Tara guessed. "You didn't learn how to do a victory roll and suddenly stop listening to My Chemical Romance or become an optimist?"

Holly's laugh ricocheted through the car.

"I did not. But now, that's who Holly is, and I don't even

know who Siobhan is anymore. She used to be an angry wild child ready to take on capitalism so no one would ever be trapped in poverty, unable to make their own choices about the life they wanted to lead. But then I guess I got disillusioned by constantly fighting what felt like an unbeatable force? Selfishly decided to opt out of the hustle myself and stopped trying to make big structural changes, instead focusing on local actions like community fridges and volunteering as a clinic escort?"

Tara shook her head. "There's nothing wrong with micro, intra-community action. Honestly, it might be the best possible choice right now. And the clinics that are left always need escorts."

"That's a very generous read on my life choices," Holly observed. "Anyway, now I'm kind of stuck being this version of me. Which is fine. It's a pretty good life."

"I'll start calling you Siobhan, if you start calling me Sloane," Tara told her. As soon as she said it, it felt way too cheesy, but Holly flashed her a huge grin.

Maybe it had been just the right amount of cheesy.

"Siobhan and Sloane sounds like a seventies detective show," Holly joked. "If we get lost in this storm, we can start a new life for ourselves somewhere in Delaware, solving crimes and baking cinnamon rolls. But okay, let's make a deal. On this trip, no matter who we have to pretend to be for anyone else, we'll only be our real selves with each other."

She took one hand off the wheel, which made Tara's heart stop for an instant, only to hold it out for a fist bump, which Tara returned.

"We might have both chosen lives where we wear masks all

the time," Tara agreed, "but we can have a little bit of our real selves when we're together."

They fell into a quiet that was less comfortable than the silences they'd shared earlier. Tara never talked about the arson, ever, even with Cole. It felt too vulnerable. She started to retreat back into herself.

Holly must have noticed, because she started to sing.

Actually, she said, "Are you ready? Are you ready?" Which is what Melissa Etheridge said to k.d. lang when they dueted live on Melissa's "You Can Sleep While I Drive." Tara knew those words very well. How many times had she watched that video, wanting a girl to ask her to drive away into the night?

Holly motioned impatiently for Tara to join. Tara laughed and picked up the harmony. They sang at the top of their lungs, steaming up the windows of the Mercedes with their breath as the scenery flew past. Tara's heart felt like it would float out of the car and be carried into the snowy sky by the swirling winds.

She felt like she could fly.

"Thank you. I needed that. Is there a reason we're heading out of Pennsylvania like we're being pursued?" she asked after she caught her breath.

Holly shrugged. "It seemed like I shouldn't waste any time getting you to Cole. I know you're not a big fan of Carrigan's, but it *is* rumored to have magical healing powers."

Not that she would ever admit it, but now that the molding wallpaper had been replaced, she was looking forward to being with her friends, even if it was in the unsettling chaos of Carrigan's.

Hell, maybe she'd misjudged it. The last time she'd been there, she and Miriam had been in the middle of a breakup, and her heart and ego had been too bruised for her to appreciate its particular brand of kitschy charm. Now that she was close with Hannah and she and Miriam had mended their friendship, she thought she might be able to let herself have fun there. Mrs. Matthews, the cook at the inn and Hannah's mother-in-law, gave hugs like a weighted blanket, to begin with, and Tara could use one. She could also probably use some fun.

"I'm sorry I took you into that," she said, because it needed to be said.

"I agreed to go," Holly pointed out. "Let's not give Cricket Bailey any more of our day than we already have. We still don't know enough about each other to convince anyone we're dating. Let's do a rapid-fire question round. You start."

Tara tried to think of a good question, and then she remembered the game the Carrigan's crew had played at Thanksgiving last year, learning each other's personalities by their pop culture preferences.

"Favorite guilty pleasure TV show?" she asked.

"I'm never guilty about my pleasure," Holly said immediately. "Except for how much Bravo I consume. I feel a little guilty about that. You?"

"Oh, uh . . ." Tara had been distracted by Holly's mention of pleasure and hadn't thought of her own answer. "I watch a lot of teen dramas in the background while I'm working. I have more feelings about *Outer Banks* than is probably healthy for me, an adult. Your turn."

Holly was shaking her head over Tara's answer, which was fair.

"Desert island Disney movie. Be honest. Don't try to be cool and say *Atlantis* or *Treasure Planet*."

Now it was Tara's turn to raise an eyebrow. "Do I look like I've ever done anything to seem cool in my life? I'm wearing vintage linen on a road trip, in the snow. Although those are both brilliant, underrated masterpieces, the answer is *Frozen II*."

"Interesting. Even though they didn't let Elsa be a lesbian?"

Tara scoffed. "Please. It's not up to Disney to let Elsa be a lesbian or not. She *is* a lesbian. She's ours."

"Mine is *Hercules*."

"Oh, now who's trying to look cool by naming an underrated masterpiece?" She rolled her eyes.

"I really love Meg!" Holly protested.

"Do people call you Merida?" Tara asked. "And, follow-up, how do you feel about *Brave* as a film separate from that?"

They bounced questions back and forth all the way into New York, trading jokes and sour gummy worms and sideways smiles. Tara's rage at Aunt Cricket and disappointment in herself slowly gave way to her anxiety about being back at Carrigan's Christmasland.

It was going to be great. She and Holly would have fun, and everyone would see her head over heels for a beautiful redhead, totally chill about the whole situation.

Well, no one would ever describe Tara as "totally chill," but maybe she could manage icily cool. It should be easy, because the more uncomfortable Tara got, the further she tended to disappear behind her armor of cold Southern politeness.

When they finally pulled through the wrought-iron fili-
gree gates at the front of the Carrigan's property, Tara did her
best to take it in with an unbiased eye. The interlocking Cs
were a pretty design, and the gate itself had obviously been
recently cared for. She remembered it as rusted, hanging from
its hinges, but it wasn't at all run-down. Now that she knew
more about Mr. Matthews, Levi's dad, she knew he would
never let the first glimpse of Carrigan's be shoddy for guests.

Because it was the middle of the Christmas season, the
front lawn was covered in decorated cut trees, while the
acreage that stretched out behind the old Victorian inn
was a sea of snow-covered growing evergreens. Carrigan's
hosted a Christmas festival starting the first of November
that included, according to Cole, reindeer races, gingerbread
house and snowman-building contests, a very intense cookie
swap, and, somehow, military battles among nutcrackers
named Steve.

Tara hadn't known Carrigan's existed while she and Miriam were together. In fact, until its previous owner, Cass Carrigan, had died and unexpectedly left part of the business to
her nieces Hannah and Miriam, Tara's ex hadn't set foot there
for a decade.

The day Cass died, Miriam had told Tara that she needed to
go to the Adirondacks to sit shiva, and she'd never returned to
Charleston. Instead, she'd fallen in love, saved the business, and
found a big, wonderful family. Tara had always empathized
with the uptight blond fiancée at the beginning of every Hallmark movie who was so obviously wrong for the main character, but she'd never thought she would become one.

The sound of the car pulling up to the front door of the inn brought Noelle out to investigate, and Tara saw her start a bit as she realized who they were.

Climbing out from the driver's side, Tara brushed herself off and extended a hand. "Noelle, thank you so much for inviting me. I appreciate that I might not be the top of your list for people you want at your wedding."

Noelle quirked a lip up, and Tara had to hand it to Miriam—the woman was smoking hot. With a high pompadour with shaved sides, suspenders over a flannel shirt, beat-up work boots, she was a fat dapper butch dreamboat, and Tara could give credit where credit was due.

"I'm grateful you were willing to come. It means a lot to Miri, and let's face it, you didn't do anything wrong at any point in the proceedings."

Tara made a so-so gesture with the hand she still had extended. "I was kind of a bitch."

"Hell, *I* was kind of a bitch. That's Miri's type!" Noelle pointed out, and wrapped Tara up in a bear hug.

Oh God. She had not expected this. She didn't have a script ready. What she ended up saying was "You smell good."

Noelle laughed down to her gut. "You too. Magnolias?"

"You can take a girl out of Charleston..." Tara said. She heard a throat clear behind her. "Oh, gosh! Let me introduce you to my girlfriend, Holly."

The word *girlfriend* rolled around in her mouth, unfamiliar but delicious, like the first time you tried something that you didn't expect to love. This was it. It was time for them to put on their act.

Holly was coming forward to shake hands with Noelle when a giant flash hurtled toward them, blond hair reflecting the lights of the Christmas trees like a halo. Tara didn't even try to brace herself, because she knew what was coming, and she'd learned long ago that there was no stopping him. She was hoisted into the air, the summer they'd spent practicing ice-skating jumps and the lift from *Dirty Dancing* rushing back, her muscle memory taking over. She extended her arms as she was spun in dizzy circles, Cole whooping the whole time.

"You're heeeeeeeere!!!!!" he shouted, finally letting her down into his arms, but not far enough down that her feet touched the ground. He carried her back over to Noelle and Holly like a kid with their favorite stuffy.

"Tara's here," he said to Noelle, and she could hear the smile in his voice.

"I noticed," Noelle deadpanned. "Holly's here, too."

"Don't pick me up," Holly warned him. "I will puke hot Cheetos and Diet Mountain Dew all over you."

"Might be worth it," Cole ventured.

Tara coughed. "Nicholas. Jedediah. Fraser. The third. I require oxygen."

Cole made a *pfft* sound like he didn't believe this, but he released her from his bear hug, spinning her around so she could rest her back against his chest, wrapping his arms around her neck and resting his head on hers.

"Can I take your luggage?" Noelle asked. "Since Fraser here seems unlikely to let go of you long enough to do it?"

"I'll help!" Holly offered. To Tara, she said, "Obviously

doesn't like you. Hi, Cole!" She waved, as she followed Noelle inside.

"Hi, Holly! Great to see you! Did you bring coconut cake? Who doesn't like you?!" Cole demanded of Tara. "I'll beat them up!" He paused. "Well, I won't beat them up, but I'll empty their bank account!"

She sighed in pretend frustration at his general too-muchness, but she breathed more deeply when he was around. Resting her head back against his chest, she told him, "You know the rules, no hacking for personal gain or petty vengeance."

"Bo-ring," Cole singsonged. He spun her around, his hands on her shoulders. "Okay, now that they're gone, how's it going? With the fake dating scheme? Tell me everything. Are you using it as a ruse to get into her pants? I feel like you could just ask. Have you kissed? I know these kinds of hijinks are not usually your scene, so if you need anything at all, I'm here to help."

She put her hands on his face. "I'm not telling you anything until you tell me what's going on with you and the hot bartender mayor," she said seriously.

A blush rose up Cole's neck, all the way up his face and down his bare chest.

Wait.

"Cole, why aren't you wearing a shirt? Or socks? Boat shoes are not appropriate for this weather!"

He shrugged happily, smiling his lopsided smile that was meant to make people forget whatever trouble he was up to. "You cannot deflect from this conversation about your *fake dating.*"

This last part was nearly yelled.

"Fraser, I can deflect from any conversation. Don't underestimate me. And keep your voice down! This won't work if you announce it to the whole Adirondacks!"

Cole looked at her skeptically. "Do you not trust me, a professional secret keeper for, like, world governments, with whom you once committed felony arson that I told no one about for decades, to keep this secret for you? Because I'm going to be very offended."

She narrowed her eyes at him. "Who did you already tell?"

"Sawyer, but he's not going to tell anyone! He was there when I talked to you." Cole shrank, his shoulders rolling in and his smile turning into a grimace. "I'm sorry! But I swear, it's actual state secret time from here on out. Forgive me? Because I'm keeping it a secret from Mimi and you know I would never do that for anyone else."

He glanced over her head and said dramatically, "Mimi! Look who's here!"

Tara turned to see her ex-fiancée.

Miriam Blum was a tiny, elven force of nature. Standing five foot on a tall day, her wild mass of dark brown curls gave her another couple of inches in every direction. She was wearing a pair of paint-spattered skinny jeans, a hoodie so big she must have stolen it from Cole with the cuffs rolled up to fit her arms, and ancient Doc Martens Tara had never seen before. She supposed you rarely needed to wear Docs in the heat of South Carolina.

They'd seen each other since their breakup, although sparingly. Miriam had come to Charleston earlier in the year to pack up her warehouse of art and the rest of her stuff, and make her apologies for the way things had ended. Tara had gotten over the situation easily enough, since mostly her pride had been wounded. She and Miriam had entered into an engagement of convenience, with the clear purpose of never falling in love, and the engagement had ceased to be convenient for Miriam.

She'd been hurt, as a friend, that Miriam hadn't been more honest with her, but with some distance she acknowledged that most people wouldn't have known how to handle the situation Miriam had found herself in, especially in the middle of grieving.

How do you call your partner and say, "Hey, good news/bad news, I met my soulmate"?

Still, Miriam hung back, looking nervous. A small part of Tara wanted to be a little mean and let her squirm, but her training was too ingrained. "Miriam!" she said, putting on her brightest smile (not even a fake one!) and offering a hug that Miriam accepted. "It's so wonderful to be here. You look incredible."

This, too, was genuine. Miriam's skin was brighter, her eyes less sad. Tara would not have described her as haunted before, or even dulled—she was one of the most vibrant people Tara had ever met—but the difference, between then and now, was striking. Carrigan's, and love, suited her.

"You look..." Miriam paused. "Cold. Beautiful, but cold! Let's get you inside."

She wanted to say the cold didn't bother her, but she was a Southern girl through and through. Give her 90 degrees and 100 percent humidity over a white Christmas any day. Following Miriam into the warm foyer was a relief.

Until she was hit by the wall of noise, color, and light that was Carrigan's at Christmas.

Why were there real trees inside the inn?! Were there not enough on the front lawn? Why was every single tree decorated in a different theme, none of them coordinating with the one next to it? Every tree was lit up like a lighthouse, and not a single white bulb anywhere to be found. As Tara tried to process this onslaught of visual information, the Chipmunks started playing overhead, imploring Christmas to not be late (How could Christmas be late? It was always on the same day), and the trees began blinking in unison.

Cole's familiar weight at her back might have been the only reason she didn't faint.

"Oh God," she said, and found she had actually clutched her actual pearls, "this is . . . really something."

Miriam snorted. "It's not exactly your aesthetic, I know. But look! We completed the installation of the wallpaper!"

"I don't know how I would be expected to see the wallpaper behind all the trees, garland, tinsel, and other varied holiday ephemera," Tara said flatly, "but I can certainly no longer smell it, which is a wonderful sign."

"You know," Miriam observed, "for a woman who has spent all her life in a place that mildews like it was the city's vocation, you're very picky about this issue."

There was simply nothing to do but ignore that remark. Miriam, who knew her well, would expect that of her, so she wasn't even being rude.

"Noelle took Holly upstairs to your room if you'd like to get settled. Hannah is in the kitchen with Mrs. Matthews." Miriam gestured to the left, where a swinging door opened to the dining room and kitchen. "Levi is helping his dad fix something in the reindeer enclosure."

She'd only met Levi in person for a few minutes, when he had, at her request, come to kidnap Cole off her couch this past summer, but she was looking forward to seeing him again. And eating his food. Why be friends with a famous chef if they don't feed you, after all?

A cat of enormous size, with ear tufts as wide as a normal cat was long, sauntered through Cole's legs to wind himself around Tara's.

"Oh, and Kringle is, apparently, here, although he's supposed to stay in the Carriage House."

Kringle chirped at them. Cole gathered him up and flipped him upside down, carrying him like a baby, if babies weighed thirty pounds and had tails the length of an adult human arm.

"Come on," he said, though Tara wasn't sure if he was talking to her or the cat, "I'll show you to your room."

Chapter 10

Holly

Carrigan's Christmasland felt like taking an acid trip in an abandoned 1960s department store. Holly had expected it to be wild, because Miriam's upcycled antique art business, Blum Again Vintage & Curios, had a strong whiff of that energy, and Holly suspected Miriam had gotten it from her great-aunt Cass. Still, even after looking at the social media feeds for the farm and scrolling over photos and videos posted by guests, she wasn't prepared for the full sensory experience. She wondered how Tara was handling it—Holly had noticed that Tara dealt best in minimal sensory environments.

"So, uh...Tara really likes women with a huge amount of curly hair, huh?" Noelle asked, shoving her hands in her pockets.

She looked so uncomfortable with this situation, escorting

her fiancée's ex-fiancée's new girlfriend around. Holly had felt some general indignation on Tara's behalf, about how Miriam and (perhaps unfairly) by extension Noelle had handled the whole situation last year, but watching Noelle squirm made Holly soften a little toward her. Besides, Tara hadn't brought her here to fuck with Miriam and Noelle, so Holly decided to behave herself and try to put Noelle at ease.

She smiled. "I would have said sassy power bottoms, but I'm sure the curls help."

Noelle sputtered, clearly laughing in spite of herself. There, now she wasn't overthinking anymore.

From outside the door, she heard Tara's and Cole's voices coming down the hall. "I booked you in here," Cole said, and the door opened, right into Noelle's back.

Tara walked past Cole into the room and cut a suspicious glance at him. "I see you've booked us both into this beautiful room with one bed," she said, her voice dangerously even.

"Well, it only made sense," Cole explained gleefully. "The rooms with two beds are needed for families arriving together, and you'll obviously be sharing a bed. Since you're dating."

Internally, Holly cheered.

"It's so cozy and perfect!" she exclaimed, pulling Tara to her by her dress and snaking an arm around her waist. "We've been talking about how excited we are to have a few days away together, so don't be surprised if we hole up for some quiet time. It's so hard to get quality alone time in the city."

Tara's voice dropped to its most syrupy drawl. "We can't wait. But y'all must have a million things you need to do! We won't keep you any longer."

Noelle obviously got the message, although Cole looked like he wanted to pretend he hadn't understood Tara's unspoken direction to get the hell out. Tara pinned him with a stare that made him actually shiver. He scuttled out after Noelle.

When they were gone, Holly cleared her throat. "This is a beautiful room."

It really was.

Unlike the public areas (what little she'd seen), which were full of kitschy wallpaper and tacky antiques, this room had obviously been decorated by someone with an eye toward quiet minimalism—from what Tara had told her, Holly guessed it was Hannah. She also guessed that Cole had chosen this room specifically, of all the rooms with one bed, because he knew that Tara would need somewhere with less visual stimulation to escape to. He had, after all, spent many long hours in Tara's Charleston house, including a stint crashing on her couch, so he understood her need for aesthetic quietude.

This room wasn't white, like Tara's house, but a muted, dusky rose. All the fabrics were a variation on the same shade, with greens sprinkled throughout, like leaves peeking through the petals of a rose. It should feel dated. The palette, in theory, was reminiscent of a 1980s office, but the lines and furniture choices were modern enough that it looked fresh.

Tara nodded in agreement, but she was biting her lip. "It's very small." She had kicked off her shoes at the door and set her purse down on the dresser and was now walking around the bed, which took up most of the room.

"It's a converted Victorian mansion," Holly pointed out. "Not exactly known for gigantic rooms."

"Oh, I know," Tara said, sounding distracted, "I just...don't know where we're both going to sleep."

Holly frowned at her. "In the bed?" Why was this a confusing concept?

"Do you think that's a good idea?" Tara worried, smoothing the already perfectly smooth comforter. "We're already not doing a great job of keeping our hands to ourselves."

Here it was. This was Holly's chance to convince Tara that they should have a fling.

They'd already bonded, been through hell (aka Aunt Cricket) together, told each other their darkest secrets. They had cemented the "friends" part of Friends with Benefits, so why not move on to the benefits?

"I think it's an incredible idea, actually. I personally think we should stop keeping our hands to ourselves," Holly told her, sitting down on the bed so that she could look up at Tara with big eyes, and Tara could see down her shirt. "I haven't stopped thinking about that kiss. Have you?"

Instead of answering, Tara turned partly away so Holly couldn't see her face. Holly was about to push a little, when a horrifying yowl came from outside, and something began rhythmically thumping the door. Because she was nearest, Holly went to open it, if only to stop the thumping. The most enormous tortoiseshell cat she'd ever seen sauntered in, tail twitching, and sat at Tara's feet to yell at her. It was larger than Holly's childhood family dog.

"What *is* that?" she asked. She'd known the farm had a cat, from her deep dive into their social media, but this was not a farm cat. This was a mutant.

"That's a Kringle," Tara said, looking down at the beast.

"He's a Norwegian Forest cat. No one knows where he came from. If you ask the people who live here, they'll tell you he's magic because he's a boy tortoiseshell, but obviously there's no such thing as magic cats."

The cat in question continued screaming at her. She sighed and picked him up. He wrapped himself around her neck.

"Mostly he belongs to Levi and Noelle, as far as I can tell, but he goes wherever he wants, if his humans are to be believed," Tara continued. He purred, whapping her in the face with his tail. Watching the perfect Tara Chadwick splutter as a pony disguised as a cat tickled her was a sight Holly would always remember.

"I think you may be too quick to dismiss the idea that he's magic," Holly told her. "That's a forest spirit, obviously."

A lanky man with a tall swoop of brown hair topped with a floral satin yarmulke stuck his head through the still-open doorway. He was wearing a fringed leather vest and smudged eyeliner. "Hey, Tara, I'm so glad you're here! Have you seen— Oh, yep, you *have* seen Kringle. I heard him yelling and thought he was in trouble, but obviously he was being dramatic. Wonder where he gets that from?"

This last sounded like it was a joke, although Holly wasn't sure what the joke was. The man, who she recognized as Levi Matthews from both Instagram and the several magazines he'd recently graced the cover of, turned to her. "You must be Holly! Hi!" He stuck out his hand.

"It's great to meet you," she told him. "I hear you also recently had a wedding."

He grinned, and his face turned from interesting to breathtaking. She didn't watch food TV, or find men attractive, but she suddenly thought she might be wrong on both fronts. No wonder his cooking show was such a runaway hit.

"Which Tara did not make an appearance for. My wife may never forgive her," he joked. "Speaking of unforgiving, dinner is almost served and my mom does not look kindly on people who are late. Do you want to head down with me?"

Holly looked at Tara, who shrugged under her cat scarf.

"We'll finish the other discussion later," Holly promised with a wink, and she heard Tara draw in a sharp breath.

To Levi, Tara said, "You told me about the wedding less than twenty-four hours before it happened."

"More than enough time to hop a flight," Levi observed, and Tara huffed. From around her neck, Kringle huffed, too. Her huff turned into a squeak when Levi hugged her. "I'm glad you're here. Hannah's really glad, and, you know, Hannah's happiness is priority number one."

Tara pulled back and gave him a Lawyer Look, one that Holly suspected compelled many people to tell her the truth.

"Now," he amended. "Hannah's happiness is priority one now."

"It's good to see you, too, Matthews," Tara said. "I like the show."

Holly wouldn't have guessed that those two would get on well together, since from everything she knew about Levi he was pure unbridled chaos and Tara was the dictionary definition of Lawful Good, but they seemed to enjoy one another, walking arm in arm down the stairs, chatting about a recent episode of *Living Bold* that Levi had done featuring knishes.

There was not an empty chair in the dining room, and diners were spilling over into the high-ceilinged great room across the hall. Cole was acting as a waiter, and a short brunette who vaguely resembled Miriam was directing traffic.

"Who is that?" Holly whispered to Tara. She didn't recognize the person from the Carrigan's Instagram feed.

Tara looked puzzled. "I've never met them. Levi?"

"Oh, that's Gavi," he said. "They're a Rosenstein cousin we poached from B and P."

"Bread and Pastries," Holly told Tara, who seemed confused. "That's a real Davenport insider thing to call it." To Levi, she said, "I grew up about half a mile from the home office."

"For me it's a 'married into the family and it's confusing that my in-laws and their business have the same name' thing," Levi countered. "But let's chat about old B and P recipes sometime. I bet you grew up eating some things I'd love to be able to reproduce."

Rosenstein's Bread and Pastries, begun in the 1800s by a Ukrainian immigrant, was a nationwide chain of bakeries focused on traditional Jewish recipes, but it was also her hometown business success story. She'd have to ask if Gavi had been at the home office and see if they could bond about Iowa. Not that Holly had a lot of positive feelings about Davenport, personally, but it wasn't a bad town for other people, and the Rosenstein's flagship store was one of the best things about it.

Tara nodded, her face clearing. "The new guest services manager!"

If Holly remembered correctly, Hannah had previously been in charge of both guest services and event planning, so they must have hired on extra help.

"Holly, I'm going to leave you with Cole to find a place to sit, and take Tara to say hi to my mom," Levi told her.

Tara's eyes widened and she mouthed, *Help me*, at Holly, but Holly was not going to save her from being well-liked by very lovely people.

She was, however, going to use the cover of being a loving girlfriend to get some more kissing in.

Before she could be drawn away, Holly swung an arm around Tara's neck and kissed her hard. "Come back to me soon, babe," she said before releasing Tara and watching her walk off. Maybe it was Holly's imagination, but she did look a little disoriented. Good.

Meanwhile, Cole slung an arm around Holly's shoulder and led her toward a table, where he introduced her to Sawyer, who might or might not be his boyfriend.

Holly wasn't sure what she'd expected from the man who had—according to Tara—made Cole realize, with one hand-shake, that he was gay, but somehow she was unsurprised that he was the opposite of the typical Charleston bro. Slight, with a waxed mustache and long hair in a French braid, he looked like he had a lot of thoughts about whiskey and might own a pocket watch.

Years of waitressing had made her very good at talking to strangers, which stood her in good stead as she was seated next to a family that told her they had been visiting Carrigan's for generations. The grandparents, in fact, had gotten engaged at Carrigan's one Christmas. Holly learned that, every year, on December 23, the Christmasland hosted a special anniversary dinner for all the couples who'd been engaged or married at Carrigan's over the years. It was supposed to be good luck.

Holly, who was as interested in either good luck or marriage as she was a hole in the head, found herself immensely charmed by all of it regardless. Still, she kept one eye out for Tara to return from the kitchen.

Cole leaned over Sawyer to stage-whisper to her. "Okay," he said, gesturing with a roll. "I hate to plot against my oldest and dearest friend, who is basically my sister—"

"You do not hate it at all, Nicholas Fraser," Holly interrupted.

Sawyer snorted. Cole smirked. "Of course I don't. And anyway, I'm not plotting *against* her. I'm plotting *for* her. And what I want is for her to have some damn fun."

"I'm not plotting with you to get your best friend laid."

He didn't appear convinced.

"Oh," she clarified, "I'm definitely plotting to get your best friend laid, no question, but I'm doing fine on my own. I don't need your help. It would be weird. It doesn't feel great."

"She's right, Cole. It's weird," Sawyer said, stealing the roll from Cole's hand and biting it.

No adult had ever sighed so dramatically. "Why does everyone have so many morals on this farm?" Cole whined. "If you regret this choice and need my help, you let me know."

"You an expert in romance now?" Holly asked skeptically. "From what I hear, you've seriously dated one person, ever, if in fact you two are seriously dating." She pointed between them.

Cole flushed. Sawyer rolled his eyes. "You can tell people I'm your boyfriend, Nicholas."

"I can't," Cole said, this time actually whispering, his voice serious, "say that to anyone until I've said it to Tara. She has to be the first to know."

Sawyer squeezed his hand, and Holly found her eyes unexpectedly wet. Something about this massive goofy man who was never serious about anything being so deadly serious that he had to tell Tara about his love life first pierced her. Maybe it was because she knew that Tara did not believe she held that space in Cole's life, or even deserved to, because Tara believed that she herself did not deserve to be anyone's other half.

"Does she know how much you love her?" Holly asked.

Cole looked confused. "Obviously. Why wouldn't she?"

That made her heart ache, because even the person who knew her best didn't truly see her. Hadn't noticed what she wasn't saying.

"TARA, FINALLY!" Cole shouted, and Holly turned to see her walking up to the table. "You know how much I love you, right?"

Tara blinked at him and smiled a small, pained smile. "Yes, Cole. I know exactly how much you love me."

Holly didn't know Cole well enough to know if he heard what she was really saying, but she thought she saw him stiffen a bit. Maybe something real and serious would come out of this fake dating shenanigan and they would have a real talk.

Sawyer rose.

"Tara, I would know you anywhere, based on Cole's description," he said, embracing her once Cole had released her and then holding her at arm's length to look at her.

Her eyes widened. "Oh no."

He grinned.

"Stunning blonde, eyeliner wings so sharp they could kill a man, always dressed like she raided Chanel's archives."

"Cole, you know I don't wear Chanel," Tara objected. "Coco Chanel was a Nazi."

"So is your aunt Cricket," Cole pointed out.

Holly laughed so hard tea shot out of her nose.

Once they were seated, Tara put an arm along the back of Holly's chair as if it were the most natural thing in the world, and Holly reached up to weave their fingers together. She turned to Tara, who gave her a little smile, and on her other side, Cole winked at her.

"So," asked the wife who had gotten engaged at Carrigan's, "how did you two meet?"

Holly stared at Tara, her eyes wide. How had they not come up with a cover story? Two weeks to prep and two days on the road, and neither of them had thought to wonder how they were meant to have gotten together?

Tara squeezed her fingers reassuringly. "Let me tell the story, babe. I love it."

"You *are* better at it." Holly smiled in a way she hoped read as beguiled. They should be able to wing this—they were both professionally trained at reading people. Defense attorneys and diner waitresses had to be good storytellers.

Taking a deep breath, Tara looked around the table, obviously assessing her audience. "Holly is a waitress at my neighborhood cafe, and I went there a lot for cake and coffee, and to talk to the beautiful redhead. I know it's cheesy to have a crush on someone who's paid to smile at you, but what can I say? She was so snarky, and funny, and she bakes a killer pastry. I couldn't stop thinking about her."

"What Tara's not telling you," Holly interrupted, "is that she was far too honorable to flirt with someone who was paid to smile at her, so I kept mooning over her, bringing her pastries, and desperately trying to get her to ask me out, for months."

The husband clasped his hands to his heart. "So what happened? How did you break the stalemate and get together?"

Under the table, Holly kicked Tara, urging her to finish the story. This was the part where reality diverged from make-believe.

"Well, one night I was leaving as Holly was getting off work, and she asked where I was headed. I said home, to open a bottle of wine and watch a Bravo marathon, and she asked if I wanted some company," Tara said, winking at Holly.

"I do love *Vanderpump Rules*." Holly nodded.

The wife laughed. "So you invited yourself over to Netflix and chill, and the rest is history? That's fantastic."

It did sound fantastic, Holly thought. A little bit of her wished it had happened that way.

They stayed close all through dinner, Holly leaning against Tara while they waited for dessert, Tara leaning over to whisper in Holly's ear when coffee came. It didn't seem to affect Tara at all, this dance they were putting on for her friends. Apparently, she'd been right that she didn't need practice—she was an absolute natural at having a fake girlfriend. Every time their skin brushed, a bolt of lust shot through Holly. She studiously ignored how much she didn't hate the handholding, either.

This is make-believe. Keep your head on straight. You don't even like all this stuff—your goal is short-term, hot sex.

As she thought this, Tara reached over to push a curl off her forehead and then "lovingly" caressed Holly's ear. Their eyes caught, and Holly almost got lost in a very dirty fantasy. How were they going to keep it up for several more days? It had only been a couple of hours, and Holly already felt like she was going to combust.

If this fake dating thing was going to work, they were going to need to actually sleep together. It was the only way Holly would get through this weekend without tearing off her skin from lust.

Back in their room, Holly had a plan, and that plan was to look so hot coming out of the bathroom that Tara threw her on the bed and took full advantage of her. The problem with this plan was that she had not accounted for Tara's skincare regimen.

Holly said, "I'll just wait for you to be done before I use the bathroom."

Tara said, "Oh, it will take me absolutely hours before I'm done. I insist that you go first."

As a result, Holly was relying on plan B, which involved lying seductively across the bed. It wasn't as satisfying as plan A, or as subtle. A person could, theoretically, happen to come out in sexy pajamas and saunter toward the bed. It was difficult to nonchalantly lounge in a seductive manner.

Still, she had tiny shorts and willpower, which had to get her somewhere.

The longer she sat propped up on the pillows, her legs extended over the covers, getting colder and colder, the more she suspected that Tara was staying in the bathroom until she thought Holly was asleep. Even with a fire burning, the room was too chilly for her to stay as she was.

It was time to resort to plan C.

She braided her hair, because having to untangle it tomorrow morning was not worth the potential sexy factor tonight, crawled under the blankets, and pretended to be asleep. She heard the door to the bathroom creak open, and then open all the way. Light footsteps crept to the bed, and then Holly felt Tara's weight sink down. On top of the blankets.

Well, if she could stand the cold, Holly guessed Tara had won this round.

This was what she thought, until she woke up in the middle of the night with Tara's silky legs tangled with hers, Tara's sleek head tucked up under her chin. She could smell Tara's breath, feel her heartbeat, and she tried to focus on her own breathing but she couldn't go back to sleep. She lay there, getting intimately acquainted with Tara's skin as Tara, in her sleep, turned into a very handsy octopus.

When one of Tara's hands closed over her breast, she couldn't stop herself from squeaking as her nipple immediately became so hard it was painful.

She heard Tara's breathing change, and then the hand was gone. "Oh my God, Holly, I'm so sorry!" Tara jumped up, taking the top blanket with her in her rush to get out of the bed.

"Please come back to bed," Holly said, rubbing her eyes. She was nearly vibrating with sexual frustration. She'd planned to be cool, to act unaffected and hard to get to pique Tara's interest. Instead, she whined like a needy puppy. "Tara," she begged, "please. If you don't let me fuck you, I'll die."

Tara laughed, which was perhaps not the response one hoped to get from this kind of declaration.

"I'm not sure what concerns me more," Tara said, wrapping the blanket around herself, but not coming back to bed. "That you think you can die of sexual frustration, or that you think *you* would be fucking *me*."

"Explain to me why we're not having sex right now," Holly pleaded. "Like, this exact moment."

"Well, at this exact moment, we're not having sex because I haven't brushed my teeth, but in the larger scope of things, we're not having sex because we can't date."

Holly nodded thoughtfully, fully awake now and ready to argue her case. "And we can't date because we can't get married, right?"

Tara nodded.

"But here's the thing, I don't want to get married again. Ever. I'm not built for it, and if I were, marrying into any family that includes your aunt Cricket would be strictly outside my boundaries." Holly moved to sit up on her knees, aware her nipples were still pointing directly at Tara, like they were trying to hypnotize her. "I'm not asking you for anything, except your enthusiastic participation in a fling. Unless you wouldn't be enthusiastic about participating, in which case, we can table the whole discussion."

Tara sighed and looked up at the ceiling, and then she flopped back onto the bed. It was the least stiff movement

Holly had ever seen her make, like all the marionette strings that normally kept her posture upright had been cut.

"I would obviously be enthusiastic. My physical interest in you is not the issue here," she said finally.

"Tara"—Holly shook her lightly—"we could be having hot gay sex in this bed at this instant. Don't we owe it to our fore-mothers, those Daughters of Bilitis who worked so hard to bring us sexual liberation, to be liberated?"

This earned her a grin. "I can't tell if I'm appalled or impressed that you just used lesbian history to try to get down my pants."

"Please. Herstory," Holly joked.

"Touché." Now Tara was laughing again, but this time, thankfully, not at Holly's seduction attempts. Progress! "Although that's a very gender essentialist, second-wave feminist term. But being clever won't win your argument."

Holly's stomach dropped, although she'd been briefly distracted by how hot it was when Tara got precise. If they weren't going to have sex at all, this whole weekend, she was going to need to sleep on the floor. Or the bathtub, like in "Norwegian Wood." That song was about lesbians, right? Or maybe in the reindeer enclosure. Somewhere she couldn't even smell Tara.

"However," Tara said, a mischievous grin on her face, "if there's absolutely no possibility that either of us will want anything more out of this, I don't see why we couldn't have a fling."

Holly's brain took a minute to catch up to what Tara had actually said, and then she wanted to punch the air in victory. *Yesssssss*. She started to reach out for Tara, who held up a hand.

"We'll have to have an ironclad agreement."

"Really? You're going to lawyer our sexual encounter?" Holly asked, not sure why she was so turned on by this. She raised her right hand. "I solemnly swear not to fall in love with you or expect anything from you at the end of this weekend."

"And as soon as we leave Carrigan's, we're back to being friends, without benefits," Tara added.

That was the perfect situationship for Holly. A whirlwind romance with a defined end date and no hard feelings so she wouldn't need to do a runner.

She held out the hand she'd raised. "Shake on it?"

Tara grabbed her hand and pulled her in for a blistering kiss. Their tongues tangled, and Tara's hands ran up and down Holly's body, leaving a trail of heat that pooled in her center. Then, suddenly, her hands were gone and Tara's mouth was saying, "We can't get started now, though."

What?!

"Why not?" Holly cried.

"We have to be at breakfast, bright eyed and bushy tailed, in two hours," Tara said breezily. "Which is not nearly enough time for what I have planned. In the meantime, you need to get some sleep."

Holly stared at her. "You think we're going to be able to sleep now?!"

"Oh, no, I won't, but I don't need very much sleep to operate. I'm going to shower, and then get ready for the day. But you should sleep." She hopped out of bed, grabbed the dress she'd ironed the night before, and carried it into the bathroom.

"We could shower together!" Holly called after her.

Tara's laugh rolled out and around her, surprising her again with its earthiness. She always expected it to dance in the air like icicles tinkling. "Haven't you ever heard of delayed gratification?"

Holly pouted. "I've already delayed my gratification!"

THE PACT

December 21-22

Chapter 11

Tara

There was no way in hell Tara should have agreed to what she just had. If she hadn't woken up from a deeply illicit dream to find herself groping Holly—and Holly not minding—if she hadn't been driven to distraction by Holly's miles-long legs and the curls escaping from her braid, she wouldn't have agreed to any kind of fling, parameters or no.

As she stood under the scalding water, she wondered if Holly would hear her if she had a quick, tiny orgasm. Probably. It was a *very* small room.

She needed to clear her head, because she couldn't spend the entire day obsessing about what would happen when they finally got into bed together that night. She was here to celebrate Miriam and Noelle, and she was not going to make their big day about her. More to the point, it was December 21, which meant it was Miriam's birthday, and she had some shitty birthdays to make up for.

Through the bathroom door, she heard Holly's voice murmur and then Cole's shout. Well, it was Cole's normal volume; it was just several times louder than anyone else's.

"Everyone is needed at breakfast immediately! It's Mimi's birthday and Mrs. Matthews has prepared a surprise! It's blintzes! Which I think is a weird surprise but apparently Mimi loved them as a child!"

He knocked, then yanked the door open without waiting for an answer. Only because she'd been prepared for him to do this did she not burn herself on her flat iron. "Your hair is straight enough!" he declared. "We must celebrate the perfection that is Miriam Blum! MOVE YOUR CUTE BUTT!"

Tara looked down and realized she was still in her bra and slip. She sighed. "I don't have clothes on."

Cole pouted. "But we'll be late, and I won't see Miriam's face when she sees the blintzes! You can't do that to me!"

"Well, go without me. You don't need me to go down to breakfast," Tara said, unplugging and stowing her flat iron and checking her mascara while they talked. She'd spent most of the past two hours on her makeup, but a femme needed her face on, after all.

"I do need you! I have been without you for months! *Months!* I have not touched your beautiful face since *May!*"

Tara shook her head, patting a tiny bit more cream blush into the apples of her cheeks. "You know I don't like it when you touch my face. You have to stop touching people's faces."

"That's not what Sawyer says!" he singsonged.

She watched him in the mirror. He wasn't going to budge. "You're standing in front of my dress."

Reaching back over his head with his immense wingspan,

he whipped it at her. She pulled it over her head, and he zipped her up while she put on lipstick. From the room outside, Holly said, "Wow. Y'all are truly one person in two bodies."

"Unkind," Tara accused, patting Cole to get him to move out of her way. She sat on the bed to slip on her flats and noticed that Holly had dressed and fixed her hair while Tara had been in the bathroom. Disappointing.

Reaching into her suitcase, Tara produced a ceramic doll nearly the size of Kringle. It had a cap of frizzy blond hair and giant blinking green eyes, and wore a lavender dress with layers of lace in the petticoat. She set the doll on her lap to straighten its dress, and both Cole and Holly recoiled.

"You stole the doll! Wait, you stole from a Daughter of Bilitis?!" Holly sounded both proud and horrified.

"You met a Daughter of Bilitis?" Cole asked. "Wait! Back up! You stole? Without me?! I thought you were on the straight and narrow. Also, importantly, we need to immediately call a priest for an exorcism. Never mind Miriam's birthday."

These two. Tara shook her head. "I paid Barb for this doll, fair and square. I don't steal anymore."

"We stole a truck last Thanksgiving!" Cole reminded her.

She glared at him. "I don't steal from nice lesbian ladies who offer us hospitality. And we can't exorcise whatever ghost is probably in this doll before celebrating Miriam's birthday, because the ghost *is* the birthday gift."

Many birthdays, Tara had dragged Miriam to some society party or law firm dinner in lieu of celebrating, because the holiday season was peak schmoozing time. Even when she'd taken Miriam out for a nice birthday dinner, it had been somewhere she could see and be seen. Because they hadn't been in love, Tara had told herself it was fine to not do anything romantic, but she'd also been a bad friend.

This year, she was determined to make amends. With a ghost.

"I'm mad that this is a much better birthday present than mine," Cole told her.

"I'm mad that you didn't tell me it was Miriam's birthday," Holly added.

She shrugged. "We can say it's from both of us. It was your idea, after all, and that's a couple thing, right? Joint gifts."

Holly eyed the doll. Its eyes blinked lazily. She shook her head. "You take all the credit, actually."

Having grown up in a city haunted beyond imagining, one creepy doll barely registered for Tara.

As they left the room, Holly whispered to her, "I get to *un*zip you from that dress, right? Also, what's a blintz?"

Mr. and Mrs. Matthews were waiting for them in the dining room along with the guests and the rest of the Carrigan's staff. A perfectly matched pair of outdoorsy silver foxes, who must be Tara's parents' age, the Matthewses had aged gracefully into their love and bodies instead of turning into gin-soaked, Botoxed, fake-tanned wax statues. They were both a little soft and faded, with wrinkles that spoke of laughter, like a perfectly worn flannel. Tara had been deeply jealous, when she'd met them last Thanksgiving, of every kid who got to grow up with them as parents, real or surrogate. Which, according to Hannah, was every kid they'd ever interacted with. To hear her tell it, Ben Matthews had never met a child he didn't try to be a dad to.

Tara's own father, like Miriam's and Cole's, had never met a child he didn't actively try to avoid parenting.

The squeal of delight Miriam let out when she walked into a dining room full of singing people and fresh blintzes was very sweet. Her shriek of pure joy when she saw the doll was very gratifying. Kringle came over to investigate, hissed loudly at the doll, and ran away to hide around Levi's neck.

Levi laughed. "It's nice to have some real ghosts in this hotel, not just the ghosts of our pasts."

His wife shook her head vigorously. "Hard disagree, babe. Put that thing out in the Carriage House, Mir."

Miriam pouted, hugging the doll. "But I love her and I've named her Lisa."

Leaning down, Noelle peered at the doll. "I like her. She looks like she might murder us in our sleep."

Noelle had a tattoo of Lizzie Borden, so this was probably genuine praise.

"Fine!" Miriam said. "I'll put her in the Carriage House. If she curses the main house in retaliation for you all kicking her out, though, it's not my fault!" She smiled at Tara. "You're my favorite ex-girlfriend."

Tara held up a hand for a high five, which Miriam returned on her way outside with Lisa. Noelle gave Tara a thumbs-up. This was admittedly surreal, after last year. Noelle had been jealous, Tara had been hurt, Miriam had been a hot mess, and none of them could have foreseen this easy camaraderie.

"Are they...always like this? All of them?" Holly asked, but before Tara could answer, she realized Holly was talking to Mrs. Matthews and including Tara in "all of them." Tara almost objected, but she found she sort of liked being lumped in with this ragtag group of hooligans. It was a hell of a lot more flattering than the other groups she usually got lumped in with. She might not really be part of this tight-knit chosen family, but she wouldn't mind if she were.

Mrs. Matthews nodded. "Oh, they're often much worse. I suspect you'll see it as the wedding events ramp up. This crew never misses a chance for trouble."

Levi rubbed his hands together. "We do love a dangerous, reckless idea."

From her seat at the breakfast table next to Tara, Hannah grumbled, "He always acts like the Shenanigans mastermind, but we all know it's me."

Tara snorted. "Cole does the same thing to me." She turned to Hannah and dropped her voice. The whole group had stuffed themselves into one of the circular tables in the dining room, but they were so loud they couldn't hear anything. "How are you feeling?"

Hannah shuddered. Tara noticed that she was wearing a lot more foundation than usual, but it wasn't quite hiding the fact that her beautiful olive complexion was noticeably green around the gills. "Pukey? Tired? I always have to pee, and I hate everyone? Also my boobs hurt *so much*."

"Yeah, it's ridiculous that no one has noticed. They're *much* bigger than usual. Spectacular—"

Hannah nodded. "Thank you, aren't they?"

"But really, obviously bigger." Tara dropped her voice even lower, knowing there were interfering family ears all around them. "When are y'all thinking about telling everyone?"

"Can we not tell them?" Hannah asked ruefully. "Is that an option? Can we just mysteriously have a baby one day?"

Tara raised an eyebrow at her.

"I know, I know, in some ways it would be easier if everyone knew," Hannah explained, picking at the tablecloth, "but I don't have the energy right now to deal with everyone's opinions, which they're all going to have. Especially our moms. I don't usually mind working with my mother-in-law but even the best woman in the world may get weird about her grandbaby."

Putting a hand over Hannah's to stop her fidgeting, Tara said seriously, "I think it's going to be amazing." Then, to distract her friend, she asked, "Do you think he's trying to talk my girlfriend into something nefarious?" She inclined her head toward where Levi was talking to Holly.

Holly was nodding thoughtfully as he gesticulated wildly. Tara thought the two of them might get along a little too well. She suspected Levi would approve of a fake dating scheme.

Eventually, the guests wandered off to do whatever activities Hannah had scheduled, the room quieted, and Miriam insisted on hearing the entire story of Barb, her dolls, her vintage menu (this was of more interest to Levi, who was updating the Carrigan's menu), and her lesbian activism.

"It sounds kind of epic," Noelle observed.

"It was a very different experience than the next day at Cricket's, I'll say that," Holly agreed.

As one, Cole and Miriam turned to Tara.

"YOU TOOK HER TO CRICKET'S?" they both yelled.

Tara winced.

"Who's Cricket?" Hannah and Levi asked in unison, looking like they wished they had a bucket of popcorn.

"Were you trying to get her to break up with you?" Miriam asked, sounding horrified.

"Let me guess," Cole said, pinning her with an uncharacteristic glare from his ocean-blue eyes. "It seemed like the only option at the time."

That was the thing. She could think of a million lies she could have told her family now, but it *had* seemed like the only option. It always did.

"Believe me, I know I was wrong."

"I would have forgiven you for dying in a snowdrift and ruining my wedding," Miriam told her, "if I'd known it was to avoid your aunt Cricket." Under her breath, she muttered, "This girl must like you a lot."

Tara didn't want to think about the fact that she'd exposed Miriam to Aunt Cricket's bigotry, and would, someday, do the same again with a real girlfriend. Assuming she wanted her family to keep speaking to her, which was the only reason she was trying to get married to begin with.

She wondered idly if she could pay an actress to pretend to be her wife a few weeks a year.

Her family would eventually find out. In Charleston, everyone eventually found out everything.

After the blintz breakfast, Cole insisted that he needed to go into Advent for Best Man Duties. And he needed Tara, but not Holly, to come with him. Tara was deeply suspicious about this.

"We can't just leave Holly here. It's rude," she explained patiently to Cole. "She's my guest. And my *girlfriend*."

Cole balled his hands on his hips, chewing on his lip. "Well, there's the library. I mean, there are two libraries, the one in the inn and the one in Advent. Collin's diner is a good place for her to hang out."

"Alternately," Mrs. Matthews interjected, "you could hang out and bake with me."

Cole made huge puppy-dog eyes at Tara, and she sighed.

"I'll hang out and bake!" Holly insisted. "And if Mrs. Matthews kicks me out, I'll go hang out in the library or at Collin's. All great options."

"See!" Cole said, gesturing at Holly. "She's fine. And when you come back, she can welcome you with extra kisses. Absence makes the heart grow fonder!"

"Yes," Holly teased, "I will happily welcome you back with extra kisses."

Reluctantly, Tara followed Cole downstairs and out of the inn, although at least half of her brain was trying to talk her into digging in her heels and going back to kiss the hell out of Holly.

Once she and Cole were in the truck on the way to Advent, she turned to him. "What is happening right now? I'm sure you don't have a best man emergency."

He drummed his fingers on the steering wheel. "Well. Here's the thing."

Then he stopped talking.

She waited.

"You're the only family I have left."

She kept waiting. Where was he going with this?

"That sounds like a consolation prize, but you've met the rest of my family. You were probably the only family I ever had, and you're certainly the only one I'd ever choose to keep."

"Miriam is your family," she told him. "This whole group here. They're thrilled to have you."

"No, I know, but like. Not to ever dismiss the importance of queer found family but...there's something irreplaceable about someone who grew up with you and knows all your shit. Miri has that with Hannah and Levi, and that's their whole, like, unbreakable bond thing." He waved with one hand, and she bit her tongue to not tell him to keep both hands on the wheel in case the road was icy.

She wondered if he really needed her, or if anyone who had grown up witness to his family dysfunction would do. "Okay, so you need a family member, why?" she asked instead of voicing this.

It felt maudlin, and she didn't want to ask him for reassurances. Plus, she'd noticed he hadn't ended a single sentence with an exclamation point for several minutes, which meant he was serious about whatever this was.

He scrunched up his shoulders, in that way he did when he was nervous. "I need you to meet Sawyer."

She'd kind of been expecting this, but still, she was surprised that he was placing so much weight on it. "I've met Sawyer, remember? At the bar, the night Miriam and I broke up? The same night *you* met Sawyer. Also I had dinner with him yesterday. He was very lovely and hilarious."

Nodding, he said, "Yes, but I need you to meet *my boyfriend* Sawyer."

Bless Cole's nostalgic sentimentality (and, as he'd pointed out, absolute lack of other viable family)—if he believed he needed her for this, she would be there for him. She'd be his stand-in family, even if it was destined to be temporary. He was building a new life here, and eventually he wouldn't need to hang on to his childhood attachment to her.

Why did that make her tear up? It was ridiculous, to feel both jealousy and grief that her best friend was falling in love. She was committed to showing Cole only joy, so she looked out the window for a second, blinking until she could smile brightly at him with no hint of more complicated emotions.

They met up with Sawyer at Ernie's, the dive bar where he bartended. It was, as far as Tara could tell, the only bar in Advent, and she remembered the food being good and the owner lovely, even if it was the scene of her most humiliating breakup.

The owner came out to greet them. Ernie was a young Black woman who had, if Tara remembered correctly, inherited the bar from her grandmother, her namesake and the original Ernie. She had on an incredible red lipstick and giant Bake-lite earrings in the shape of monstera leaves. She was wearing beat-up Chuck Taylors, ripped skinny jeans, and a Bad Brains shirt. It was almost exactly what she'd been wearing when Tara met her a year ago. Tara respected a work uniform.

"Ernestine!" Cole cried, holding his arms out.

"Nicholas Jedediah, I told you that if you insist on calling me by my full name, I will revoke your invitation to this establishment," Ernie said, hugging him tightly.

"This is my best friend Tara," he said, turning to introduce her.

Ernie cocked her head at this. "I thought Miriam was your best friend?"

"In the immortal words of Mindy Kaling, best friend is a tier, not a position. But Tara is my sister-cousin-heartbeat-half-of-my-soul. Miriam is my..." He paused, gesticulating. "Platonic life partner. It's different. I don't know how to explain it!"

"I am very curious about what the other half of Cole's soul is like," a voice said behind her.

"Well-ordered," Tara said without thinking as she turned.

The night they'd all met Sawyer, she'd been overwhelmed by the loud chaos in the bar and focused on watching the way Miriam and Noelle looked at each other when they thought no one was watching. She hadn't noticed her soulmate's life changing forever, because hers had been, too. Later, when they were back on good terms, Miriam described the moment Cole met Sawyer as like watching someone be struck by lightning. He had, up to that point, thought of himself as a staunch ally who happened to never be able to get emotionally attached to the women he dated. It had not occurred to him, until the day he met Sawyer, that this might be because he was meant to fall in love with men.

To be honest, it hadn't occurred to Tara, either. She'd wondered if he were aromantic, although he seemed very interested in finding romance. This was something that had never made sense to her, as she felt romantic attraction but didn't really want to. She'd thought that, given the number of queer people he was surrounded by and the openness with which he embraced the community, if he'd been queer, he would have said so.

She'd underestimated his desire to never have uncomfortable conversations, even with himself.

Last night, she'd been distracted by Holly and trying to be polite to all the various people being thrown at her. She'd been off-kilter from being treated, by everyone, as if she were part of the core Carrigan's team. So, she still hadn't focused on Sawyer and taken him in. The picture she carried of him in her mind was of a very small man with a giant handlebar mustache and a ponytail.

The man standing before her certainly seemed short next to Cole. He did have an extraordinary mustache, but it wasn't as cartoonish as her brain had painted it. His hair was high up on his head in a sloppy bun, and he was wearing skinny jeans and a giant cardigan that she was certain used to be Cole's over a button-down and a tie. Honestly, he reminded Tara a great deal of Miriam, which she was sure neither Miriam nor Cole had clocked.

"Sawyer!" she said, holding out a hand. He held out his arms for a hug in response.

Shrugging, she gave in. Of course Cole had fallen in love with a hugger.

Sawyer pulled her to the bar and told her he'd been trying a new mint julep recipe and needed her input as a Southerner, since Cole didn't drink. He talked about his childhood and how he'd ended up running for mayor of a tiny tourist town in the Adirondacks, and Tara told him stories about their childhood that didn't involve them lighting anything on fire.

"I'm still not sure I understand how you two are related," Sawyer said, making easy conversation in a way that spoke to his years of bartending. "I thought you were cousins, but if Aunt Cricket is only *your* aunt..." He trailed off, the question implied.

Tara looked at Cole. "Oh, we're not blood related," she clarified. "Although to be fair, neither are Cricket and I."

"You said she was your sister-cousin, literally moments ago," Sawyer reminded him.

Cole blinked, unfazed by having his own words mirrored

back to him. "Yes. Our mothers are best friends who were pregnant at the same time."

She turned to Sawyer. "We were raised in each other's pockets. We're family."

Sawyer nodded. "I mean, we're all gay here, it's not like we're new to found family. Y'all just didn't find each other."

Tara laughed. "I wouldn't have been who Cole chose, if he'd had to go further than his crib to find me."

Cole hummed. "I did choose to find you, though. Remember?"

She did.

Cole had come for her once. After the fire, she thought their friendship was as dead as the grass on the country club lawn, but he'd found the tiny embers that were left and refused to let them die.

She'd never been able to figure out why.

"Enough sappiness!" Cole said suddenly, like the hypocrite he was. "We have errands to run! I need to pick up the boutonniere made out of book pages that Mimi asked the librarian to make for Noelle, and then I need to stop by the diner to get the sandwich platter Collin made for today, and then we need to get back to the Christmasland for more birthday celebrations!"

"Can I help?" Sawyer asked, slipping his arm around Cole's waist.

Cole smiled down at him. "You can show up this evening for the festivities."

Ernie waved at them as they left. "I'll see you tonight! And then on the twenty-third *and* the twenty-fourth. I'm going to take a day in between to sleep. Why would anyone have a birthday, then a rehearsal dinner, then a wedding all in a row?"

Tara had the same question, but the answer was, Miriam Blum. A woman who loved glitter and sparkle but hadn't been allowed to sparkle most of her life and was now running at fun full tilt.

She hung back behind Cole and glared at Sawyer. "If you harm a single hair on his head, I will string you up by your toenails over a vat of spitting acid. I am not exaggerating. You will not survive my wrath."

Sawyer grinned. "It's amazing how close that is to what Miriam told me. Although her threat involved glitter glue and Mod Podge. Believe me, all my intentions are to make that man the happiest he's ever been."

Tara narrowed her eyes. "Good. Then we have an understanding."

Stepping out of the dark, narrow bar, Tara glanced down at her phone. There were several texts from Holly.

Holly: Hey, wondering when you'll be back

Holly: Not that I miss you

Holly: I'm having a blast with Mrs. Matthews

Holly: But I don't want to get her naked

Holly: Actually she's kind of a MILF, I probably would, but she seems happily married

Holly: I do want to get *you* naked, though

Holly: You should come back so we can make that happen

Tara was in the middle of contemplating both Holly's texting style and her naked body when Cole's voice interrupted her.

"So?" he asked, his face tight. She wasn't sure she'd ever seen him this anxious before. "Did you like him?"

She held his face in her hands.

"Wow, this is actually kind of weird," he said. "I should stop touching people's faces. Why didn't you tell me?"

She nodded but didn't let go. "He seems wonderful. I can't wait to get to know him better."

Cole sighed like a 1950s teenager who'd just seen the Beatles on *Ed Sullivan*. "Yeah. He's the best."

Chapter 12

Holly

When she'd envisioned this time at Carrigan's, Holly had thought about the opportunity to hang out more with Miriam's extended group of interesting loved ones, whom she'd seen featured on the Blum Again Vintage & Curios Instagram account. She'd envisioned spending a lot of time with Tara, naked or otherwise.

She hadn't thought about how chaotic weddings were, or how quickly Tara would get sucked into a tight-knit group of friends she hadn't seen for a long time. Partly this was because she was used to being on the periphery of things, and it didn't bother her. She preferred observing, without expectations.

And partly it was because she primarily understood Tara's relationship to the Carrigan's crew through Tara's own perspective, and now that she'd seen them interact, she had a strong suspicion that, much like with Cole, Tara's version of their friendships didn't match anyone else's.

Holly was surprised when the Carrigan's circle opened up and absorbed Tara as if she had been a missing piece of their puzzle, and even more surprised to find herself a little lonely at being left out. In the car, they'd been a team—together, meeting Barb, facing down Aunt Cricket, trying to get through the snow.

Ironically, now that they were actively pretending to be together, they felt less like a couple.

She was telling herself that this uncomfortable sense of being left outside the circle was why she'd sent Tara an absolutely mortifying series of texts. It had been like an out-of-body experience. Instead of the couple of flirty, suggestive messages she'd meant to send, when she didn't hear back from Tara right away, she just...kept...texting.

It was the most embarrassing she'd been around a cute girl since she'd had a crush on Kelsie Kramer in the eighth grade. Although, come to think of it, she and Kelsie had ditched gym to make out, so maybe she hadn't been that embarrassing. Unlike now.

She didn't even have a crush on Tara. Sure, she liked Tara, and she wanted her, but in a friends-with-benefits way. Except they still hadn't gotten to the benefits yet, unless you counted those toe-curling, reality-altering kisses. Holly did *not* count them as a benefit, because they had left her incredibly sexually frustrated.

Her phone pinged.

Caitlin: OMG the inn looks so cute! And is that Chef Levi Matthews? Has he cooked you anything yet?

Holly was about to text her back when another text came through.

> **Tara:** I'm going to tell Levi you called his mom a MILF.

> **Tara:** Also we'll be back in half an hour, according to Cole, so it may be 3 hours. Impossible to tell.

> **Tara:** It's adorable that you think you'll be the one getting me naked.

Holly couldn't decide if she was more turned on by Tara's cocky top energy or her commitment to punctuation. It was like, as soon as Tara had agreed to hook up, she'd taken control of the seduction. Holly was very happy to let her.

"I don't understand why Collin is making the sandwiches," Levi said to Hannah, walking into the kitchen where Holly was helping Mrs. Matthews get cinnamon roll dough ready to rest for the next morning. It had been wonderful, baking and gossiping, sharing recipes and stories. "She's *my* best friend, and I'm, like, I don't know if you know this, kind of good at cooking."

Like Cole, Miriam had multiple best friends, and Levi was, apparently, trying to assert his space as one of them.

His wife patted him on the arm. "You *are* good at cooking, babe. You're famous in Australia for being good at cooking."

"Hey! I'm famous here, too!" he objected, pouting a little.

"Wait, didn't he *lose Australia's Next Star Chef*?" Holly asked.

"But," Hannah continued while her husband feigned being wounded by this, "Collin is good at *sandwiches*, and your best friend wants Collin's sandwiches for her birthday."

Levi huffed, and his mother handed him a cup of coffee. He poured enough sugar in it that Holly, watching him, began twitching. She could imagine the sugar sludge at the bottom of the cup, left there for whoever was stuck with the dishes.

Although, possibly his mother would make him do his own dishes, in which case, he could drink his gross coffee syrup in peace. He must go through more sugar in a month than her family had been able to afford in a year when she was growing up.

"Who's Collin again?" she asked, trying to distract herself from comparing her life to the ones of everyone around her. "Mrs. Matthews said something about a diner?"

Hannah reached past Levi to grab her own cup of coffee and settled on a kitchen stool. "He owns the diner in Advent, which, other than Ernie's bar, is the only place to get food. He's married to the woman who owns the boutique. Levi actually is friends with him and respects his cooking. He's just grouchy because he wants to make Miri's birthday dinner."

Mrs. Matthews added, "Miri wants Levi to *participate* in her birthday dinner, and me as well, which is why she's outsourced the cooking."

"Oh, that's very sweet of her," Holly said. "Do you need an extra pair of hands to wait tables? I'm a pro."

Hannah gasped. "You're our guest! You're here for us to get

all the dirt on your relationship with Tara. And to get to know you."

Levi pouted more, but Holly could see a gleam in his eye that told her he was doing it to get a rise out of his mother. "I get put to work all the time."

Mrs. Matthews flicked him. "You work here."

He sighed, then turned to Holly. "Holly, you obviously know your way around a yeast dough. What other kitchen skills do you have?" He changed the subject with the flash of a smile and a twinkle in his kohl-lined gray eyes.

She'd underestimated how powerful his charisma would be in person, even when he was sitting in his mother's kitchen whining. She was understanding more and more how he became a global TV sensation so quickly.

"Well," she told him, "I've worked in a lot of diners, so if you need a perfectly fried egg, I'm your girl, and I can hash-brown a potato like magic. But mainly I bake."

"Finally," Mrs. Matthews said, "we have a baker in the family! You should see her cinnamon roll skills."

Holly was taken aback by already being assumed part of the family. She hadn't even known Tara was part of the family.

"You can't bake?" she asked Hannah. "Aren't you a Rosenstein?"

Levi laughed. "She's the only Rosenstein who can't bake, but I'm a classically trained chef and I also can't bake, so we're a matched pair."

They clinked their coffee mugs together.

Holly watched them and felt a twinge of…not envy, exactly. Longing? Wistfulness? The two of them, she knew from Tara, had been through the wringer together, falling in love, then breaking up catastrophically before finally finding their way back to rebuild their marriage. Now they seemed at complete ease with each other, peaceful in their love.

There was a way that everyone here was with each other, not just the couples, but also the friends, that Holly had rarely seen. Even Tara and Cole, taken out of the constraints of Charleston, seemed to relate to one another more easily. Holly was close to her sister (and loved her brother fiercely, as annoying as he was), had a decent relationship with her parents (even if she was currently avoiding their meddling), had friends (sort of), but she didn't have a person, any person, platonic or otherwise, who felt like her ride-or-die.

This morning, she would have said that didn't bother her.

With a noise like a tornado, Cole burst through the swinging kitchen door. "LEVI!" he shouted, picking Levi up and swinging him around in a bear hug.

"I saw you two hours ago," Levi said, his voice muffled in Cole's arms.

"HANNAH!" Cole put down Levi and picked up Hannah. She made a noise like she might puke on him, which he probably deserved.

Holly turned to Tara, who had come in quietly behind Cole. "He seems like he's dialed way up, even for him."

Tara nodded. "He just introduced me to his boyfriend. He's on a high."

"That's fucking adorable," Holly said, and then, when Cole turned to her, held up her hands. "Do not pick me up, Nicholas."

He turned to Mrs. Matthews. "FELICIA!"

"You know what else is adorable?" Holly asked Tara quietly,

pulling gently on the skirt of her dress until Tara was standing closer, so close their bodies were brushing against each other.

Tara looked down the front of Holly's braless shirt. "Yes."

"Rude! Those are not adorable! They're majestic." She held her shirt closed. "Keep being mean and you won't get to see them later."

Tara smiled wolfishly. "Oh, I will." She turned to whisper into Holly's hair, and Holly shivered. "In fact, I think there are several hours until dinner, if you'd like to try to escape now."

Oh yeah, she was totally okay with Tara taking the reins on this situationship. Nodding enthusiastically, Holly took Tara's hand and turned to lead her out of the kitchen, still wearing the *I'm Not Irish, Kiss Me Anyway* apron Mrs. Matthews had loaned her, but she bumped into Miriam coming in the door.

"Ow!" Miriam laughed, rubbing her forehead where they'd run into each other. "It's my birthday! Be nice to me!" Coming farther into the kitchen, she exclaimed, "Ooh! Are we making cinnamon rolls?!"

Noelle followed behind her, her face lighting up at the words *cinnamon rolls*.

"Unlike these brats"—Mrs. Matthews gestured at her son and daughter-in-law—"Miriam can bake."

Miriam nodded. "Usually at three a.m. You're always invited," she told Holly. "Maybe you can show me your coconut cake recipe."

"But you're not baking today," Noelle reminded her, "because we're all going outside to build snowmen."

"That's true," Hannah agreed. "Wedding and birthday week or no, guests expect a snowman competition, and we're going to give it to them."

Tara sighed. "They're not going to let us get out of this. I should go change into something warm." She rested her forehead on Holly's, and Holly got a little dizzy from the smell of magnolia and star jasmine.

"I can come with you?" Holly asked hopefully. She'd been so close. She wanted to find out if *all* of Tara smelled like a Southern summer in bloom.

"You are coming with me!" Cole announced. "We're going to be on a team! Because Tara is very bad at building snowmen!"

Tara gasped in indignation. "I'll show you, you little shit," she said, and stomped off to get changed.

"Now she'll try really hard," Cole told Holly, bringing his finger to his lips like his ploy was their secret. "Pretending you think Tara will be bad at something is the best way to get her to do it."

Hmm. That was good information. Holly tucked it away for later. Competitive orgasms? She could get on board with that.

"Is this everyone?" Levi asked the room. "Who are we waiting for?"

Hannah counted on her fingers. "Esther is around somewhere. She said she'd meet us outside. Elijah and Jason are supposed to be here with the twins. Lawrence said he was bringing that new girl he's dating."

"They broke up," Levi updated her.

"Oh no, I liked her! Okay, so just Lawrence, unless he's at home moping. Ernie's supposed to be here. And Marisol."

Holly vaguely knew who some of these people were from Instagram, but she was a little overwhelmed at the idea that this tight-knit friend group was apparently even larger.

Noelle must have seen the panicked look on Holly's face,

because she started explaining. "Elijah Green is our lawyer. Jason is his husband and the drama teacher at the local high school. They have twin six-year-olds, Jayla and Jeremiah. Cutest kids on the planet. Lawrence is Levi's friend from culinary school. Ernie owns the bar in town, and Marisol the boutique. She's married to the guy who owns the diner and is supplying the sandwiches."

"Ahh, yes," Holly confirmed, "I heard about the sandwiches. Are there, uh, more of you? Than that?"

Noelle threw back her head and laughed, and everyone else in the kitchen turned to look at them. "Wait until you meet all the Rosensteins."

Holly's eyes widened. "All of them?"

Noelle nodded. "They'll be arriving tomorrow and the day after." Holly's face must have shown her panic, because Noelle laughed again. "You didn't know your new girlfriend came with a massive extended social circle, huh?"

"I did, but only the shitty ones in Charleston," Holly explained. "I don't think *Tara* knows she comes with this group. She would never describe herself as being part of Team Carrigan's."

"Carrigan's is like the Jewish Olive Garden. The pasta is unlimited, except during Passover, and once you're here, you're family," Noelle told her. "So, welcome to the family!"

Holly felt a little guilty about lying to this very nice woman who was going out of her way to open her home to someone she didn't realize she'd never see again. Except in her wedding photos, where years later people would point and say, "Wait, who's this redhead?" and someone else would say, "I think she was Tara's date. Does anyone remember her name?"

"All of those people can meet us down by the pond!" Miriam exclaimed, and hustled everyone out the door.

Because she'd only seen the front lawn so far, Holly had expected the snowman building to happen there, although she hadn't known where they would fit any snowmen among all the decorated trees, reindeer, Santas, sleighs, and various other holiday detritus.

Instead, they all took snowmobiles down to a frozen pond near the back of the acreage. This meant Holly clung for dear life to Cole's back while he drove way too fast through the trees, whooping at the top of his lungs. She would have liked to look around her at some of the beautiful winter wonderland they were hurtling through, but she mostly closed her eyes and prayed.

The snowmobile came to an abrupt halt, and she banged into Cole's back. Rubbing her nose, she finally took in their surroundings. They were near a frozen pond, on which a few guests were skating. Around the pond, people had staked out spots to build their snowmen. They were blowing on their hands and stomping their feet, trying to stay warm while they waited for Miriam, Hannah, and Noelle to announce the start of the competition.

"It seems like you've acclimated well to Carrigan's, despite the cold. Was it everything you'd hoped?" Holly asked Cole.

He'd posted an Instagram video last year about all his hopes and dreams for the place, now that Miriam was finally taking him to the fabled Christmasland. Those hopes and dreams had included falling in love and meeting the real Santa.

Cole managed to both shrug and nod while bouncing on the balls of his feet. "I love it even though it's nothing like I imagined!" he said happily. "I came here planning to meet Santa, but instead I became a homosexual and fell in love with a bartender, despite the fact that I don't drink."

Holly looked at him, her head cocked. "Cole, has it ever occurred to you that *you* might be the Santa of Carrigan's?"

He stopped moving and blinked at her, gesturing for her to continue.

"You're giant, with pale hair and a distinguishable costume."

He looked down at his trademark lobster shorts (now snow pants; how had he even found those?) and fleece-lined boat shoes. "Huh."

"You appear and disappear at will. You have mysterious, seemingly unending sources of income. You quite literally, if you wanted to, could see anyone when they were sleeping or awake—and you know who's been bad or good. Also, your name is Nicholas."

He grinned. "You're *right*. This is the greatest thing ever. I AM SANTA! I have to tell Sawyer he's going to be Mrs. Claus!"

She watched him run off, presumably to find his boyfriend. She wondered how Sawyer felt about Cole's apparent easy assumption that they were permanent. He seemed to have skipped over any of the "dating" parts of dating.

Tara came up behind Holly and put her arms around her neck. Holly leaned back against her, wondering if Tara realized how closely she was mirroring how Cole had held her the other day. No one that Holly had seen in Tara's life, except Cole, showed her any physical affection, and Holly suspected the two of them had taught each other how to love people.

Not that Tara loved her. They barely knew each other; they were acquaintances who were attracted to each other. Like, very, very attracted. They were going to bang it out, and then Holly would have done everything she wanted to do in Charleston and would be ready to move on to her next adventure. Tara was only cuddling her for show, to sell their fake relationship.

And maybe a little as prelude to tonight, Holly hoped, as Tara breathed into her ear, "Sorry I left you alone with these hooligans again."

"I don't think Cole should, legally, be allowed to drive any vehicle," Holly told her. Tara's laugh vibrated behind her. *Mmmm.*

"He's very good with a sailboat, strangely," Tara said. "We used to race them when we were kids."

Holly would give a hell of a lot to see Tara Sloane Chadwick, ice queen, racing a sailboat, wind whipping her hair, eyes alight with competition.

"Why'd you stop?" she asked. She knew they still sailed together sometimes.

Tara gave her a pained smile. "I gave up reckless endangerment after I almost killed us both. It seemed the least I could do."

That was clearly not the whole story. Did she still want to race? Did Cole still go, or had he stopped when he lost his partner? Did he miss it? Was it really that dangerous, if Cole was at the helm? Why did Tara bear all the responsibility for the fire they had ostensibly both set?

She didn't have the right to ask any of those questions, but she wanted to. Their pact might expire when they got back to Charleston, which was best for everyone, but that didn't stop Holly from wishing there might be a little more time to find out more of the tiny, fascinating secrets Tara kept squirreled away.

A tall, thin Black man with a short Afro, wearing a large argyle scarf and holding the hands of two squirming kindergartners, walked up to them.

"You're Tara, right?" he asked. "I'm Elijah Green. We met the night we all went caroling? But I think you were distracted."

Moving one of her arms from around Holly's shoulders, Tara held out a hand to him. "It's nice to meet you under better circumstances. This is my girlfriend, Holly."

Holly held out her own hand to greet Elijah. Then, sinking on her heels, she held out her hand to shake those of the children.

"I'm Jayla," said one of the coat-swaddled children. "This is my brother. He's not important. I like your hair."

"*Dad*," whined the brother, whose name, she remembered, was Jeremiah, "when do we get to build snowmen?"

Elijah raised an eyebrow at his son. "When your papa gets here. But you won't get to build one at all if you're rude."

The child extended his hand to shake Holly's, and Jayla told him, "Come on, let's go find Grandma Vaunda!"

They ran off, chasing each other. She wasn't sure how they could run in those snowsuits.

Elijah turned back to Tara. "I've heard you're one hell of a lawyer, and friend."

A blush rose up Tara's cheeks, and Holly immediately liked Elijah. Tara might not believe her friends when they told her how amazing she was, but maybe she would believe a colleague.

"I hear the same about you. Cole says you're working on his trust fund," Tara returned. "You know once he has access to it, he's going to give most of it to community aid organizations."

Elijah nodded. "He told me, after I get paid, the list starts."

Now Holly *really* liked Elijah. She was going to become friends with him.

Holly cocked her head. "Isn't Cole...a criminal?"

"He's a very ethical criminal." Tara laughed. "I'm glad you know you're doing all this work for him to basically turn around and give it away."

"Friends!" Miriam shouted over the noise of conversation. "We have been hosting this snowman competition for years, and we're so excited that this year it coincides with so many other celebrations! Today, in addition to being my birthday, is the anniversary of the first time Noelle and I kissed, on this very pond."

"Wow," Tara said, sounding surprised, "they waited a month after we broke up to kiss? That's...kind of sweet, actually?"

Holly found it interesting that although Tara talked to all of the crew regularly, including Miriam, she'd apparently never asked for the details of Miriam and Noelle falling in love. She had instead allowed herself to assume the worst, that they'd hooked up as soon as the ink was dry. Refusing to have difficult conversations seemed to be her MO.

Holly couldn't exactly judge, given that she was currently lying to her family about a girlfriend instead of forcing her mom to listen to her boundaries.

"You are very unbothered about the breakup," Elijah noted.

"Well, I've had a lot of time, they're clearly in love, and we never were. I was frustrated with Miriam because I felt like

I deserved honesty from my friend, but it's water under the bridge now."

Except that her pride wouldn't let her come without a fake girlfriend, Holly thought. Tara might talk a big game about being over the whole thing, but her heart had been bruised, and she needed a shield. Holly vowed to be a good one.

Cole bounded back up to them. A gaggle of preteens followed like little ducklings, trying to get selfies with him. He looked slightly panicked. "Will someone? Help?"

"I thought you loved being Instagram famous," Levi remarked, ambling up to the group. "Elijah! You're wearing the scarf I gave you! Children! Do you want a selfie with a guy who has his own TV show? Come with me," he said to the preteens, then led them off.

"Levi is my hero," Cole whispered. "Even I am no match for that much energy."

"Wow," Tara said, "we found Cole's Achilles' heel."

He held a finger up to his lips. "We will never speak of this again. *Okay.* We are going to build the best snowman in the history of Carrigan's Christmas— Oh, Lawrence is here!"

With that observation, he bounded off as suddenly as he'd come.

"Do you ever get used to that?" Holly asked. "The thing where he's never where you expect him to be? He just appears and disappears?"

Tara shook her head. "Never."

"I guess that means it's the two of us? For the snowman building? Unless you want to go skating, or wander back to the inn while everyone is busy?"

Tara raised an eyebrow. "You keep trying to rush us into

bed, but I promise, when we get there, it will be worth the wait."

"We have limited time for this affair," Holly said, her mittens on her hips, "and I, for one, would like to have as much sex as possible during that window."

She reached over and tugged on the lapels of Tara's coat. Tara raised an eyebrow but came willingly, bringing their bodies flush. "I hear this pond is great for kissing."

"Oh, you do, do you?" Tara asked, her voice a sexy rasp. She wrapped an arm around Holly's waist and ran her hand lower, until Holly gasped, her whole body lighting up. "I guess we should test that out."

Their lips had just met and begun to sink into each other, Holly's tongue teasing into Tara's mouth, when a snowball hit them.

Tara pulled away from Holly to whip her head around and glare at Cole, already gathering snow for another ball.

Groaning, Holly tried to pull Tara back into the moment.

Instead, Tara held her chin and looked her right in the eye. "I guarantee you that we are going to have the best sex of your life, soon, and you are not going to find any part of it unfulfilling, in quality or quantity. Now," she said, turning away, "I'm going to go kill my best friend, but after that, do you want to build a snowman?"

Holly did not want to build a snowman. She wanted to melt into a naked mess with Tara, although she might melt all on her own. Parts of her were definitely turning to liquid.

"Hold that thought," Tara added, pretending to be oblivious to Holly's pout, except that she had a little smirk. She ran off after Cole.

The two of them rolled around like blond puppies in the snow, laughing and kicking and tumbling as if they cared about nothing but joy. It was the most carefree Holly had ever seen Tara.

Cole had managed to free himself from their childhood training, but Tara was still willingly behaving the way she was expected—except when she was here. God, Holly wished Tara would stay here. Move to Advent, run around getting into trouble with Cole. Give up talking to her family.

And if she were here, maybe Holly would stick around for a little while, too. She *had* been planning on getting out of Charleston, and Advent was basically on another planet. Maybe they could be friends with benefits for a little longer than a weekend. If Aunt Cricket and the Southern Charm Rejects weren't in the picture.

Not for good, obviously. Holly would eventually need to leave, because she wasn't built for long-term. But for just a little longer.

Chapter 13

Tara

Holly was killing her. She was wearing a long black sweater that hugged her body over fleece-lined leggings covered in little pink skulls, her hair caught in a low ponytail under a beanie. She was always incredibly hot, but Tara was finding that, when she wasn't dressing for work, Holly's personal style leaned into her emo girl roots, and it was irresistible. The more she dropped all the characters she was playing and let herself get a little messy, the more Tara wanted her.

She also did a thing that Tara was pretty sure she didn't know she was doing, which was whine a little in the back of her throat every time Tara exhibited any top energy. Which made Tara lean into it more. By the time they actually got to bed tonight, Tara was going to be a powder keg, and the only recourse she had was to light Holly on fire.

She was trying to stretch out the anticipation and cool

them both down by insisting they make these snowmen, even though she was terrible at it and she hated to do things she was terrible at. She didn't expect either of them to try very hard, since obviously the returning Carrigan's guests were in it to win it.

Holly, however, was seriously gathering and piling up snow, and Tara's competitive streak immediately kicked in.

"Okay. Here's the thing about building a snowman when you're not skilled," Holly told her. "You don't want to build up. It takes too much time to get it stable. You want to do something close to the ground, like a . . . turtle."

They built a very mediocre turtle, in between sneaking snowballs down one another's shirts and sharing glances that should have melted all the snow in New York. Tara was deeply grateful for how distracting Holly was. This was the first time she'd been around Miriam and Noelle as a couple.

Tara and Miriam had been together for years, and in some ways, Miriam was still frozen in her memory that way. Enough that there was some cognitive dissonance at seeing her happily engaged to another woman. They were adorable together, in a way that made Tara's heart hurt. Not out of jealousy, but awareness that she didn't have that and, if she got the life she was planning for, she never would.

It helped that this Miriam, a year out, was so clearly different from the one who had left Charleston "for a week to sit shiva." She held her body more loosely, laughed more easily. She was less prone to disassociate in the middle of conversations, a little more frenetic. This was, Tara guessed, what she would have always been like, if not for her trauma.

There was something very unsettling about the idea that

trauma had been what made Miriam a good match as a wife
for Tara. Thankfully, she was saved from delving too deeply
into this by Holly sticking an ice-cold hand up the back of her
sweater.

"That's it!" Tara grabbed Holly's hand and dragged her
toward a snowmobile. To Noelle she said, "I'm going to get
Holly out of these wet clothes."

Noelle grinned knowingly. "Wouldn't want her to catch a
cold, after all. Try to be back down for the cake, okay?"

"We'll try," Tara told her, though she had her doubts.

She thought she heard Noelle say something about the pond
having magical Cupid powers but she had to be joking.

The two of them held hands and walk-ran through the
near-empty inn. Mrs. Matthews poked her head through the
kitchen door at the noise, but when she saw them, she just
waved and winked. It wasn't clear who was pulling whom,
and Tara wanted to stay in control, but she was willing to let
herself be a part of this tug-of-war as long as it got them to a
bed sooner.

Inside their room, Tara locked the door and began stalking,
slowly, toward Holly. She was going to slow this down, take
back control. Because it turned Holly on when she was bossy,
and because she had made certain promises and she intended
to keep them.

Holly launched herself, like a spider monkey, at Tara, and
they tumbled to the floor in front of the fire, Holly's legs wrapping around Tara's waist. Their mouths fused together, hands
going everywhere. Tara tried to strip Holly out of her sweater,
but her hands began to wander once they met skin.

Holly was trying to unbutton Tara's jeans, the button stuck

because of the cold and wet. "I want to undress you," Holly complained.

"I want to do the same, but I think it's going to take all night if we do it this way." Tara laughed, and sat up, pulling Holly with her so that she sat in Tara's lap. "Let's start with this sweater."

Slowly, one piece at a time, they peeled leggings and boots and socks off, leaving them in a damp pile on the floor that Tara was, for once in her life, too distracted to hang up in the bathroom so it wouldn't ruin the carpet. She watched Holly's long limbs come uncovered and ran her hands along the black and gray tattoo work that covered her thighs. Holly shivered under her touch.

It was almost too much, the tan where her work clothes didn't cover, one arm darker than the other from driving in the summer and fall, the pale, freckled redhead skin she usually kept covered. The scorpions and spiders, skulls pierced by knives and bottles of poison scattered across her torso and thighs. Tara wanted to catalog them all. Later.

Holly's eyes were on her, too, laser focused on her breasts as she unhooked her wet bra and peeled it off. This part... she always got off track at this part. The part where someone else had to see her, and she had to let herself be seen.

The fire in Holly's eyes went a long way toward vanquishing that fear, but nothing could make it go away completely. No matter how badly she wanted to be naked with this woman—and she wasn't sure she'd ever wanted to be naked with anyone more—she still wished they could do this in darkness, hands and tongues making perfection out of flawed human flesh.

Not that Holly was flawed. Holly, naked, was life-altering. Jesus Fucking Christ.

Holly raised her eyebrows as if to say, *Your move*, and Tara pushed her back onto the floor, taking control and taking her brain out of the equation.

She'd promised Holly the sex of her life, and she was intent on delivering.

Reaching up, she grabbed a pillow off the bed and wedged it under Holly's hips. Smirking, she began kissing down Holly's body, spending as much time as she wanted on every part that caught her attention. She did love the curve of a woman's hip. Her gaze, then her fingers, then her tongue moved lower, until she was where she intended to spend the next several hours.

They didn't make it down for cake.

When Tara checked her phone, her texts were full of filthy emojis from her friends and smirks from Cole.

She wanted to tell Cole that she and Holly still weren't dating, just friends doing each other favors that involved orgasms, but she was worried Miriam or Hannah would read his texts over his shoulder. Besides, if he'd decided that because he was living his own love story she must be as well, she wouldn't be able to convince him otherwise. He would have to see it to believe it.

From inside the tangle of their bodies, Tara ran her fingers lightly down Holly's spine. "We should make an appearance before everyone goes to bed."

Holly peeked up at her through a curtain of hair. "You don't think us very obviously disappearing for sex is going to convince people that we're dating?"

"Oh no, I do think they're convinced about that," Tara said. "I also think it's rude that we're here for a wedding but missing the wedding events."

Holly groaned but rolled over to start finding her clothes. "I'm only leaving this bed because I adore your Carrigan's friends, and I hate your Charleston friends, and I want you to consider abandoning them to move here."

"You don't even know my Charleston friends," Tara protested. Not very convincingly.

Holly looked up at her while pulling her jeans up. "Are they not terrible?"

They weren't *all* terrible. She was friendly with queer activists and community organizers, and other people doing the work to try to reform—or deconstruct—the South Carolina legal system. Admittedly, she mostly socialized with people she hated, and it wore on her.

It wore even more on the people she dated.

"I'm never moving to Carrigan's," Tara said instead of answering. "I may love these weirdos, but there's no way in hell I'm leaving my beautiful port city for the snow and woods and nothingness."

She couldn't figure out why everyone suddenly seemed to think that she, a dyed-in-the-wool Southern belle, from her perfectly pedicured toes up to her blond highlights, might want to leave a place so deeply ingrained in her identity. Carrigan's was the polar opposite of her life, practically a mirror universe. It wasn't for her.

Holly stared at her for a long moment, and Tara tried not to get distracted by her in her lacy bralette. "Even if Cole stays here for good?"

Tara sighed, her heart constricting.

It was ridiculous to think she couldn't live without Cole. No one couldn't live without their childhood best friend. Except Hannah, maybe, but she'd fallen in love with hers. Tara had been fine the year she'd gone to boarding school, and the months that Cole was in New Zealand and off the grid. Sure, she'd come back from school with some self-destructive habits. And she'd been an absolute fucking mess while Cole was gone, but that was because she was in the middle of a breakup.

Cole could live without her just fine, and she wasn't going to need him more than he needed her. So, she would survive.

"I'm not throwing away my whole life plan because Cole fell in love."

Holly made a noise in her throat but didn't say anything else. Instead, she pulled on a hoodie, and Tara was finally able to look away and start putting on her own clothes.

"Okay!" she said. "Let's go put on another show."

"I don't really get why you're pretending," Holly said. "Or, I guess, why we are. I don't see your friends as the kind of people who would judge you for coming solo."

Tara blew out a breath as she tried to tame the hair that had gotten frizzy when she pulled her sweater over it. "I know, I shouldn't have panicked to begin with, but now that we're here and they're being so damn nice, and working so hard to make me feel welcome...I can't tell them I lied to them. They would be so disappointed. Please, I can't face that. They can never know."

The only thing more humiliating than coming to her ex's wedding single would be her friends finding out she'd faked a relationship. If she became a problem they felt they needed to fix, at best they would pity her, and at worst...they would decide she was too much work. She already wasn't good enough for her friends; she didn't need to also be a burden.

"Okay," Holly said, shrugging like she didn't agree, but this wasn't her life. It was Tara's. "They'll never know."

Chapter 14

Holly

There are so many people here.

Holly scanned the dining room the next morning, having emerged from the room only because Cole texted Tara to say they were going to miss breakfast.

They had gone down the night before to eat leftover cake and be sociable for a little while but had quickly run back to bed. Thankfully, Miriam had wanted Noelle to do "that thing I like" for her birthday, Levi and Hannah could barely keep their hands off each other (she suspected they'd had sex in every room of this hotel), and Cole and Sawyer were always sneaking away to make out, so no one was too upset when the party broke up early.

They hadn't gotten any sleep. At all.

Holly had had a lot of sex since her divorce, even if she hadn't had any relationships, and she'd never, in her life, had sex like this. It wasn't that everything was easy, or they were an immediate perfect fit. Things were still sometimes awkward, they were still learning each other's bodies. But even when they wound up in a giggling pile because something they tried had gone off the rails, Holly was still more turned on than she'd ever been. The chemistry between them was like a forest fire.

Yesterday morning, she'd thought it was hard to drag herself out of the room because of the promise of getting Tara naked. This morning, it was almost impossible because Tara *was* naked, and Holly wanted to trace every inch of her skin in the dawn light.

"Do you think," she'd said, leaning against the bathroom doorway, watching Tara put on her blush, "that they would deliver breakfast to our room?"

Tara winked at her. "Normally, yes. This is a full-service inn. This morning, though? No. I think Miriam will have our heads on a platter if we don't go down, and maybe Cole, too. Today is the first day of official wedding activities."

"Isn't the wedding still two days away? Tomorrow's the rehearsal dinner, and then Christmas Eve is the ceremony?"

"Hannah's an event planner," Tara reminded her. "Give her an event to plan, she's going to plan it within an inch of her life."

Holly pouted. "Why do they need us? They have a million people more important to their lives than an ex and an ex's new girlfriend. Who would even notice if we were gone?"

Even as she said it, she knew the answer. Cole would notice, because even if Tara didn't know it, there actually wasn't anyone more important than her in Cole's life. And he would always notice when she was gone.

Tara, who believed herself as tertiary to the proceedings as Holly had made her out to be, didn't argue that she was needed. Instead, she said, "It wouldn't be polite."

Groaning, Holly pulled on her own jeans and wondered how she could convince Tara that it would be more polite to go down on her for hours.

In the dining room, all Holly could process at first was that there were *so many people* in the room.

As she dug into a pile of perfect scrambled eggs to refuel and thought about how Mrs. Matthews was a national treasure and it must be hard on Levi that his mom was a better cook than he would ever be, she watched *more* people stream in without stopping.

Some she identified as Rosensteins and some must be Noelle's relatives from New Mexico, given her excited greetings. And then a number of older guests who didn't seem to be related to anyone started arriving.

"Who are all these people?" Holly whispered to Tara, gesturing at the septuagenarians hugging each other like long-lost loves.

Tara smiled. "These are Miriam's Old Ladies. She buys junk from them, for her art. Well"—she paused—"some of them are. I think some of them might be Noelle's AA friends? They seem to have put their collections together."

"I don't understand how anyone knows this many human beings," Holly said, and Tara looked at her strangely. "What?"

Tara shook her head. "I don't think I'd be happy *not* having a village."

Holly's hackles stood up. It was pretty rich of Tara to accuse her of not building a village, when Tara actively avoided being where her village was, in favor of burning her candle at both ends, trying to make up for one terrible teenage mistake.

"There's nothing wrong with my life, Tara."

"I didn't say there was." Tara's drawl was back, and her posture was straighter, which meant she was feeling called out. She didn't have to say that she thought there was something wrong with the way Holly lived her life. She said it with her actions.

"Tara!" cried a woman holding out hands with perfectly sculpted nails, tasteful, expensive gold bracelets clinking as she walked toward them.

"There's Ziva," Tara said flatly. She put an arm around Holly's shoulders and whispered, "Get ready."

Holly put on her waitressing smile, the one she used for men who tried to peer down her dress and women who talked to her like she was three. She knew from Tara that Ziva was on a tour of amends for allowing Miriam to grow up in an abusive home, but something about her dinged Holly's alarms. Was it the way she presented herself, the blowout and freshly microbladed eyebrows and expensive athleisure reminding Holly, fairly or not, of a Certain Kind of affluent customer who never tipped enough? Was it the knowledge that Ziva had called Tara after the breakup but before Noelle and Miriam were officially together, to apologize for Miriam's bad judgment and try to talk Tara into winning Miriam back?

Tara rose from the table and held Ziva at arm's length, air kissing both of her cheeks. "This is my girlfriend, Holly," Tara introduced them. Holly did not stand up. There were people on this earth she would pause her breakfast for, but Ziva Rosenstein-Blum wasn't one of them.

Ziva scanned Holly up and down, holding out a hand. Holly shook it, refusing to react when Ziva squeezed a little too hard. Then she sat down in the empty chair next to Tara without being asked, effectively forcing Tara to turn her back to Holly if Tara wanted to look at Ziva while she talked, which Tara was too polite not to do.

"So you're not here to dramatically object in the middle of the wedding and win back the love of your life?" Ziva asked, her tone joking, although Holly was sure she heard a little bit of disappointment.

"Fortunately for all of us, Miriam was never the love of my life, and I could not be more glad that she *is* the love of Noelle's life," Tara said in that syrupy, slow drawl she used to tell people they had crossed a line. The "Bless Your Heart" was silent but implied.

Ziva tittered and turned to Holly. "So, what do you do?"

Before she could answer, Tara said, "Holly is an amazing baker, and she actually grew up right near the Rosenstein's flagship store."

Apparently "waitress" would have been too embarrassing an answer for Tara.

Ziva clasped her hands together. "Oh, so you grew up eating our products."

"Our" seemed like a stretch, given that, as far as Holly knew, Ziva was in no way involved in the family business and hadn't been since she'd married Richard Blum, to whom the family had objected because he was, well, a dick.

She didn't say this to Ziva.

Instead, she said, "I would die for the hamantaschen!"

This had the benefit of being true, so she could say it with real enthusiasm.

"I have to introduce you to some friends who work at the home office," Ziva told her. "You'll have so much to talk about."

Standing up, she pulled Holly to her feet and began dragging her to a nearby table as Holly glanced longingly at her unfinished eggs. It was clear that it had never occurred to Ziva that Holly might not follow along. Ziva seemed very skilled at moving social situations so that people couldn't object to whatever she wanted without appearing rude. It was equal parts impressive and appalling.

Holly looked over her shoulder at Tara, whose face, to her credit, was sheepish. She wanted to hang back and remind Tara that she'd known all along that Holly was a career waitress but had agreed to have Holly come along on this fake girlfriend farce anyway. Remind her that Holly didn't give a shit if her life was impressive to someone like Ziva. If Tara'd wanted Holly to pretend to be someone else, she should have said so.

Actually, she should have gotten someone else to do this. Pretending to be the kind of woman who would date someone who was ashamed of her really chapped her ass.

Instead of getting into that argument, she let herself be dragged off by Ziva, who introduced her to a lot of people whose names Holly wouldn't remember. The cousins who were close to her age exchanged details of what high schools they'd gone to and played the game of trying to figure out who they knew in common. One of the cousins had spent a summer working with Caitlin at a movie theater, so they took a selfie and sent it to her.

"Holly is an incredible baker," Miriam supplied when she joined the group. "Her coconut cake blew me out of the water the first time I had it."

This brought on a chorus of oohs, requests for recipes, and a discussion of the difficulties that Miriam had experienced when adjusting to baking at such a different altitude, here in the Adirondacks, than she was used to in Charleston.

When Holly looked away from the bright, laughing group toward Tara, she saw that she was now sitting alone, her hands clasped and her face in the polite mask that meant she was wildly uncomfortable. She touched Miriam on the shoulder and subtly nodded in her direction. Miriam nodded back and gave a tiny wave to Cole, who was busy snuggling with Sawyer and systematically shoving turkey bacon into his mouth.

Once she caught his eye, Holly watched her gesture toward Tara, all small enough that Tara, who was staring into her coffee, wouldn't notice. Cole casually steered Sawyer over to Tara's table and drew her into a conversation with Esther Matthews and Gavi, who were sitting nearby.

"You watch out for her," Miriam observed, pulling Holly into a corner, outside of the earshot of the crowd.

"So do you," Holly said.

Miriam smiled. "We might have broken up, but Tara and I were good friends for a long time. She took care of me, when I was still in shell shock from being estranged from everyone. She was gentle, and kind. I mean, you know, also kind of cold, but she always made sure I had what I needed. She financed the launching of my art career, and when I up and left to become a tree farmer's wife, she never asked for a single cent back. In fact, she bought a lot of Miriam Blum originals to help save the farm when we almost lost it."

Why did that make Holly's heart melt?

She chewed on her lip, watching Tara and Cole with their blond heads bent together. "Does she ever stop trying to save people, and worry about saving herself?"

"I think she thinks she has to," Miriam said. "Save everyone, I mean." She paused to take a sip of coffee and leaned against the wall behind them. "I never understood why, because she didn't tell me about the fire. Neither of them told me. I didn't find out until a year ago, and it made a lot of puzzle pieces fall into place."

"How so?" Holly asked.

Miriam cocked her head, giant mane of wild brown curls bouncing as she did. Holly was going to have to ask her about her conditioner. "Well, they went in opposite directions after, didn't they? Tara trying to fit in every box so she never lit anything on fire again, literally or metaphorically. Cole beginning a life of crime. Tara cutting off all her emotional ties, and Cole finding and clinging to me because he'd been cut off from the person he needed most."

Holly watched as Cole casually put an arm around Tara's shoulders, and she let her body relax in a way she never did, even during sex.

"But the Tara who wants to blow things up is still under all those layers," Holly said.

Miriam laughed. "Yeah, I'm not sure you can take the arsonist out of the girl, in this case. No matter how hard she tries to be The Perfect Lesbian Debutante, underneath she's the biggest hooligan of us all. So she has to keep her lid on super tight."

"I'm afraid she's going to explode," Holly said. "Like a pressure cooker."

Nodding, Miriam said, "I'm glad she has you now. It's hard on her, all of us falling in love like dominoes. She hates to feel left out."

Internally, Holly winced. Had she made things worse for Tara by agreeing to this? Now her friends weren't worried about her, but maybe they should be. Actually, she was certain they should be—Tara worked too hard, hated half the things she was doing with her life, never slept, lived on sweet tea, and instead of using her broken engagement as an opportunity to reflect on her choices, she was planning to find another woman to enter into a marriage of convenience with her.

Holly was worried about Tara, and she barely knew her.

"We really do want her to move up here, you know," Miriam said, as if she could hear Holly's thoughts. "We'd all love to have her living close by. If you wanted to come, too, there's lots of opportunities for bakers, especially since the Matthewses are talking about retiring."

It didn't seem worth pointing out that it would be weird to move in with Tara this early in their supposed relationship, especially since Miriam had lived with Noelle since before they started dating.

Also, it had to be said, they *were* lesbians. It made sense that Miriam assumed she would U-Haul it to wherever Tara was.

"She's dead set on staying in the South, but you should keep asking her. I think moving up here would be so good for her that it scares her," Holly said. "You'd probably have to tell her the farm was failing and only she could save it, if you wanted to convince her."

"I'm not above that," Miriam deadpanned.

"Tell me about your Old Ladies," Holly said, turning the conversation from Tara because she suddenly realized Tara would be mortified by all her friends discussing her behind her back.

Besides, Holly was curious about this ability Miriam had to keep friends all over the country, whom she rarely saw. *Could I have built and maintained friendships with all those line cooks and fellow waitresses I left behind? Should I have?* It wasn't something Holly had ever wondered, assuming that seeing the world meant, by necessity, being a lone wolf.

While she listened with half an ear, part of her was watching Tara.

Although they'd been acquaintances for years, she'd really only known Tara for a few days, but she missed her. Missed her now, across a crowded room. Her life, with Tara in it, felt like she was driving into range of a radio station after miles of static, to find her favorite song playing. What was it going to be like when they went back to being friends, and Holly moved away? Would she just always miss Tara?

On the table in front of her, her phone buzzed with a text from her sister.

> **Caitlin:** I need a million more details about this magical Christmas tree farm

> **Caitlin:** Also are you really not coming home, even after Christmas?

Caitlin: Is it because Dustin is here? Because I can lock him in a closet for a few days.

Holly did not want to explain any of this to her family, who tended to view her with loving and supportive yet over-bearing bafflement. When she'd gotten married at eighteen, they'd helped hot-glue dollar store flowers to a plastic garden arch Ivy found on Craigslist. When she'd gotten divorced at twenty-two, they'd come over to help her pack and given her zero lectures about familial responsibility. No one had even said I told you so.

When she didn't make it home for holidays, year after year, her mom wrapped her presents in perfectly folded corners and big coordinating bows and carefully packed them with pack-ing peanuts, shipping them to wherever she was.

Apparently, she'd hit the limit of Christmases she could miss before her mom ran out of patience. Maybe it was because both of her siblings were home now, or because Dustin was whispering in their ears like Littlefinger that it was Holly's duty as the youngest daughter to take care of them. Maybe her mom's biological clock was starting to tick on Holly's behalf now that she was firmly in her thirties.

They knew she wasn't running from them, specifically. Just from...turning out like them. Rational or not, it felt like going home for Christmas was a trap, and she would find her-self drawn back into the comfort of the known. She'd end up spending Wednesday nights in the bar down the street with people she'd gone to elementary school with, in the kind of job that you couldn't skip out on to have an adventure with-out getting fired and being late on rent, and then she'd get mean. At least with her life right now, when she got fired and couldn't make rent, she could get in the car and drive.

She *should* call her family, but she was having too much fun at Carrigan's, and she didn't want to feel guilty about it.

She turned her phone over.

"Ooh," Levi said, looking over her shoulder, "who are we avoiding?"

"My sister," Holly said.

He nodded. "Sisters are complicated. Why are you avoiding yours?"

"You remind me of Cole," she said, hoping to distract him into dropping the subject, because she didn't know the answer herself. "You both have no idea where the boundary of 'not your business' is."

He threw back his head and laughed. "Welcome to Carrigan's," he said. "But also, touché. Shall I escort you back to your beautiful girlfriend so you can stop being assaulted by my various in-laws?"

She nodded enthusiastically, and she had to remind the butterflies in her stomach that she didn't actually have a beautiful girlfriend.

Chapter 15

Tara

This day was remarkably unstructured for one Hannah had planned. It seemed that even her supernatural powers of organization couldn't stand against the chaos force of the assembled Rosensteins and Old Ladies.

Everyone was milling around, chatting in the great room, noshing in the dining room, lounging on the porch. It was making Tara twitchy. She needed to do something useful, or at least with an itinerary. She thought she might be needed to babysit Ziva, but Ziva was happy as a clam (or whatever the kosher equivalent was), playing host to all the Rosensteins she'd been semi-estranged from for years.

Sitting next to Holly on a couch in the corner of the great room, Tara didn't even realize she was anxious until Holly put a hand on her bouncing knee and stopped its movement.

"I'll bet it would help Hannah out if you roped some of these people into an activity of some kind," Holly whispered, her breath tickling Tara's ear and raising goose bumps on her arm.

Tara loved that Holly knew her well enough to understand why she couldn't sit still. She laced their fingers together. "What would we do? We can't exactly go hiking, or boating, or out for a picnic in this weather."

Holly acknowledged this with a dip of her head. "There are downfalls to a white Christmas."

"Yeah, it's cold as shit, and wet, and the snow gets *everywhere*." Tara shook her body in disgust. "I'll take a low-country Christmas any day."

Holly laid her head on Tara's shoulder. "I wish we could have stayed in bed all day instead of being sociable, but your friends need you, and I know you never let anyone down when they need you. So, what can we do with a whole bunch of people before it's even time for lunch?"

"Hey! Coco!" Tara called, and Cole's head snapped up from across the room.

"Wait, weren't you complaining about everyone else here calling each other ridiculous nicknames?" Holly asked, pulling away and laughing. "Coco?!"

Tara ignored this, turning to Cole as he and Sawyer walked up. "If anyone in this godforsaken hotel knows where there's a karaoke machine, it's you."

Cole's eyes lit with the kind of glee that he usually reserved for doxxing white nationalists and exposing them to their employers after they marched with swastika flags in the streets.

"Karaoke?! Oh, my love, my light! Better half of my heart! You are a genius of epic proportions," he cried, clapping. "To the barn!"

Tara looked around at the crowd. "How are we going to wrangle them all?"

"Oh, I'm on it," Holly said, slipping out of her Docs and standing up on the couch. "Excuse me!" Her voice carried over the room, pitched to get the attention of the most recalcitrant drunk midnight diner customer. "As much as you're all obviously enjoying Mrs. Matthews's superb coffee and the variety of pastries graciously provided by the Rosensteins— you all really know how to make babka—"

A cheer rose from the crowd.

Holly continued, "—as much as you're enjoying yourselves, this old inn is about to burst at the seams. Some of us need to get out of the way so the people who live here can finish wedding preparations."

Tara heard Hannah grumble, "The wedding preparations have been done for weeks. Please. This is me."

"So, we're going to do a classic midmorning activity. Karaoke! Follow the giant blond man!"

At this, Cole waved his arms, the crowd cheered again, and at least half of them peeled off to head to the barn after him.

Hannah shot Tara two thumbs-up, although Tara wasn't sure how she knew it had been Tara's plan to begin with.

She hated karaoke. It was chaotic, and people who were bad at singing did it anyway, picking songs they thought they knew the words to but didn't actually, and everything was noise and flashing lights and people screaming over the music. She liked bars, when she could go to dance, but sitting still in sensory overload and listening to people butcher Queen songs? No.

But here she was, at the front of the barn, where a microphone stand had materialized along with the promised karaoke machine. Gavi was setting up the projector in the back, and suddenly something that looked like an old Windows screen-saver was on the wall behind her.

"Can you sing?" Cole asked Holly.

Holly shook her head. "I'm real bad."

"Great. You need to start," he told her. "Tara sings very well, and it tends to kill the mood if the first person is great. It intimidates people."

Tara nodded. "I do intimidate people." It was also true that she could sing, but she rarely let herself do so in front of people.

Holly had a moment of looking like a deer in the head-lights, but then nodded. "Nicholas, I need you to cue up the Violent Femmes."

As she started singing the opening lines of "Blister in the Sun," the crowd whooped and started jumping. By the time she got to the chorus, the whole barn was singing along. It wasn't good, but it *was* cute.

Tara was in real trouble if she thought a woman singing off-key was cute.

The midday winter sun streamed in through the open barn doors, and dust mites danced in the air as the floor bounced. It was surreal, and a little beautiful, in spite of the chaos.

When Holly was done, Tara grabbed the mic. "Y'all, I need people to sign up for slots here, or Cole is going to take over, and he knows every word to every Meat Loaf song. I would do anything for the love of him, but I won't listen to that."

Cole gasped, clutching his chest. "I will have you know," he said, taking the microphone from her, "that I am planning an ode to a great bisexual icon and hero of our generation, Billie Joe Armstrong."

That was smart. Cole also sung very well, which you might notice in a hair band ballad, but wouldn't if he was screaming a Green Day song. She relinquished the stage to him, and he began "When I Come Around."

She would have gone with "Welcome to Paradise," but it worked the way it was intended. People thought of nostalgic songs they could mostly remember and signed up.

As she listened to a Rosenstein cousin launch into "Don't Stop Believin'," she watched Holly. Her red waves had been stuffed under a Pikachu hat and she had black liquid liner ringing her eyes. She was wearing ripped-up jeans over fishnets with her big platform black Docs. Tara wasn't sure what about seeing Holly this way, completely in her element, wearing no masks, she found so damn adorable.

A tiny voice in the back of her mind whispered that if she and Holly ever dated, Holly would have to put that self back into storage, at least for family and work functions. The voice asked, *Is that fair? Is that what you want?* Tara ignored it. Obviously, she would support Holly dressing any way she wanted, and Tara would never ask her to mask when it was just them, but everyone had to mask sometimes.

No one really ever got to only be who they wanted; that was life. Plus, they weren't going to ever date. Even if a part of Tara was starting to wish maybe, in some world, they could.

While Elijah and Jason Green were in the middle of a rendition of "I'll Cover You" from *Rent* that had most of the audience close to tears (Jason must be one hell of a theater teacher), her phone buzzed with a text.

Hannah: You're a lifesaver! let's get everyone back inside.

It was time for her to shut this down, which meant she was going to have to sing.

Through a series of eyebrow movements and telepathic communications, Cole got her center stage and cued up her music. He winked at her when she saw what was on the screen. She could sing, sure, but could she sing Idina Menzel? They were going to find out. And, if she fell flat, she would be in good company.

"This has been so much fun, but Hannah tells me we're moving on to the next part of the schedule, and what Hannah says, goes." The crowd tittered at this. "So, to close us out, let's go... into the unknown."

When her nieces had watched *Frozen* for the first time, they'd said, "Auntie Tara is Queen Elsa!" and though she'd known they meant it as a compliment, it hadn't felt that way. A woman who refuses to use her power because she's scared of it, who is happier to freeze than love? That might be how Tara appeared on the outside, but she knew, inside, she was a whole different person.

The cold had always bothered her.

Right now, though, this song... Every word felt like it was being ripped out of the depths of her soul—an unnerving thing for an almost-forty-year-old to feel about a Disney princess, but many unnerving things had happened to her this week, and it hadn't killed her yet.

She poured her heart out through Elsa's words, hitting every note (apparently having a midlife crisis made you better at singing?) and finishing, breathless, to find the whole barn frozen (pun intended) and speechless.

"Wow," Holly whispered, "you really *can* sing."

"To lunch!" Cole hollered, and then wrapped an arm all the way around her body and basically carried her inside with him, which was good, because she found her knees a little weak.

He deposited her in a chair and handed her a sandwich. Apparently, though Hannah was coordinating people into vehicles to go eat lunch at Ernie's, she was also feeding them pre-lunch to keep them occupied. The sandwich in Tara's hand was pimento cheese, and as she chewed, she wondered how anyone in the northern wilds had learned how to make it well. Must be Miriam's influence.

"This egg salad is amazing," Holly said, her mouth half full, and then more quietly added, "That was the sexiest thing I've ever seen."

Tara almost spit pimento cheese out of her nose. "That was embarrassing. It was way too many feelings to be having, way too publicly, with way too many strangers."

Holly raised an eyebrow. Tara could raise just one eyebrow, because she'd spent hours staring in the mirror as a child willing herself to, but she had to concentrate to do it, and she had an irrational jealousy of people who made it look effortless. "You keep a very tight leash on the sheer power of your charisma, Tara. When you let your hair down...it's mesmerizing."

Tara shifted uncomfortably in her seat. She didn't know how to deal with being watched with as much intensity as Holly was looking at her right now, how to handle being actually seen.

"I don't have enough hair to let down," she said, sounding

prim to her own ears, "and the last time I was unleashed, a country club burned to the ground."

Holly bent her knees so that she was sitting with her feet underneath Tara's thigh, and pushed the curtain of Tara's hair behind her ear. "You can hide your face, but I'll still see you, Sloane," she said. "There are a lot of ways to unleash yourself without burning everything down, and I trust you to find them, even if you don't trust yourself."

Her breathing sped up, and her body froze. She clamped her lips shut to stop herself from saying something Southern and cutting to distance herself from the moment. Looking over Holly's shoulder to avoid her eyes, she focused on a little Charlie Brown tree (Why did they insist on bringing all the live trees *into* the inn? Wouldn't a nice pink plastic tree have fit the aesthetic better and been more hygienic?) that someone had shoved into a corner and decorated entirely in Funko Pops from *Flight of the Fordham*, the space opera show that Levi and Noelle were obsessed with.

Just then, Jayla Green walked up to them, a Belle costume pulled over her hoodie and jeans, coordinating yellow plastic heart elastics bobbing on her Afro puffs. "You didn't tell me you were Queen Elsa," she accused.

Tara looked at her, their eyes almost level from her seat on the short couch. "You didn't tell me you were Princess Belle," she rejoined, holding out her hand for a shake. "A pleasure to make your acquaintance, Your Highness."

Elijah, who had been across the room trying to keep Jeremiah from eating his weight in rugelach, winked at her. Oh, good. She'd gotten that one right. She was okay with her nieces, but she also understood the strict parameters of their upbringing. Tara had never been allowed to be much of a child, so she always felt a little at odds and ends when asked to interact with children who were allowed to be themselves.

Jayla was nodding solemnly over their clasped hands. "Your Majesty," she said. "I'm so thrilled you could join us for this royal wedding."

"Oh, is it royal?" Tara asked. "I didn't know."

"Obviously, Miriam is Aurora." The little girl told her, as if this were a known fact to everyone. Tara searched her memory, and realized Aurora was Sleeping Beauty. "She told me that before she came here, she was asleep for a long time, and Noelle was the prince who woke her up."

From behind her, her brother said, "That's silly, girls can't be princes."

Without turning to look at him, Jayla sighed the exhausted sigh of siblings everywhere tired of their brothers. Tara liked this kid so much. "People say you can't have two dads, Jeremiah, but look at us. Girls can be princes if they want to."

Jeremiah scrunched up his face like he wanted to argue with this logic but could not.

Jayla turned to Holly. "Are you Queen Elsa's prince?"

A sparkling laugh tumbled out of Holly. "I'd like to be," she said, "but Queen Elsa doesn't need a prince, does she? She has her family, and they all save each other."

Jeremiah, who was obviously tired of being left out of this conversation, said (through his missing front teeth), "I think Elsa falls in love with the nice girl she meets in the magical forest."

"Well," Holly said, "we *are* in a magical forest. Maybe I'm the nice girl Tara falls in love with in between saving the world."

"That makes sense," Jayla concurred. "After all, Carrigan's is a fairy-tale castle, and Aunt Hannah is Rapunzel, even though she cut her hair. The forest must be magic." The twins seemed appeased by this and went back to their father.

"Those two almost make me want kids," Holly observed, watching them go. "Not quite, but almost."

In case she tried to go back to the conversation they'd been having, Tara decided they needed another distraction. She stood up, carefully brushing crumbs off her clothes. There weren't any, because she'd learned from the time she could feed herself that a lady didn't get food on her, but it was ingrained in her to check.

"I'm going to find Hannah to see if she and Gavi need help getting these people wrangled." She bent down, intending to drop a kiss on Holly's cheek, but Holly moved her head so their lips met.

"Come back to me soon?" Holly asked, reaching up and running her hand down Tara's sleeve, then squeezing her fingers before letting go. It was the same thing she'd done the first night they got here, which was the only thing that reminded Tara that she was acting for the benefit of their friends, no matter how sincere her eyes looked.

THE PREP

December 22–23

Chapter 16

Holly

Some of the Rosensteins and Old Ladies were settled for rest (Seriously, where were they all sleeping? Did Carrigan's have secret extra rooms that only magically opened when you needed them?), while Hannah finally got everyone else in the shuttles to go to lunch at Ernie's. Some of them were grumbling about not being able to eat here, where there was a famous chef, but Holly knew Mrs. Matthews must need the kitchen desperately for wedding prep. Therefore, lunch had become a Wedding Event.

Cole and Hannah, who were jointly in charge of this as the best man and matron of honor, took attendance at Wedding Events very seriously. Holly knew this, because she'd tried to sneak Tara off for a midafternoon quickie and been hauled back. How was she ever going to get enough of Tara, so they could go back to being just friends after this weekend, if she couldn't get *any* of her?

"We're going to the bar," Hannah said in a tone that brooked no argument.

Hannah was kind of scary, in a hot way. This trip was teaching Holly a lot about her attraction to terrifying women.

"Isn't one of the brides a recovering alcoholic?" Holly asked. "Why are we going to a bar?"

"It's a small town," Noelle explained. "If we don't hang out at the bar, we hang out nowhere. But, trust me, I'll be surrounded by three-quarters of the sober alcoholics in the greater Adirondacks. I'll be fine."

Holly raised an eyebrow. "What happened to the other quarter of them?"

"I don't like them so I didn't invite them," Noelle said, shrugging, and walked off to herd Old Ladies.

Holly was still confused. "What are we going to do at the bar? At two in the afternoon?"

Hannah looked at her like this was a ridiculous question. "Eat lunch."

"We literally just ate lunch," Holly pointed out.

Hannah laughed. "Oh no, that was a light nosh. You haven't spent a lot of time at Jewish family gatherings, have you?"

"I mean, not none. I did grow up in the Quad Cities, which has a long history of tight-knit Jewish community, so I went to a lot of b'nai mitzvahs," she countered. "But I'm also Midwestern, so I understand the concept of the meal before the meal. Still..."

"Go with it," Miriam advised. "We had to come up with something to get them all to Advent, and they won't fit inside Collin's diner."

Ernie's was dark and narrow, lined with wood that had soaked in generations of cigarette smoke. It felt like home.

Sawyer was behind the bar, while a woman Tara introduced as Ernie, the owner, was taking tickets and looking frazzled.

"The girl who's supposed to be on the grill tonight is at home vomiting, so I need to be on grill, but I also need, like, three more waitstaff," she explained, pulling out a pen and pad to take their order.

Holly gazed around their table thoughtfully. "What if I could get you one killer waitress and a line cook who's famous in Australia?" she said, and Levi's eyes lit up.

"Yes! Put me in, Coach!" He rubbed his hands together. "I will fry so many pickles."

Ernie looked skeptical.

"I've been waiting tables for fifteen years," Holly assured her. "I can get all these people served before Levi even has the tickets."

"Oh," Ernie assured her, "I'm not worried about you. I'm not sure I want to let Chef Angst over here near my griddle, lest he decide to start serving deconstructed tapas or something."

Levi gasped in indignation. "I would never besmirch the name of your sainted grandmother Ernestine by soiling your deep fryer with fine dining."

Ernie glared at him.

"Okay, I would," he admitted, "but not right now. You're way too swamped."

She handed Holly her pad and paper. "Can you take this table?"

Holly saluted. "Roger that."

Pointing at Levi, Ernie said, "Don't screw this up."

Levi grinned, and his beauty freaked Holly out.

"Why does his face look like that?" she asked Hannah. "It can't be good for him."

Hannah held her finger up to her lips. "He knows he's beautiful, but he doesn't actually know how beautiful, and we choose not to tell him. He's already insufferable enough."

"I don't think he's that handsome," Noelle said, and they all stared at her. She shrugged. "He has too much hair. And his smirk is asymmetrical."

"Have you met your soon-to-be-wife?" Hannah asked. "Because if anyone on this earth has too much hair…"

"Okay. What are you all eating?" Holly interrupted, and began taking orders.

She was dropping off drink tickets with Sawyer when he caught her hand. "Thank you."

"It's fine. Y'all needed a waitress. I'm a waitress. This saves me from awkwardly making small talk with a bunch of people I barely know."

Sawyer shook his head, the curls on the ends of his mustache turning up as he smiled slightly. "That's not what I meant, although Lord knows it's appreciated. Thank you for making Tara more comfortable this week. It was critical to Cole that she be here. He doesn't ask for much from the people he loves, but he needs them."

While he said this, he released her hand to do a complicated bottle flip, then measured whiskey into a shaker, never taking his eyes off Holly. He'd obviously been bartending long enough that it was ingrained in his muscle memory, and she felt a kinship with him. He would never judge her for her job, and Cole obviously didn't judge him for his. Maybe Cole could work on Tara, get her to see that being involved with a waitress wasn't shameful.

Holly bit her lip. "But who's taking care of Tara, while she takes care of Cole, and the rest of the world?"

Sawyer pointed at her. Oof. Even he, who knew they were faking it, seemed to have been convinced that she would be good for that job, and she didn't know how to tell him she wasn't available. She wanted to be, but she couldn't. He handed her the drinks she'd come for, and she went to deliver them to the table.

Then she stuck her head in the passthrough. "I need fries, Matthews!" she shouted.

"Order up!" He smiled at her, dropping a platter of various fried foods in front of her. "I don't suck at this, remember? Culinary school?"

"I bet culinary school didn't prepare you to cook a perfect plate of poutine," she argued, "or how to run a packed bar kitchen."

He shrugged. "That's why I spent four years cooking around the world. But you shouldn't knock what you haven't tried—have you ever thought about pastry school?"

She glared at him. "Did Tara put you up to this?"

"I don't take orders from Tara," he corrected her.

"Ah, Hannah put you up to it." She nodded. "You should all stop meddling."

She walked off with the plates, some of the high she'd been riding wearing off. Cole might not judge Sawyer for being a bartender, but he was, after all, also the mayor of this little town. Collin and Ernie both owned their businesses. No one in this group was ever going to accept someone who didn't have a real career and didn't want one.

Of course, she reminded herself, she didn't need to be accepted by this group. After this weekend, she would never see these people again.

While she was delivering Fried Everything Platters, Cass Style (a secret menu item where everything was kosher), Ernie stood up on a chair and yelled for everyone's attention.

"All right, you hooligans! Miriam over here is obsessed with pub quiz," she said, and Miriam whooped. "That means, while all of her friends and family are gathered, you're going to fulfill one of her life dreams and let her beat you all at trivia."

"Hey!" Miriam shouted. "They're not going to let me beat them! I'm going to beat them fair and square!" Then she turned to Tara and said, "You're on my team."

Tara smiled a smug smile. "Oh, we're going to kick everyone's ass so hard."

They high-fived each other. And then proceeded to absolutely destroy everyone in the bar at trivia—the winning question was about women's basketball.

Elijah Green, who appeared to take trivia as seriously as Miriam, looked at Tara with an appraising eye. Holly watched them all play, laughing and throwing straw wrappers at each other and arguing playfully over answers. She watched Noelle step in to settle disputes like she was breaking up squabbling siblings, and laugh until she cried when Tara said something hilarious.

Holly hadn't even known Tara could *be* hilarious, and honestly it was really hot. This version of Tara, that let her shoulders down from around her ears and unclenched her jaw and played, was like a magnet whose pull Holly couldn't resist.

A couple of hours later, when everyone was packing up so they could explore the rest of Advent, Ernie flagged her to stay back. Tara hung back, too.

Ernie handed her a cup of coffee and tried to hand her tips.

"I'm not taking these," Holly said, pushing them back across the table.

"You earned them," Ernie offered. "You hustled your ass off, and we would've been lost without you. You're a hell of a waitress."

Holly acknowledged this with a nod. "I'd better be, after all these years, or it would be time to find a new job."

"Well, if you ever want to spend some time in a small town in the mountains, I'd give you an apron in a minute."

"That's very kind." It would be easy to take Ernie up on that generous offer. She liked it here, and Ernie would be an amazing boss. "I just left a job because I wanted to do more baking, though."

"Not a lot of need for baking in a dive bar," Ernie conceded. "Collin might need a baker. But what *you* need is to take these tips."

Holly shook her head and sipped her coffee. "I don't take money when I do favors for friends."

"Are we friends?" Ernie asked, a laugh in her voice.

Holly nodded emphatically. "We're going to be."

"Okay, friend, do you want to do me one more favor?"

"Hit me."

Ernie suddenly looked much shyer than Holly would have

guessed she could. "Will you find out for me if the hot chef is single?"

Holly was taken aback. "I'm pretty sure Levi is, like, very married."

"Ew! Not that guy!" Now Ernie laughed full-out. "Lawrence. He's so cute."

"I will absolutely put in a good word for you if I meet him," Holly assured her.

They had a moment where Holly felt they were kindred spirits, a friendship immediately formed. Her heart clenched. Maybe Tara was right, and she did need friends.

Tara had been watching all of this with a little smile on her face. Holly leaned over and kissed the edge of it, startling her. It seemed to Holly that outside of the bedroom and shows for public consumption, Tara wasn't that comfortable with being shown affection through touch. She wondered if it was because no one but Cole ever bothered to touch her, or if she genuinely didn't like it. But then, Tara smiled full-on at her, and leaned back in for a real kiss. Her eyes, locked with Holly's, were crinkled with pleasure at the edges.

"You're always doing kind things and hoping no one notices," Tara told her.

"I'm not doing it for kindness's sake," Holly said. "I'm doing it because it needs to be done, and I can. No notice necessary."

Tara looked at her for a long moment, those blue eyes boring into her, as if she wanted to say something else, but she seemed to think better of it. Instead, she picked up Holly's hand and kissed her palm.

"Get a room!" Sawyer said.

"We have one!" Tara laughed. "And I think getting back to it is the exact right idea."

Holly loved this plan. The family and friends were still exploring the town, and dinner was not for hours.

They hauled ass back to Carrigan's and, once there, Holly pulled Tara into their room, tugging at her clothes and running her hands up Tara's stomach.

"Sloane," she whispered, "let's get this off."

Tara grabbed her hands, interlacing their fingers. She held them up above Holly's head before leaning in to kiss her. Nipping on her lower lip, she pulled away.

"I promised Miriam and Noelle that we would actually make it to dinner tonight, which means we are not taking our clothes off."

Holly pouted.

"What we *are* going to do, is take your shoes off. Because you have been on your feet way too long."

This, Holly couldn't argue with. She sat down on the bed to pull off her boots, and Tara pushed her back against the pillows. Taking Holly's feet in her hands, she pulled off the socks and began massaging her feet.

At first, Holly was appalled. This perfectly put together, never mussed woman with the impeccable hair, eyeliner wings that could cut someone, and unstained white sofa was rubbing her dirty, aching feet. She let her head fall back and moaned.

"Does Miriam know you can do this? Because I'm starting to question her judgment in choosing Noelle."

Tara gasped playfully. "You weren't already questioning it? I'm obviously the superior catch. I mean, except that Noelle is hot, funny, well-read, successful, emotionally mature, and went to Yale."

"You went to Duke law," Holly reminded her. "And you're all those things."

"Maybe not emotionally mature," Tara said wryly. "I'm still trying to both rebel and win my mother's approval at the same time."

Holly acceded to this point with a little nod. "Noelle might be further along her self-knowledge journey, but it's not like Miriam was any great shakes in that area. And she does seem to be smack-dab in the middle of trying to figure out her own mom issues."

"Meanwhile, all of them are trying to figure out their Cass issues, whether it's rebelling, seeking her approval, or some mixture," Tara conceded.

"I don't really understand the whole Cass thing," Holly admitted after a couple minutes of being rendered unable to speak by Tara working the pain out of her calves.

"Just wait. I guarantee that now that everyone's here, dinner will turn into the Cass Carrigan remembrance hour. I only spent, like, twenty-four hours here a year ago, and if there's one thing I know, it's that these people love to talk about Cass. They don't even know they're doing it. I don't think I've ever had a phone conversation with Hannah that didn't invoke her name."

"How often do you talk to your ex's cousin on the phone?" Holly asked. She knew they were friends, but she couldn't gauge how close they were, because once again she was caught between Tara's version and everyone else's.

"A couple times a week?" Tara guessed. "We always talk on Tuesdays when Miriam and Noelle are at trivia, but sometimes we talk other days, too. We're each other's outside-the-bubble friends, and we can be as petty as our hearts desire together."

Holly stared at her in horror. "Why don't you text like normal millennials? Or send voice memos?"

"We do." Tara moved from her feet up to her calves, and Holly shut her eyes, dropping her head back against the headboard. "Plus, they added me to the Carrigan's group text, and they keep adding me back every time I take myself off. But sometimes it's nice to hear someone's voice."

Shuddering, Holly shook her head. "I'll take your word for it." It was truly extraordinary that Tara's belief in her own unlikability had managed to, thus far, survive the love onslaught that was the Carrigan's friend group. "Now. My feet feel wonderful, but do you think you might want to make the rest of me feel wonderful, as well?"

"Hmm," Tara said thoughtfully, "I do charge more for full-body massages."

"Oh? And what could your payment possibly be?" Holly asked, running her hands up Tara's arms as Tara crawled up from the bottom of the bed to hover over her, boxing her in.

Tara smiled wolfishly. "I charge in kisses. And my prices are very steep."

"Gosh, it's a hard call, but I think I'm up for paying it." Holly wrapped her arms and legs around Tara and brought their bodies flush.

Dinner was, in fact, a flood of reminiscences about the Carrigan matriarch. After dancing around the world under the stage name Cass Carrigan, Rivka Rosenstein had decided that, rather than joining her family's bakery business, she wanted to own a Christmas tree farm and Christmas-themed inn, because it would allow her to contain most of her business to a few months of the year and leave the rest open for travel. She'd opened Carrigan's Christmasland in the early sixties and then, in the late seventies, Ben Matthews and Felicia Cohen, teenagers from Advent, had come to work for the summer. They fell in love—with the farm, with each other, and with Cass—and they stayed and raised a family there.

The stories everyone told painted a picture of an eccentric misanthrope, an Auntie Mame type who arrived auspiciously in people's lives to save them from drowning (usually emotionally or financially, but at least once literally). She collected misfits, loners, weirdos, and revolutionaries.

Holly noticed that, while Mr. and Mrs. Matthews and the younger Matthews twins, Joshua and Esther, listened with happy smiles, Levi stood in the corner, his head buried in his wife's shoulder and, judging by his shaking, weeping. Noelle walked up to them and enveloped both him and Hannah in a hug, rocking them gently. Holly wondered if there wasn't more complicated grieving going on, with the last generation of children who had grown up here.

It wasn't any of her business, but it helped her remember that this place, magical though it might seem, was built and run by humans—fallible, difficult humans who loved and hurt and lived and died like everyone else.

Kringle yowled at her feet. Well, fallible humans and a perfect cat. She gathered him in her lap and kissed his head.

"Do you miss her?" she whispered into his gigantic ears. He rubbed his cheek against hers and chirped mournfully.

It was a shame that Kringle couldn't stand up and tell his own Cass stories. Holly would bet his were wilder than anyone's.

She sent a picture of him to her sister, with a chair for scale, and instead of a text back, she got a call. Slipping into a hallway corner, behind a garishly decorated tree, she answered.

"What is this wild place?!" Caitlin asked. "I need to hear everything, especially about Tara."

Holly smiled involuntarily. "She's...pretty amazing. I don't think I've ever met anyone easier to like but harder to get close to."

Her sister barked out a laugh.

"What?"

"You're describing yourself, Holly!" Caitlin told her. "Everyone likes you, but as soon as anyone tries to breach those impenetrable walls, you pull out the knives and throw them as you run. You won't even wear the clothes you really like in case someone guesses who the Real Holly is."

"Yeah, yeah, yeah." Holly couldn't argue, because that was definitely what she did. "It doesn't matter with this one, though. She just...she hates her life, and I don't think I want to be a part of it."

"Sounds like an excuse to me! Maybe if you really like her, she'll make you actually put in the work."

What the hell? That, she could argue with. "I work my ass off, Caitlin. I have since I was twelve and got my first under-the-table job, remember? So we could get new backpacks for middle school?"

"You do work hard, at your job. And not at all at anything that involves emotional vulnerability," Caitlin said. "Which is kind of ironic for someone who says they don't dream of labor!"

It was a low blow to quote James Baldwin at her.

"Look, I know you don't want to hear this, but most people aren't naturally good at friendship or romantic relationships. Lots of people get mean when they're scared or feel threatened. And they work hard to stop. You can be a different partner this time, but you have to actually try. Or you can be a jerk to this girl, too, and mourn her for ten years like you have with Ivy."

Caitlin wasn't saying anything Holly hadn't begun to ask herself as she spent more and more time with Tara. She kicked the tree in front of her in frustration, and a shiny pink ball fell to the ground and shattered. Shit. She hadn't meant to break their ornaments.

"I'm hanging up now, Cait. I'll call you never!"

"I love you!" Caitlin said as Holly hit end on the call.

She rested her head against the wall and closed her eyes, not ready to go back out into the crowd. It was true that she was scared she hadn't changed. But that wasn't the real issue.

The real issue was she could change into a whole different person, one who was kind, emotionally generous, open, loyal, and she would still never be Marriage Material for Tara. So why try?

Chapter 17

Tara

"Can I tell you something kind of awful?" Miriam asked, sitting next to Tara on the porch swing.

She'd come outside because the energy in the dining room was a little too romantic for her to handle, and it was starting to give her traitor brain ideas about how she and Holly could, next year, be celebrating their anniversary at Carrigan's. If they really got together. Which they obviously couldn't, even if she wanted them to. She didn't even think Holly was interested in a real relationship.

Holly had a whole world to see, and she hadn't said anything to make Tara believe she wanted anything past their agreed-upon weekend.

Tara startled at Miriam's voice. "Please! I love a terrible confession."

Miriam sighed. "I want to be unreservedly happy for Cole

and Sawyer, but I'm feeling a little...jealous. That I'm going to have to share him with a romantic partner."

"I get it." Tara nodded, although in actuality she had lost Cole's affection years before, when she'd walked away after the fire, and when he'd met Miriam. Miri had never, really, had to share Cole with Tara. "And I feel better that I'm not the only one."

"Hmmm, I mean, he became friends with me, and he didn't stop loving you. It will probably be okay? Cole's very big—he has a lot of room for love in his body."

"I'm not sure it's the same thing," Tara argued, though she should leave it be, since Miriam was only trying to make herself feel better. "I was never the most important other person in his life."

"Are you sure?" Miriam asked skeptically. "Because the way he tells it, you were his other half, and then after the fire, you pulled away and he was floating around desperate for a life raft when he happened to meet me."

As if he had been summoned by his name being spoken, like the chaos demon he was, Cole appeared. "What are we talking about? Is it me?"

"Not everything is about you, Nicholas," Tara said, but Miriam threw her under the bus.

"We were talking about how you love Tara the most of anyone."

His blond waves bobbed as he nodded emphatically. "Not just of anyone, of anything. Oceans, sailing boats, lobster pants, international crime, bad decisions—there's nothing and no one on earth I love more than this one."

He pointed at Tara, and his tone was melodramatic and ridiculous but his eyes were serious as they held hers.

That was the most absurd thing she'd ever heard, and she wouldn't—couldn't—entertain it as an option. Even the possibility that it might be true overwhelmed her, gutted her, and tried to rewrite her, as if Cole were able to hack her most basic wiring. If he loved her that much, as much as she loved him, she had been dismissing his love for half her life, refusing to believe in him. If he had been serious every time he effusively adored her, and not joking, as his manner implied, he had offered her his heart and she'd rejected it, and she could have spent the last twenty years with a soulmate but instead she'd sent him off to sea alone and hurt them both.

Her version was safer. "You love me like a blankie," she said, but she couldn't meet his eyes.

She felt herself be swept up, and then she was sitting on his lap. It was unfair, how fast he could move, and also how strong he was. He settled her against him, his arms around her waist. "Your ass is way too bony to be a good blankie, Tar."

She wiggled her butt bones against his thighs to make him yelp, because messing with him was much, much easier than dealing with what he'd said.

"Where's the rest of your crew?" she asked, changing the subject. "Don't y'all usually travel as a pack these days?"

Miriam picked at an imaginary loose thread on her overalls. It was, Tara knew, one of her tells for when she was uncomfortable and trying to hide it. "They're having some Feelings about Cass and it's best if I give them space for that."

"You don't have feelings about Cass?" Tara asked, nudging Miriam with her knee.

"I do"—Miriam shrugged—"but I didn't exactly have feelings at all for ten years, so I'm still kind of in the training-wheels phase." She looked up at the sky, like she was trying to figure out how to phrase her next words. "Plus, like, not to invalidate how they're feeling, but I'm so much more mad at my parents that Cass's idiosyncrasies barely register. Is that terrible?"

It was Tara's turn to shrug. "It's a feeling. It doesn't have moral value. I probably wouldn't tell it to Levi, but..." Tara had heard a lot about Levi's Issues with Cass from his wife.

Miriam laughed. "Noted."

"Speaking of your parents..." Tara grimaced.

"Oh my gosh, is my mom being awful?" Miriam asked, clutching at Tara's sleeve. "She promised she would behave."

"She implied I should object to the wedding and try to win you back *My Best Friend's Wedding* style."

Miriam's eyes got huge in her tiny, elven face. "That rat-fink."

Tara had forgotten that Miriam said shit like *ratfink*, and how charming it was. God, she was glad they were getting back to being real friends again. She would never want to lose one of the few people she genuinely liked in this world because they'd had the bad sense to try to date. "The weird thing is, I think she genuinely adores Noelle. It's like some sort of compulsion, to set you up with the wealthiest person in the room."

"I know!" Miriam threw up her hands. "Since she found out Cole's getting his trust fund, she's been trying to suss out if he's gay or bi, and whether we ever slept together and might do so again."

"*Ew*," Cole said. "You slept with Tara! That would be like incest!"

"You're so weird," Tara said, but then remembered a story she'd meant to tell Miriam. "I forgot! When he came out, my mom told me, 'Oh that's great, now you can get married and you won't get in each other's way.'"

"WHAT?!" Miriam screeched, almost falling off the porch swing with laughter.

Cole gasped. "You never told me that! Ew times a thousand."

"It's a good thing that we never introduced our mothers," Miriam said when she caught her breath. "We wouldn't have survived their scheming."

Tara wiped tears of laughter off her cheeks and shook her head.

"It turns out, I'm glad we didn't get married." Although she was fairly certain Miriam knew this, she felt it still needed to be said.

"Me too," Miriam agreed.

"Third!" Cole agreed. "We always needed Noelle in our karass."

"Although," Miriam mused, "we did make a good team. You're going to make some lucky girl a hell of a wife someday. Maybe soon?" At this, she elbowed Tara gently.

Tara grimaced. "I really like Holly, and I think she would make an amazing wife, but I'm not sure she wants to be one. I think I've been hiding my head in the sand a little about whether or not I could ever fit her into my life, and vice versa."

There, that was true, if not the entire truth.

Cole snorted. "Where there's a will, there's a way, my friend. Look at Hannah and Levi! He wanted to see the world, she wanted to stay at Carrigan's, he left her alone for four years in a remote hotel in the woods with his parents while he wandered off on a boat to find himself, and yet, here they are. Two little peas in a pod, living their best lives. You like her, that's what matters."

"It's more complicated than that, baby, you know it is," she told him. And herself.

He made a dismissive noise. "Is it? When was the last time you liked anyone this much?"

Honestly, maybe...never.

Tara did really, *really* like Holly. She was quick, and funny, thoughtful and always down to help. She was a freaking clinic escort, and what was sexier than a girl who rode hard for reproductive rights? The sex was so hot it felt like her brain was melting.

"What if I like her too much?" she asked, not meaning to speak out loud.

Miriam whooped and pointed at Tara. "I told you you were going to get turned ass over teakettle by love when you least expected it!" she crowed.

Tara glared at her. She would have glared at Cole, who was shaking with laughter underneath her, but she couldn't twist her head far enough.

"I'm changing the subject," she said, trying to keep the laughter out of her voice. She secretly loved how much her friends wanted to meddle. "Tell me what's happening with your names? Are you keeping Blum, after everything?"

When they were engaged, Miriam had been ecstatic about legally becoming Anything-But-Blum, even if she needed to keep her maiden name for her art business.

Miriam shook her head. "No. I can't keep his name, no matter how much time I've spent making it my own. Noelle doesn't feel particularly attached to hers, although she loves her parents' memories. There's something a little too on the nose about being a Christmas tree farmer named Noelle Northwood, after all. Plus, we both want a shared name."

"So, what are you going to do, become Carrigans? Go extremely millennial and combine Rosenstein and Northwood?"

"We thought about Rosewood, actually!" Miriam agreed. "Which is very lovely."

"But?" Tara asked, hearing the unspoken word.

"But it's not Jewish enough!" Miriam exclaimed. "Too many of my ancestors had to give up their names in the diaspora, and I'm lucky enough to have this long family tradition stretching back generations. Even Cass never legally changed her name. She was born and died a Rosenstein."

Tara smiled. This was another thing that Noelle could give Miriam that she could not have—she wouldn't have been able to give up the Chadwick name, without giving up the power and influence that came with it. The power to do good, with a terrible legacy.

"So, you'll be Miriam and Noelle Rosenstein, then. Is your family thrilled?"

"You should have heard them!" Miriam's eyes sparkled, actually sparkled as if happiness were surrounding her like pixie dust. "The cheers were absurd when we told them. Noelle is going to keep North as a middle name. And I . . ."

"Are going to finally, really be Mimi Roz," Tara finished for her.

Miriam nodded, so much weight in the action.

Mimi Roz had been the name Miriam had used for the paintings she'd done right after college. Her father had burned most of them, but a few had survived, and the sale of some of those remaining pieces had been what helped save the farm a year ago. The deepest part of Miriam, her truest artistic self that Tara had never truly known, was attached to that name.

"I'm going to take Sawyer's name," Cole said, though he'd been quiet up to this point—probably because he knew all this. "We're not getting married, we don't believe in it, I'm just going to change my name because I hate my family. I'll be Cole Bright. I like it."

Tara and Miriam looked at each other and started to laugh again. Then they caught up on each other's lives. She'd noticed before how different Miriam seemed. It was part of why she'd been okay with the breakup (or, mostly okay), because even a year ago, Miriam had been obviously so much happier here. After a year of growing freely into herself, though, she was like a whole different woman. Someone mischievous, hilarious, strong-willed.

Tara had always thought of Miriam as sassy and sad, but she wasn't particularly sad anymore, except around the edges where the loss of Cass still haunted her, and her personality had blossomed to fill that space and beyond. Tara was, honestly, thrilled for her, even emotional at the sight of it. And, speaking of terrible confessions, jealous. Not that Miriam was marrying someone else or had fallen in love, but that Miriam had found herself.

Eventually, Holly stuck her head out onto the porch. "There

you three are! Hannah says we all have to sleep, because there are so many more wedding activities tomorrow."

Miriam groaned. "I should have eloped! Hannah is using my wedding to make up for the fact that she had zero wedding hoopla, either time she and Blue got married."

"I assumed she was using the fact that you have millions of social media followers to market Carrigan's as a wedding venue," Tara said.

Huffing, Miriam pushed up from the swing and crossed her arms. "I have, max, half a million followers. They're just very...intense."

Miriam's followers, self-named the Bloomers, were intense, for sure. Tara had gotten a few hateful messages from them after the breakup, which she'd forwarded to Miriam, who she assumed had gone scorched earth on them because no one had bothered her at all in months. Except that every once in a while, someone would stop her at Emma's for a selfie.

Miriam leaned down and took Tara's hand to pull her up.

Holly made a gimme gimme gesture. "Come on, I have plans for you, and they don't involve being out in the middle of the night in the freezing cold with your ex-girlfriend."

Miriam flashed her a smile. "Go with the hot redhead who's trying to seduce you."

Cole squeezed her, extra hard, for just a moment, his head against her back, before he let her go.

Tara paused on her way inside.

"You made it possible, you know," she told Miriam, gesturing to Cole. "For him to fall in love with Sawyer. You gave him the safety and solidity to face the scariest thing in his life, actually trusting in romantic love, because he knew he'd always have somewhere to land."

Cole shook his head. "She wasn't the one who did that, Tar."

Back in their room, Holly pulled her in by the lapels of her shirt dress. "Hey," she said, dropping a slow kiss on Tara's lips. "What were you and Miriam talking about?"

Tara smiled, leaning in to prolong the kiss. "Oh, our...Cole called it a karass? What the hell is that? Did he make it up?"

"He did not, although Kurt Vonnegut did," Holly said. "He defined it as a group of people brought together to do God's work, but I've always thought of it as a sort of... spiritual caravan. A group of people predestined to travel through the human experience together."

"That's pretty deep for Cole," Tara observed, pulling away and flopping on the bed.

Holly flopped down next to her, and they lay on their sides, looking at each other.

"What's actually bothering you?" Holly asked.

Tara pushed a wave of hair out of Holly's face. "They both keep trying to tell me that I'm loved here and it feels...hard to believe."

"Why is it hard," Holly asked, running a hand down Tara's arm, "to believe that your friends like you?"

People trying to love her shouldn't make her lungs seize up. She wanted to pick it apart, to find all the reasons she didn't deserve their love.

Blinking, Tara tried to articulate what was patently obvious to her. She never talked about this with anyone, mostly because it seemed like saying the sky was blue. "I mean," she said, "I'm not very likeable."

"Who says?"

Holly's tone wasn't demanding, or accusatory, just curious. It made Tara give her a real answer, instead of the flippant "everyone" that was her first impulse. How did Holly keep getting real feelings out of her?

She held up the hand she wasn't lying on, which caused the bed to shift, and she wobbled a bit before resettling. She began counting on her fingers. "One, my parents."

"Okay, your dad would be a Civil War reenactor, on the Confederate side, if he didn't hate grass stains; your parents are fundamentally unlikable. What else do you have?"

Tara didn't know how Holly knew that about her dad, although it was true. She kept counting. "Two, all the kids I grew up with—"

"Except Cole," Holly interrupted.

No one ever interrupted Tara when she was in the middle of her patented intimidating Argument Lists. It was disconcerting. Holly wasn't intimidated by her at all.

"Except maybe Cole, but I have no way of knowing."

Holly blinked at her this time. "You could believe him when he tells you, constantly and specifically."

She waved this off. It was too close to what she'd been contemplating earlier, and she still couldn't look at the thought straight on. "He's too good, you see. At his core, he's too good for this world, and he would never break my heart by telling me the truth."

"Okay." Holly sounded unconvinced. "Who else?"

Tara held up a third finger. "My law colleagues."

"The rich old cishet white men whose entire system you want to see dismantled don't like you? Seems like a good sign, actually."

Tara blew out an exasperated breath. "Most people don't like me when they first meet me, Siobhan. They think I'm cold, and prickly, and kind of a bitch."

"Well, I like you *because* you're cold and prickly and kind of a bitch," Holly said, "but also, your friends didn't just meet you. They've known you for a long time, and they've learned all the other wonderful things you are."

"You like me?" Tara whispered. Her brain had caught on that part of what Holly said and wouldn't move on.

Holly smiled a little. "I do. I like that you argue in lists, that you match your handbags to your suits, that you eviscerate bad people for money but also for fun. I like that you're slyly funny and you don't think anyone notices. I like that you always, always try to do the next right thing, even when I think you're wrong about what that is."

"I like you, too."

"What do you like about me?" Holly asked. Her hand had moved from Tara's arm to tracing the neckline of her dress, and it was very distracting.

"Is everything a reasonable answer?" Tara asked, and Holly shook her head.

"You're good at lists. Make me a list."

Tara traced the freckles on Holly's face with her eyes, trying not to lose her focus to the whisper-soft fingers undoing the buttons of her dress. "I like that you don't take shit from anyone, even when it seems in the moment like it would be easier to. I like that when you see something that needs to be done, you do it. I like that you're proud of where you came from. You know yourself. You don't have inhibitions. You're always the brightest thing in any room, like you're lit from the inside out."

"Oh God, don't say I light up a room," Holly groaned. "That's a surefire way to get me murdered and talked about on *Dateline*."

Tara giggled.

"But," Holly said, "I think you might be the one rewriting reality to make it kinder."

"I'm not. You're brave. Much braver than I am."

Holly smiled sadly. "I'm not brave, Sloane. If I were, I would visit my family more, but I'm afraid if I go there and stand still, I'll somehow get caught in the trap of turning into my mother. And my mom has a really good heart, but it's not the life I want!"

"You don't ever have to be like your mother if you don't want to be like your mother," Tara told her.

"That's not the only thing," Holly argued. "If I were brave, I would have a food truck."

Tara gasped. "You *do* want something more permanent!"

If Holly wanted something permanent, maybe she'd want culinary school? A pastry chef and successful small business owner could fly under the radar at social events, so she wouldn't be eaten alive by the debutante sharks.

"I do, if it was something where I could make my own hours, get to decide where I go, where I park, who I feed, and if I could pick up and leave whenever I want. I want it, but it's too risky. Most food trucks fail, and I can't be broke again. I can't lose my meager savings on a pipe dream."

Tara began to speak, and Holly stopped her. "Don't tell me you'd finance it. I can't handle that. I don't want your family's money, and I don't want our...whatever is between us...to have that kind of debt in the middle."

She wanted to argue that it wouldn't be a debt, it would be a gift, or an investment, but she could see that, no matter how she felt, to Holly it would be charity. Besides, she didn't want to argue and ruin this moment, especially when Holly had just admitted that there was something between them, and it could maybe exist outside of these walls.

"You're much braver than I am," Holly told her. "You're the bravest person I know. You're bearding the lion in its den; you've faced the worst mistake you ever made and decided to make good for it instead of letting yourself off without consequences. You keep loving your friends fiercely even though your brain is convinced they don't love you back."

Tara shook her head, then rolled onto her back and covered her eyes, because she couldn't look at Holly while she talked about this. "I'm not brave at all, either. I do have all these things I've always wanted to do, like sing in a band, and volunteer for the Innocence Project, and learn to cook, and all I do is what I've always been told, but I tell myself it's a long con. I'm not even brave enough to fall in love! I put one foot out of line one time, and it exploded, and now...I'm living this life that matters to me, that I fought for, that I chose, yes, but that I don't think can ever make me actually happy."

She felt Holly lift her hand from where it was covering her eyes and peer down at her. "I think you've been expanding your circle pretty damn well this weekend," she said, dropping a soft kiss on Tara's forehead.

"But what happens when I go back to Charleston?" Tara asked. "I'm going to go back to my little bubble. *I'm* going to be just like my mother."

"Tara Sloane Chadwick," Holly said seriously, "you couldn't be your mother if you tried."

Chapter 18

Holly

Sometime past midnight, Holly woke up to find herself lying sideways in bed, on top of the comforter, tangled in both it and Tara's long limbs. When had they fallen asleep? Why was she still wearing her jeans?

She rolled out from under Tara's arm, having been awakened by something she couldn't pinpoint. She changed into a pair of Tara's pajama pants, which were too long on her but were the most delicious raw silk. The fire had gone out, and the room was freezing, so she dragged a hoodie over her head and stepped into the hall.

As she emerged, she realized what it was that had woken her out of a comfortable sleep snuggled up with a beautiful woman. The air smelled like cookies. Not just any cookies, but Rosenstein's original recipe mandel bread. She would know that smell anywhere. Following it down the stairs led her to the kitchen, where she found Miriam and Levi, in their own pajamas, baking and laughing and drinking coffee.

"Oh my gosh, I didn't mean to intrude," she said, turning to leave.

Miriam waved a hand to stop her. "Please, we always welcome guests to our Witching Hour Baking Parties."

"Do you do this...often?" Holly asked in amusement, slowly moving farther toward the kitchen island.

Levi shrugged. "It's our thing—well, it's Miriam's thing. She keeps collecting people in the kitchen in the middle of the night."

"It's not me," Miriam protested. "It's Carrigan's! Well, maybe it's Kringle, but you know what I mean. It's the magic!"

Holly scooted up onto a stool, and Levi slid her a cup of coffee. She looked between the two of them. "The magic, huh? I thought Tara was kidding when she said you all believed this place was magic."

"Oh no"—Levi shook his head—"we absolutely all believe it's magic, whether we want to or not. If you ask Miri, it's pure concentrated Cass, baked into the walls. If you ask Hannah, it's all of the love from the past sixty years."

"And you?" Holly asked.

"My best guess is a forest spirit manifested by the cat," he said, handing her a cookie.

She chewed for a minute. "This is wrong. You left out something." Thinking for a minute, she said, "Almond extract. The original has almond extract."

"Ha!" Miriam pointed at Levi. "I told you people would notice, but no, fancy chef man said no almond extract."

"Well, fine. Holly can make the next batch!" he said, handing her a mixing bowl. She was more than happy to do so.

"So what does the magic *do*, exactly?" she asked, scooting off her stool and moving behind the counter so she could work more easily.

"It brings people here. People call it the island of misfit toys, but it's not any misfits," Miriam explained. "It's people running from home or looking for one. People who have lost their way back home or never had one. If the thing wrong with your life is, at its core, not related to home, I don't know, I assume you end up at some other magical inn to get fixed."

Kringle, who had wandered in and settled on the stool Holly had abandoned, chirped at them.

Holly considered this. "So, Tara's here because she … needs to leave home? Because Cole is her real home?" She checked the recipe, which was, for unknown reasons, written on an airplane napkin.

Levi raised an eyebrow. "The real question is, why are *you* here?"

Holly was surprised. "Me? I'm just keeping Tara company."

"Incorrect! No one shows up in this kitchen at three a.m. unless Carrigan's brought them here. So. Tell us. Why aren't you home for Christmas? And, second question, equally important: You're obviously a talented baker—why don't you work in food?" Levi pointed at her, in mock accusation.

"Miriam's a very talented baker and she doesn't work in food!" Holly protested.

"Not everyone is a weirdo who makes their whole life and career revolve around an art they're passionate about like us, Blue," Miriam told him. "Maybe Holly is in love with waitressing."

They looked at her, right as she took a bite of cookie. "Um," she said, chewing carefully, "it's more, like, poverty trauma and not wanting to participate in capitalism? Also some wanderlust?"

Miriam and Levi seemed to have a wordless conversation, which ended in them both speaking at once.

"Is waitressing making you enough money to outrun the poverty trauma?" Miriam asked.

While Levi said, "Baking is a pretty primal, pre-capitalist urge. Feeding people, creating bread?"

She answered Miriam first. "I'm broke now, but I'm never stuck without options, and I'm never hungry. It's not, I'll admit, a perfect system."

They both nodded, as if they deeply understood not wanting to be stuck, if not from poverty.

"As for why I'm not baking as a career..." She stirred the cookie dough harder than it needed, trying to be as brave as Tara thought she was and tell the truth. "I guess I started waitressing as a temporary step, something I knew I could always fall back on, and then my plan B became my plan A. Because if I started a business, it could fail and I'd lose everything. Right now I have nothing to lose."

"That's depressing," Levi said.

Miriam threw a ball of dough at him. "Be nice. I spent a lot of time with nothing to lose while I was healing. Holly probably has her reasons for living a life she doesn't really like."

What the hell, these people were brutal.

"You're mean, and I'm taking your cookies," Holly said, pulling the plate toward her.

"You can't," Miriam told her seriously. "They taste wrong, and you need to get this last batch in the oven. While you're working, tell us your reasons for living a life you don't really like."

Ugh, these people were going to make her talk about feelings. "You won't understand. Everyone here is so kind to each other."

Levi and Miriam exchanged another wordless conversation. "Us?" Levi asked. "The two of us, specifically, are two of the most self-centered people you'll ever meet. We just learned how to not give in to our most self-centered impulses so we could be part of our family."

"Anyway," Miriam said, "why do you think you're not kind?"

Holly tried to explain, because something about this blue delft kitchen glowing in the middle of the night felt like a sacred space, where she shouldn't lie. "When I was younger, I would get scared when anyone started to get close, or relationships started to get hard. I'd lash out with the meanest things I could think to say, and then run while people were bleeding. I don't like that about myself, so eventually I stopped letting people get close as a way to stop doing it."

She slid a cookie sheet into the oven and portioned out more dough, not meeting their eyes.

"Soooo..." Levi said, leaning on the counter next to her and crossing his feet, "instead of deciding that you didn't like the way you interacted with people and changing your response, you decided you were going to just…not have friends? That seems like the hard way around. Even I have friends, and I'm the worst."

Miriam nodded. "He is the worst. But couldn't you not have friends, while being a baker? I'm confused about how the one is related to the other."

"I want to see the world," Holly said, as if this explained everything.

Levi blinked at her. "Yes. I'm familiar with the concept. I spent four years on a boat, seeing the world. And yet."

"But when you have close relationships, they tie you to one place. To a suffocating, domestic life," Holly argued, but saying this out loud, to a man who had a million close connections and, from what she could tell, the least stifling domestic life imaginable (he filmed his show around the world, after all), made it sound ridiculous.

She looked between Miriam and Levi. "It's possible this is a me problem," she said eventually.

"My bride-to-be likes to quote Mary Oliver—" Miriam began.

Levi interrupted. "You're marrying such a nerd!"

She shot him a withering glance. "You wooed your wife with spreadsheets and a PowerPoint."

He shrugged happily.

"*Anyway*, as I was saying, it might be time to listen to our great queer poets and ask yourself, Holly, what do I want to do with my one wild and precious life?"

Well. When you put it that way.

"I think I want to bake, and love people, and be kind."

They nodded. When they moved in unison, it was clear they'd been close all their lives, and it made her aware that she didn't have that with anyone, except maybe Caitlin.

It felt momentous that they easily folded her in, and she let herself relax, chatting easily until the oven timer dinged.

"Do you want some of this batch to take with you?" Levi asked, pulling out the first tray of correct cookies.

She walked back up the big curved Carrigan's staircase in a daze, munching on perfect mandel bread and thinking about how she was going to bake for a living, but much more importantly, how she was going to learn to let her walls down, to love people. To be kind.

"Where going?" Tara mumbled as Holly walked into their room.

"Nowhere," Holly whispered. "I'm coming back to bed with you."

Yawning, Tara rolled back over. "Mmm-kay."

God, she was cute. Holly leaned down to brush the hair off her forehead and place a kiss on her widow's peak before shuffling off to the bathroom.

She kicked off Tara's pajamas and slid back into bed in her underwear. Holly hissed as her bare legs brushed up against Tara's, and suddenly, Tara was above her. In the dark, her eyes flashed hot.

"We fell asleep in the middle of a very maudlin conversation," Tara said, brushing kisses down Holly's collarbone. "And we never even got naked."

Holly reached up behind Tara's neck and brought their lips together. "Well, I'm not asleep now, and we can't miss an opportunity to take advantage of this beautiful bed."

Before she got completely carried away by Tara's lips and hands, it registered that this slow, intense lovemaking in the middle of the night was going to be very hard to let go of once they were back in Charleston. Holly liked waking up in Tara's bed more than she wanted to.

If only Tara would give up on this idea that she could only do her job the way she wanted to in South Carolina and would look at the broader picture. Thousands of people in the country needed a dedicated, progressive defense attorney who would represent them regardless of their ability to pay. There was no shortage of injustice in the U.S. justice system, and a lot of ways for Tara to show up for the work, without having to live for her family's whims.

Last night, they'd had this incredible conversation, unlike any Holly had ever had with anyone but Ivy, and Tara had all but admitted that she was unhappy. But even then, she'd only said she wanted to widen her circle, not explode it. How could she get the arsonist inside Tara to burn down her own life, for her own good? And for theirs, if there was ever going to be a Them?

She kissed Tara desperately, hoping that maybe whatever this was between them could convince Tara to walk away from her family, toward something healthier but just as impactful.

When they woke up later that morning, Holly surreptitiously looked up how lawyers got jobs with the Innocence Project while Tara was in the shower. Surely it couldn't hurt to make them aware of Tara's amazing work, right? Tara might not be ready to take the leap, but if they presented themselves, she might be able to imagine new possibilities. And she could start out volunteering if that made for a more comfortable transition.

She drafted an email, only to decide that it would be highly unprofessional and pushy to send it. Suddenly there was a frantic knock on their door.

"Holly!" Cole's voice called. "I need you!"

Cole needed her? What the hell was going on? She opened the door, and Cole's giant frame and floppy hair fell through.

"*Holly*," he moaned, gripping both of her forearms. "*The cake.*"

"What about the cake?" Holly asked, breathing slowly and deeply to try to get Cole to mirror her.

Cole started to cry. "It *melted*."

"Jesus, how?!" Holly gasped. She knew that the giant Rosenstein's-baked cake had been residing in the walk-in refrigerator, waiting for tomorrow to get its finishing touches.

"We left the door open a sliver by accident, and the fan overheated trying to keep the temp down, and then it exploded, and Blue says it's going to need to be completely replaced."

If Levi Matthews thought they needed a new walk-in, they did.

"Fuck, can y'all afford that?" Tara asked, coming out from the bathroom and toweling off her hair.

Cole was breathing hard, trying to get himself under control. "I'm going to pay for it. Sawyer and I...were making out in the walk-in and didn't shut the door all the way. It's my fault."

"Oh, Cole," Tara breathed. "And now you're trying to figure out how to fix it."

"Holly, you can bake. I would never ask you, with all the Rosensteins here—"

Holly interrupted him. "Miri's family is here to celebrate her marriage. They already baked her a cake once. I'm more than happy to do it."

"That's too much work for one person," Tara objected.

"Oh no, it absolutely is," Cole agreed. "Esther's going to help you. She bakes almost as well as her mother, and before Gavi came to work for us, they worked at Rosenstein's, so they're both going to pitch in. But will you please please please come lead the effort?"

Holly looked back at Tara, trying to gauge how she felt about this idea. It would put Holly in the kitchen for most of the day, and the reason Holly was here was because Tara didn't feel like she could face this party by herself. Still, over the past few days, Holly had watched Tara become more and more comfortable being a part of the group.

"You should do it," Tara said. "If you want to. I should probably try to spend some time with Cole, anyway. He's getting weird about the distance between us, and who knows how long it will be before I see him again after this."

"I am not *getting* weird about it," Cole argued. "I've *been* weird about it. But I know how long it will be, which is no more than two weeks. Because that's as much as I can handle."

If Tara loved her, and she didn't get to see Tara's face every day, she would be whiny about it, too. Hell, she was maudlin about the idea of leaving Tara when she inevitably left Charleston soon, and they didn't love each other.

She couldn't very well tell Miriam she wouldn't fix her wedding cake because she didn't want to lose one of her only days left with Tara, that she was desperate to hold on to every second of their remaining time together, to hoard it like a dragon. As far as Miriam knew, they were going back to South Carolina to continue their love story, likely heading toward moving in together, and then marriage, because that's where all Tara's relationships went. They had all their lives ahead of them to spend romantic weekends in the woods together, in their fiction. Besides, Cole was looking at her with desperate puppy-dog eyes. She smiled as warmly as she could and said, "Of course I'll help!"

Cole's face lit up like, well, like a Christmas tree. Tara came up behind Holly and squeezed her shoulder, dropping a kiss on the top of her head. "Thank you," she whispered.

Gavi Rosenstein was in full general mode when Holly arrived. They had laid out all the basic cake ingredients on the countertops, rolled up their sleeves, and tied a handkerchief around their short hair.

"I see the relation to Hannah," Holly observed, and Gavi grinned.

"What a lovely compliment! We do all tend to be formidable."

They were not kidding. Holly respected that every person in this family, or at least on this farm, seemed intensely passionate about their work. It didn't make much sense to her, even after talking to Levi and Miriam, because she'd always been unwilling to make her work her identity, but it seemed to give them fulfillment.

She surveyed the kitchen. "Do you have a recipe, or am I on my own for that? Because I have several, although I'm famous for my coconut cake, which seems risky for a wedding. Some weirdos hate coconut."

"I'm weirdos," Gavi said, raising their hand. "I have recipes you can peruse, or you can use one of your own. We have a nut allergy, so avoid them. I do know that Noelle is crazy about citrus."

"Hmm," Holly said, tapping a pen against her chin. "And I know Miriam will always choose chocolate if given an option. Maybe a dark chocolate Valencia orange situation?"

Gavi was flipping through a massive binder on the kitchen table.

Holly watched over their shoulder. "Is this the Rosenstein's bible?!" she asked, awestruck.

"The Torah is our bible," Gavi deadpanned. Holly snorted out a laugh. "But yes, this was very generously loaned by the aunts, and it has recipes going back to the very beginning, some of which haven't been made in decades. Here's a lemon white chocolate?"

"White chocolate is gross. But we could probably modify it. I like the base recipe."

Gavi grimaced. "So the original cake was vegan, because apparently a bunch of Noelle's Old Ladies convinced a bunch of Miriam's Old Ladies to go vegan a few months ago. Can you . . . replicate that?"

"I can if I have the right ingredients." Holly chewed on her lip. "The dairy part is easy, but…" She opened the kitchen door and yelled, "CHEF MATTHEWS!"

Levi materialized. "You rang?"

"Are you taking lessons from Cole in mysteriously appearing? Never mind. Talk to me about egg substitutes you already have on hand."

Within a half hour, they had a game plan and an assembly line set up. Cakes were going in the oven, then into the freezer to cool enough to ice. While they baked, they sang along to Holly's favorite baking playlist.

"I appreciate the Dolly to Black Flag transition," Gavi yelled over the music.

"You have to keep it unexpected!" Holly yelled back.

The kitchen door burst open, and Esther Matthews ran in. "I'm so sorry I'm late. I heard there was a cake emergency, but the lab called with a samples emergency! Does anyone have an apron?!"

When Miriam came to check on them, they were dancing to "I Want You to Want Me" while the KitchenAids whipped frosting. Holly saw her give a speculative look to Gavi, who was dipping Esther. Lord, did anyone on this farm ever stop matchmaking? She pulled Miri into a swing and then paused the music when the song was over.

"Do you want marmalade inside the layers, and, if so, how do you feel about cardamom?" she asked, showing Miri what they were doing. Miriam was a baker herself, and probably would have insisted she could bake her own wedding cake if her friends hadn't restrained her.

"Yes, and enthusiastic," Miriam answered.

Holly smiled. "Great, because I already made Levi make some."

"My aunt Shoshana has been making noises about how this cake cannot possibly be as good as the one they sent over that Cole callously ruined, but I think she's going to have to eat her words," Miriam said, sneaking a spoon into the frosting and licking it happily.

Grabbing a small bowl, Holly layered a sliver of cake, a spoon of marmalade, and a dollop of frosting. "She can eat the cake if she wants. See what she thinks."

Miriam cradled the bowl. "I'm going to take this to Noelle since it's her wedding cake, but I'll let Aunt Shoshana know it's an option."

Aunt Shoshana arrived with alarming swiftness, followed by Tara and Cole.

"I heard there was cake," Tara said.

Holly waved her off. "There's not cake for you—you can have some at the reception."

"Aunt Shoshana," Gavi said, "let me show you the original Rosenstein's recipe that we lovingly adapted to fit the couple. I'm thinking it might actually be something we want to bring on the menu."

Aunt Shoshana made a disbelieving sound in the back of her throat but accepted the bowl she was handed. She chewed it slowly, like a sommelier with a mouthful of wine.

"She reminds me of the judges on *Australia's Next Star Chef*," Levi whispered.

While she was chewing, Noelle burst into the kitchen, which

was now full to bursting with people and cakes. "Holly, this is the best cake I've ever eaten. In my life. Do you want to marry us? I'm open to having two wives."

"Hey!" Tara objected. "If polyamory was an option, why didn't we all end up together a year ago?"

Before anyone could respond, Aunt Shoshana cleared her throat and they all turned. "This cake is delicious. In fact, if you can bake like this, Holly, I have an opening at Rosenstein's. I don't know how you feel about living in Davenport, Iowa, and the position requires you to have graduated from, or currently be attending, culinary school, but I'd love it if you applied."

Holly could feel Tara's eyes on her.

"That's so kind of you, Ms. Rosenstein," she said carefully. "I'm actually from Davenport, and my family is still there, so I have no issues living there"—this was a lie, she had several issues—"but right now I'm not looking to settle in one place, and I don't have a lot of interest in culinary school. It's a lot of debt to take on, when I'm not sure I want to work in baking long-term."

In the middle of the night, she'd asked the universe how she could bake for a living, but now, in the light of day, when an opportunity was being presented to her, it seemed too scary. Too big a leap of faith.

Tara made a noise like she was about to speak, but Shoshana spoke over her. "Well, I'm sure we could figure out the finances, if it came to that—we have a scholarship program for promising young bakers—but I can understand how you might not want to leave Tara, who does seem quite settled in Charleston."

"She does, doesn't she?" Holly agreed, smiling tightly. "Although I'm sure there are people who need good criminal defense in Iowa as well."

From the corner of her eye, she saw Tara's lips tighten a fraction, so subtly that anyone who wasn't paying attention wouldn't notice.

Shoshana patted her on the cheek. "Well, I'm sure your family would love to have you close by." They would freak out, actually, and Holly could feel her panic rising as she thought about her mom being able to interfere in her life from down the street. "It's a standing invitation, you can always call if you change your mind."

Chapter 19

Tara

While Holly was baking, Tara was trying to put out work fires. Technically, she was on vacation, and also technically, the offices were closed for Christmas, but only the senior partners actually got to turn their phones off during things like weddings, trips, or national holidays. Her law clerk had been keeping her up-to-date on everything going on in the office, which she'd been surreptitiously checking in on when no one was watching.

Every time Cole caught her with her work email open, he threatened to install nanny software on her phone and laptop that would allow him to cut off her internet after too many hours per day.

He was a menace, but currently, he was a menace who had been distracted by trying to keep the brides from panicking about their cake situation. So, he wasn't there when a text came in from her clerk that she needed to call *immediately*.

She'd specifically hired this woman because she never, ever overstated or overreacted to any situation, so Tara knew whatever she needed to say was a big deal. She hid in the library (choosing the window seat and not the big cushy armchair where she knew for a fact Hannah and Levi had had sex; why did her friends tell her so many things?) and called Charleston.

"Boss," Lucy said as she picked up, her voice neutral.

"Lucy," Tara said, "please tell me you have great emergency news, not terrible emergency news."

"Should I lie to you?"

Tara growled, banging her head lightly against the window. Outside, snow fell in beautiful swirling flakes that danced around the evergreens as if on fairy wings. It was the snow globe Cole always described Carrigan's as, but it didn't make her feel warm and cozy, only trapped. "Tell me."

She could hear Lucy grinding her teeth on the other end of the line. "The judge was seen at a party in Hilton Head doing Jell-O shots with the prosecutor."

Tara didn't have to ask which judge, or which prosecutor. She had one huge, potentially career-altering case coming up that she'd been working to bring to trial for two years. The prosecutor had thrown every absurd obstacle under the sun at them, including trying several times to get the case reassigned. Now, apparently, he'd sunk to trying to sway the notoriously fair judge by other means.

"I should never have left town," Tara groaned. "I would have been at that damn party, and I could have kept an eye on them."

"I have photos," Lucy said. "I'm emailing them now. I can start drafting a motion for him to recuse."

Tara tapped her nails on her iPad, where the email from Lucy had come through. She gritted her teeth.

"Draft it in case we need it, but I think this may require a bit more . . . finesse."

If she were in Charleston, she would happen to stop by the judge's favorite brunch spot and surprise him by sitting down at his table. She would lean over and set her chin in her hand, smiling innocently at him, and ask how his night had been. Of course, if she were in Charleston, she would never have allowed this to happen.

"I'm never going on vacation again," she muttered.

"You have to, boss. You were starting to get jaundiced from the office lighting," Lucy told her flatly. "You can fix this. I believe in you."

She could fix this. She would call up the judge on his home phone, which she happened to have the number to because he played golf with her dad, and she'd mention casually that she'd seen some interesting photos from a party last night, and that she hadn't known he was a Jell-O fan. Whatever ground the prosecution thought they'd gained in the judge's favor would disappear, because he knew that if he stepped a foot out of line, Tara would be there, watching.

He liked his shots, but he *loved* his reputation as a man above corruption.

"You're the best, Lucy," she said genuinely. Lucy was way too good, and too moral, for this job, and eventually she'd take a job as a public defender or something that let her look herself in the mirror every day. Tara would miss her when that happened, but she would understand.

"Back at ya, boss. Have some fun, yeah?"

Tara sighed, looking again at the freezing wilderness outside the window. "Yeah. I promise." She was having fun, and she would pay for every second away by having to work twice as hard when she got back.

She called the judge before Cole could find her and stop her.

Like clockwork, he arrived as soon as she hung up, looming in the doorway. He was probably trying to lean insouciantly, she assumed because he was jealous that Levi looked so cool when he did it, but he was taller than the old Victorian doorway, so he was more lurking than anything.

"Why are you staring at me like you're worried I'm going to spontaneously combust?" she asked. "You're freaking me out."

He closed the door behind him but didn't move fully into the room, just leaned back against the door. His face, normally alight with mischief, was still and drawn, and he kept pushing his hair off his forehead. It was a nervous gesture of Levi's that Cole must have picked up while here, because she'd never seen him do it before. Of course, he was so rarely nervous.

It was strange to see him with new mannerisms, but she guessed the longer they were physically apart, the more she wouldn't know his every move. She wondered, when that happened, if any connection would still exist between them, or if they would become people whose parents were friends. Could whatever invisible string held them to each other hold up when it wasn't reinforced by habit and proximity?

"Fraser, get in here," she said. "Say whatever it is you're standing there trying to force yourself to say."

He walked toward her, his long legs covering the small library in a couple of steps. Folding himself in half, he sat down on the floor in front of the window seat, hugging his knees.

"I need to ask you something," he said, and his ocean-blue eyes were the gray of an incoming storm.

She motioned for him to continue. "Ask away."

"You're going to get mad at me."

Oh, Cole. "I think you'll live."

"I need you to do me a favor, and you're not going to like it, but I know you won't do it for yourself so I'm asking you to do it because I need you to."

She put down her phone, moved her iPad off her lap, and really looked at him. Now she was getting nervous. Maybe she *didn't* want to hear whatever this was.

"Spit it out, baby doll."

"I need you to start taking care of yourself." He had stopped pulling at his hair and was sitting with his hands on his knees, the most still she'd ever seen him. "You're burning yourself out as fast as you can, trying to martyr yourself to prove you deserve the oxygen you take up. And I get it. Your fucking parents, they made you think you needed to earn every breath. But I can't let you burn up. Not again."

Tara knew what he wasn't saying.

While she had been at boarding school, she'd picked up some poor habits from some of the other girls. It had been a shitty time, she'd felt like she was careening out of control, and a lot of things had seemed like a good idea, from vodka to diet pills to shady hookups. But that had been during the dark time. Cole had shown up and pulled her out of that, but it wasn't fair of him to equate that time and this. That had been a conflagration. This was...a controlled burn.

"I'm more healthy, emotionally and physically, than at least eighty percent of our social circle," she protested.

Cole guffawed. "Tara Sloane, that's the worst rationale I've ever heard. Bailey Ellis has been on a juice and cocaine cleanse for the past five years. Rachelle Parkins thinks Gwyneth Paltrow is an actual prophet, and I think she's in a candle cult. And that's not getting into anyone's relationship with gin."

"Ugh." Tara crossed her arms like a toddler. "I'm fine."

Why did they have to talk about this? She thought they'd silently agreed that they were going to pretend nothing had ever happened and go about their lives pushing it under the rug with everything else from their past they never talked about. It was a big rug, there was room for a whole lot of mess.

"Fine like you're taking vitamins and sleeping? Or fine like you only ended up in the hospital from dehydration and exhaustion once this year?" he clarified. He still had her pinned with his stare.

Please. She'd never ended up in the hospital. She was very good at walking the line of burning the candle at both ends without self-destructing.

She picked at her sweater. "It's not that bad. Honestly. I work too much, but it's only for now. I just made partner."

"And then what? The goalposts move, and it's until you become a judge? Or state senator?"

This conversation fucking sucked. "Why are you asking this?"

"I don't know, Tar," he said sarcastically, throwing up his hands, "the last time you had a terrible year and we didn't see each other for a while, I had to show up and drag some dude out of your bed. A DUDE!"

He had done that. She didn't know why. She could still hear him as he dropped her back off at school, with a final warning that if she didn't get her shit together, he would move in and sleep on the floor, no matter what her roommate thought (or the administration at her all-girls college).

She did have her shit together, mostly. No one made partner without losing some sleep or destroying their stomach lining with caffeine. She wasn't out of control, because Cole had asked her not to be, and sometimes in this life, when we didn't want to do it for ourselves, we held on for other people. He'd saved her life, not just that semester of college but the night of the fire.

When she had been transfixed by the flames, then racing toward the building and trying to run in to make sure no one was there, he'd pulled her away, sheltering her body with his when the windows started exploding. He had scars on his back from where he'd been hit with burning glass, and every time she saw him in a swimsuit, she wanted to trace them with her fingers, as if she could magically erase them by will alone.

He'd told the cops, when they arrived, that he'd come up with the idea. Because he knew that his family would cover for him but hers might not.

She would stay on this side of the line, with work and everything else that might kill her, because she owed Cole her life, even if it felt like she didn't deserve to. Even if it felt like she never worked hard enough to earn that. And she would stay on this side of the line when it came to love, because she'd almost killed the only person she'd ever loved with her whole heart. He should understand that.

She was so frustrated that he was acting like he didn't understand that.

"Is that why you're so intent on getting me together with Holly?" she said sadly. "Because you think I'll be happy again, and you'll be released from your imagined responsibility to make sure I don't hurt myself? And bonus, she'll make sure I eat vegetables and sleep?" Tara looked out the window, because she couldn't look at Cole. "I release you. I, Tara Sloane Chadwick, vow to you, Nicholas Jedediah Fraser III, that I am in no danger of reverting to any of my self-destructive teenage behaviors, and I release you from any obligation you may think you have to protect me."

Cole didn't answer, just snorted at her.

She heard him stand up and brush himself off.

"Are you going to stop talking to your shitty, abusive family and working yourself to the bone? Because until you do, I'm still on the clock."

Tara bristled. "They're not abusive. Not like Miriam's parents."

"Oh, do you want me to go get Miri and ask her what she thinks?" Cole planted his hands on his hips. "I was there, Tar. You were desperate to get free of a home full of people who hated you, and you made a really bad decision—*with me.* And now you think you deserve to suffer forever in penance, and look, I do not blame you for being an abuse survivor who stays in contact with her abusers. I know it's not as simple as saying you should walk away."

When she rose and tried to speak, he held up a hand, and she let him finish because she didn't have words, and because he never talked about the fire, even obliquely.

"But it's been half a lifetime now. Can you at least think about starting to forgive yourself?"

Swallowing, she said, "How can I? How could I deserve that?"

He ran a hand down his face. "Have you forgiven me? Do you think I deserve to pay miserable penance for the rest of my life?"

Of course she didn't. She knew all the reasons why he'd done what he had, and while it didn't excuse his participation, she knew he had made, and continued to make, restitution.

He held up his hands. "Do you think it might be time for like . . . trauma therapy? We can go together."

When she didn't answer him, he sighed and said, "We're not done talking about this, but do you want to go eat cake? Because I heard there is some. Available."

She was going to take this conversational out. Anything to distract him from the fact that she had been up here, working, and that she hadn't promised him what he'd asked.

"Don't think I didn't see your iPad, Chadwick," he said as they were walking downstairs to the kitchen.

Chapter 20

Holly

The cakes were assembled, frosted, and safely chilling. Cole had been banned from setting foot back in the kitchen.

Now everyone was gathered in the dining and great rooms in a celebratory combination of a rehearsal dinner for the wedding and an anniversary party for all the couples who'd gotten engaged at Carrigan's over the years. Holly and Tara were seated with Sawyer and Cole, Elijah and Jason Green, Esther Matthews, and an ancient, terrifying woman named Annie who Holly was certain was actually a primeval magical force disguised as an antiques dealer.

As the salad course was served, Holly went to reach across the table for dressing. Her arm brushed against Tara's, and she saw Tara's eyes spark. "Do you need this, darlin?" she asked, passing Holly the silver boat full of Mrs. Matthews's famous vinaigrette.

Holly flushed with embarrassment. "I should have asked instead of reaching. I have those wrong-side-of-the-tracks manners, you know?" She tried to make it a joke.

Tara stopped in the process of passing the dressing to Holly and put down the boat. She took Holly's hand and squeezed, holding on to it instead of letting go. "Your manners are lovely. Those rules are a scam made up by people in power to keep others out of their little club," Tara said. "I know this for sure because I was born into the club." She picked up their clasped hands and kissed Holly's fingers.

Esther smiled at them both. "You two are very cute together."

"We are," Holly agreed, looking at Tara with those heart eyes she'd promised.

"And you kept it a secret from the Carrigan's crew?" Esther said. "That was probably for the best. They get nosy."

As she said this, her eyes tracked to Gavi, who was checking on guest needs.

"Nosy?!" Cole protested. "Us? We would never meddle!"

Everyone turned to look at him, and he grinned unapologetically while stuffing a forkful of salad into his mouth.

"We wanted to have some time to get used to it, time that was just ours," Tara said.

Holly remembered the two of them, singing at the top of their lungs in the car, and how she'd wished for more time exactly like that. In their little bubble, where neither of them was faking or wearing a mask, where they were two people drawn like magnets to each other with no complications. No matter how much she was coming to love this group, if they ever really dated, they would have to figure out a way to carve out some space that was just theirs.

Of course, they wouldn't date.

Tara released her hand to run a finger down Holly's cheek. "Some things don't have to be a group experience," she said, dropping a featherlight kiss on Holly's mouth.

"It's a bit ironic," Annie said to Tara over the next course, "that we never met for all the years you and Miri were engaged, but now here we are, meeting at her wedding to another woman."

Sawyer looked at Annie, and then around the room. "How do you know Miriam, again? And how does she know...all of the rest of these people?"

Annie laughed. "Don't you know about Miri's Old Ladies? We're all junk shop dealers across the country, and she's like our daughter. She checks in on us, makes sure we get to our doctors' appointments, that all our legal affairs are in order, and such. There are many people in this room who would not be in business, or even alive, if not for Miriam Blum."

"But she's based here now, taking care of Carrigan's, isn't she?" Sawyer asked.

Annie waved this off. "Oh, sure, but Noelle and Hannah both knew going in that Miriam came along with the Old Ladies and that she would have to build in time not only to make art but also to travel to all the shops. There was never any question of her abandoning her old friends for her new ones."

The way that all of the team here, not just Noelle and Miriam as a couple, had put their needs on the table and come up with a solution that fit all of them—without sacrificing anyone's happiness or asking anyone to make themselves smaller—was eye-opening. Every part of the life they'd all built here was based on that, not what was expected or what they feared.

"Lawrence!" Elijah called out, hailing a man walking past. He was average height but built stocky, with wide shoulders under his dress shirt. He had brown skin and a black pony-tail, and Holly noticed that his knuckles had tattoos that read "Chef" and "Life."

He hugged the Greens and Esther and shook hands with everyone else. "The infamous Tara Chadwick!" he declared. "Cole talks about you incessantly. I'm glad to finally meet you."

Holly wondered how Tara felt about being on the receiving end of so many people who'd heard about her.

"I actually wanted to introduce you to Tara's girlfriend, Holly," Elijah said. "Holly is an experienced waitress and short-order cook, and a fantastic baker. I know you said you might be looking for a pastry chef. Maybe we could lure them both up here?"

Lawrence snagged an empty chair from a nearby table and pulled it up next to her.

"I have actually heard about you," she told him.

He grinned. "All bad things, I assume."

"Ernie said you were the hot chef, between you and Levi," Holly said, and watched his eyes widen. "And she asked me to find out if you were single."

"Oh, I love you. I do not, however, need a pastry chef. I'm focused on staffing my camp for Mohawk kids right now, and I prioritize Native applicants for that."

"As you should!" Holly agreed. "What a rad project."

"Lawrence worked at Smithsonian's National Museum of the American Indian, we should mention," Jason Green told her. "If he's not hiring, Chef Harlow is around somewhere. She has the only Michelin-starred restaurant in the area."

From a table over, a giant red-haired man with an equally giant beard said, in a deep baritone, "A baker and a waitress? I own a cafe, and I would love to chat. Look at our hair, we're basically siblings."

Esther cleared her throat. "Actually, Shoshana Rosenstein offered her a job earlier today, along with culinary school tuition."

"No, no, no, she can't go to Iowa!" Elijah argued. "They both clearly belong in Advent!"

Jason elbowed him. "You want Tara on your trivia team, full-time."

"I need a lawyer friend," Elijah pouted. "No one will be nerdy about the law with me."

Tara raised an eyebrow, and said in that perfect drawl, "As much as I would love to get nerdy about the law with you, I would not flourish above the Mason-Dixon line. I am a delicate hothouse flower, and I can only blossom in climes where the air itself is a weighted blanket."

"We're never visiting Charleston, honey," Sawyer said, his mustache ends turned down in disgust. "Sorry."

Cole shrugged. "Tara's the only person I love there, anyway, and if she won't move here, I'm going to force her to vacation with me in increasingly remote locations without access to electricity for her flat iron until she agrees to leave that horrid place and live somewhere that doesn't suck."

"In Charleston's defense," Holly said, "it's a very lovely city, considering its origins, but there's a certain class of rich person there that's objectively awful, and everyone Cole knows is part of that circle."

"What about Atlanta?" Jason asked. "Still the South, gay as hell, tons of killer activism happening."

"The humidity is still disgusting, so it technically meets your requirements," Cole pointed out.

Holly watched Tara's face, trying to read the tiny twitches in her jaw. Atlanta actually *would* be a good compromise for Tara. The reach of the Chadwick name extended far enough that it would still open doors for her, allow her into spaces that most activists didn't have access to. She would still be working against the system her relatives had helped build for centuries, from which Tara had so unfairly benefited when she'd gotten into trouble. The problem was, Holly wasn't sure Tara was ready to hear all the different possibilities that would both fit in with what she felt she needed to do and give her some much-needed distance from her family. And allow them to be together for real, since they obviously never could while Tara was still in Charleston.

When Tara finally spoke, her voice was placating, although if you didn't know her well, you probably wouldn't catch it. Putting her arm around Holly's shoulders, she said, "Well, if I'm going to consider any kind of move, I'll have to consult Holly, although it clearly won't be hard for her to find work."

Tara was looking at Lawrence, so she couldn't see Cole's face over her shoulder, but Holly could, and she watched it fall. He knew, like she did, that Tara had no intention of going anywhere.

She was thinking about excusing herself to go back to their room and cry in the bathroom about wanting a woman who would never be right for her when Miriam and Noelle came over to their table and squished an extra chair in. Miriam perched her tiny elven self on Noelle's knee and clapped.

"How did all my favorite people end up at one table?!" she exclaimed.

Annie smiled enigmatically. "I have very powerful magic that attracts people to me."

"I believe it." Noelle laughed. "Are we all ready for tomorrow?"

"Are you ready, is the question," Lawrence asked.

Elijah answered in Noelle's place. "This one's been a wife guy since minute one. I'm shocked it took them a year to get married."

"Hey!" Noelle protested. "My best friend and Miri's best friend were having a big melodramatic Shenanigan and then *they* had to get married. We were just giving them space."

"Levi does take up a lot of space when he's got his drama pants on," Lawrence confirmed.

Sawyer leaned toward the brides. "What made you decide to get married? I think if I had to guess, I'd have put money on you all being the kind of queer liberationists who think marriage is heteronormative assimilation."

Miriam mirrored his stance. "You ever heard of a pogrom, Sawyer?" she said, sounding like she was ready to give a lecture.

"It's something that happened in Eastern Europe, right, before World War II? Riots that massacred Jews?"

She nodded. "Our Rosenstein ancestor, the one who came from Ukraine to start the bakery, came from a part of the world where once we weren't allowed to live or travel outside of certain places, our vote didn't count for a whole person, and our ability to marry was tightly restricted. I'll never voluntarily hand back a basic human right that my people were once violently denied."

Noelle added, "Besides, marriage equality didn't come from nowhere, as a fight. It came because so many of our own died alone in hospital beds, unable to be with the loves of their lives, who couldn't gain access."

Elijah snapped his fingers in agreement. "And then lost the homes they'd spent their lives in, because they had no legal right to inherit." When everyone looked at him, he shrugged. "I'm an estate lawyer for a reason. And I didn't marry solely for love, either. My ancestors weren't allowed to marry. They can pry marriage from my cold, dead hands."

"Taking the human rights you are due is not assimilation," Miriam said firmly. "We couldn't assimilate if we wanted to."

"And we don't!" Jason exclaimed.

Miriam nodded in agreement. "We don't. Queerness is an extraordinary blessing, and we are gifted to be free of heteronormative patriarchy if we choose to be."

"There was a reason queer people tried to become respectable after the AIDS epidemic," Elijah said gravely. "Because if we could be like them, maybe they would see we were human and they wouldn't let us die next time. It came out of grief and desperation. But there's no amount of normalizing that will make them not hate us. We could be just like them in every way, and they would still let us die. Or kill us."

"There are a lot of great reasons to opt out of the government institution of marriage!" Cole objected.

Miriam conceded this with a nod. "There are, and a lot of brilliant queer theorists have argued against participating in it. For me, I just think...We don't have to re-create straight marriages, we can make ours into any damn thing we want, and it's reasonable to not want a legal marriage, but we're not giving it back. We never give anything back."

Holly stared at Miriam, her giant head of curls practically electric with righteous energy. "Was she always this scary?" she whispered to Tara.

Tara shook her head. "She used to be scared. This is better."

Holly wondered how this new, more radical Miri would have held up to the scrutiny of Charleston high society, or if, in the alternate reality where she'd married Tara, she would have stayed small.

Holly wondered if there was any version of reality where she was with Tara and didn't make herself small.

That night, back in their room, Tara talked excitedly about all the job opportunities Holly had received.

"I know Shoshana offered you a job first, but would working for the Rosensteins be the best path? Imagine how many doors would open with a Michelin-starred restaurant on your CV? You could work in any bakery in the country."

She doesn't hear herself. She can't turn it off.

Instead of trying to tell Tara, again, that she didn't want to work at the best bakeries in the country, she kissed her and dragged her to bed.

Holly tried to be present, knowing how little time they had left, but there was a weight on her heart. If Tara wanted them to be together, she wouldn't be jumping to push Holly off to the Adirondacks, or the Quad Cities. Not that Tara had ever said she wanted them to try a real relationship when all of this was over. That was a dream Holly had conjured up all on her own. And she was going to un-dream it, silently, so Tara would never know.

THE WEDDING

December 24

Chapter 21

Tara

It's Christmas Eve! I'm getting married in four hours!" Miriam exclaimed.

Tara opened her eyes. Miriam was sitting on top of her and Holly, eyes wide as saucers, hair in every direction.

"FOUR! HOURS!"

Tara looked at the clock. Indeed, it was six a.m., so Miriam was getting married in four hours. But that didn't explain why she was sitting on their bed.

"Why are you sitting on our bed?" Holly asked groggily. Tara was glad someone else thought this was strange.

"It's so weird and I need someone to talk to and I can't talk to Cole because he's staying at Sawyer's and Hannah is already super busy and Levi is cooking and, I mean, have you *met* my mother?"

"I'm glad I rank above your mother on the list of people you can talk to," Tara said, shifting to rest against the headboard, "although I'm still not clear on what you're doing in our bed."

Miriam sighed dramatically, throwing up her hands. "You can't judge me! I'm the bride!"

"Get off me, I'll come help with…whatever it is you need right now. But close your eyes, because I'm naked." Tara nudged her gently and rolled out from under her.

"I've seen you naked," Miriam said, her hands dutifully over her eyes.

Holly cleared her throat. "Not to be hopelessly monogamist, but I personally would prefer if you did not continue to see her naked, and I think your soon-to-be-wife would agree."

"Ah! Wife! I'm going to have a wife!" Miriam squealed. "I'm going to *be* a wife!"

Tara pulled a sweater over her head and reached for a pair of leggings. "You were definitely not this giggly about marrying me."

"That's why I didn't marry you!" Miriam said, bouncing onto her feet and hopping off the bed. "Okay! Let's go find coffee and muffins, and the hairdresser is supposed to be here from Lake Placid soon. Do you know the hairdresser? He cut Hannah's hair. He's the only person who can deal with my curls. And then you can make sure that I didn't miss any wrinkles in my jumpsuit when I steamed it because I should not be allowed to steam things but I couldn't let my mom do it because I'm pretty sure she would ruin it on purpose to get me to wear the dress she thinks I don't know she snuck in and—"

Holly looked at Tara. "Don't let her drink any more coffee."

"Come on, little bit," Tara said. "Let's feed you. Tell me what you're envisioning for your hair."

This was her comfort zone, and why she had come. Finally she could help, and maybe earn a little bit of the space her friends had made for her here.

Following happily after her, Miriam started talking about Cher going to the opera in *Moonstruck*.

After steaming the jumpsuit, Tara left Miriam in the hands of the hairdresser, whom she of course did not know, having not been at Carrigan's in more than a year, but who had, she admitted, done a killer job on Hannah's hair. She stuck her head out into the hall and was immediately snagged by Cole.

"You have to come help Noelle. She won't let me fix her hair *at all*."

"Why would you fix Noelle's hair?" Tara asked, allowing herself to be pulled into the room Noelle was using to get ready. "She has much better hair than you do."

Noelle met Tara's eyes in the mirror she was sitting in front of. "*Thank* you. That's what I told him."

"Okay," Cole argued, "that's fair, but you've been messing with it for forty-five straight minutes and according to Hannah's minute-by-minute itinerary, you were only allotted thirty-nine minutes, and now you absolutely have to get into your tux."

"Wow. Do you think Hannah will plan my wedding?" Tara said, flipping through the multipage document Cole had been waving.

Cole's eyes lit up. "She will if you get married at Carrigan's!"

She leveled him with her best "are you fucking kidding me" look, but he was immune. Putting her hands on her hips, she turned to Noelle. "Can I fix your hair? I guarantee I will make it hot as shit."

Noelle regarded her seriously in the mirror, then nodded. "I probably should not let the woman whose girlfriend I stole do my hair for my wedding, but I can't get the yarmulke to sit right and you do have excellent hair yourself."

"Fiancée," Tara reminded her. "You stole my fiancée. But I owe you for that. It would have been a really shitty divorce in a couple of years. And I would never, ever fuck up a butch's hair on her wedding day."

Cole looked between them. "Is there, like, a lesbian code of honor I don't know about?"

They both laughed at him, and Tara fixed Noelle's hair and then her suspenders.

"I need you!" Hannah said, bursting in.

"Me?" Noelle and Cole both asked, each pointing to themselves.

"Hell no." Hannah looked appalled. "I need Tara."

Tara shrugged, and Hannah pulled her out into the hallway. "Rabbi Ruth needs you to—"

"TARA!" Miriam shouted, her head popping into view in the hallway. Her hair looked amazing. "My zipper is stuck and I can't get my eyeliner wings right!"

"Don't you people have a wedding planner?" Tara asked. "What were you going to do if I didn't come to this wedding?"

"Not get married," Miriam said, as if it were obvious. "Fix my zipper!"

Sighing, she ducked into the room. "Can someone else help Rabbi Ruth?" she called back to Hannah.

"I got it," Hannah said, her eyes looking only a little panicked. "Somehow."

Cole was right behind her. "Mimi, is there a secret lesbian code of ethics?" he whined. "*Oh*, you look incredible. But is Tara going to fix your eyeliner wings?"

"How would I know?" Miriam asked him. "I'm a bisexual. The bisexual code of ethics is, like, don't sit correctly in a chair and all cops are bastards. The lesbians tell me nothing."

"Should I be a bisexual?" Cole wondered aloud.

Both Tara and Miriam looked at him.

"No, it won't work." He sighed. "I'm too gay."

Cole had come to his understanding of his own homosexuality late and was trying to make up for lost time by jumping all in as hard as he could. Tara was, obviously, thrilled for him, and also secretly entertained.

"Okay, Mir, turn toward me. I'm going to fix your eyeliner."

"Cole," Miriam said over Tara's shoulder. "I love you. Go away."

"Should I find someone who needs something from me?"

"*No*," they both said at once.

Cole pouted. "I'm going to go make out with Sawyer."

"*Not* in the walk-in," Miriam joked.

"As if Levi would ever let me back in his kitchen," Cole scoffed.

Miriam grimaced. "Someone should probably keep an eye on him, but it can't be me."

"I'll text Holly," Tara said. "She can make sure he doesn't leave any doors open in Noelle's work shed or anything."

Miriam paled. "Please try to get him to get dressed?"

"What are the parameters?" Tara asked. "Is he allowed to wear pants embroidered with lobsters?"

Laughing, Miriam nodded. "In fact, I have special ordered him brand-new lobster pants *with* a matching suit jacket. All he needs to do is put it on."

"You love him so much more than I do," Tara observed, her eyes wide with horror.

"Hmm," Miriam said, smiling a little. "I don't think that's true."

"It's weird that you're insightful now," Tara told her. There had been a lot of years when Miriam barely noticed the world around her.

"Isn't it?" Miri turned back to look at herself in the mirror and gasped joyfully.

Tara's eyes absolutely did not well up with happy tears. Nope. Not even a little. "Your eyes are perfect, your face and hair are perfect. Are you ready? What's next?"

Hannah opened the door. "You ready for photos?"

"Can one of you put on my shoes? I can't bend over in this jumpsuit. I wanted to look sexy, and I flew too close to the sun," Miriam said, sticking out one leg and pointing her toes.

Tara sighed, picking up her foot and slipping on her bedazzled Chucks. "This is a bit far, even for a lesbian. You know this is not what normal people ask of their exes on their wedding day, right?"

Miriam blinked at her, mascaraed lashes sweeping down onto her elven cheeks. "We're not normal people. We're Team Carrigan's."

"Speak for yourself," Tara said, horribly aware that she wanted to be Team Carrigan's, even if she felt she didn't deserve to be. "I'm going to go check on Holly and finish getting dressed, okay?"

"I literally don't know what we would have done without you today," Miriam said, squeezing her hand.

Tara tried to smile. "You know me. Indispensable."

Because she made herself that way, because she had always been certain no one would ever love her enough to keep her otherwise. That was too much introspection for the middle of this wedding.

She managed to get back to her room without being waylaid by anyone else needing her for anything, and slumped back against the door once it was closed behind her.

"Sloane." Holly smirked from where she was sitting on the bed and zipping up her boots. She looked stunning, long burgundy lace sleeves falling past her wrists and hugging her body.

"Siobhan," Tara acknowledged, pushing off the door. "Those people are so needy."

"You know they're going to want you for pictures." Holly pushed off the bed and walked toward her. "Let's get you into your dress."

Tara shook her head. "Why would they want me in pictures?"

Holly blinked at her. "Uh, you're family?"

She blew out an exasperated breath, although she was secretly what Miriam would have called verklempt. These five days had been healing in a way she could never have expected, allowing her a glimpse of what it would feel like to be unconditionally accepted in a family. That glimpse was going to sustain her for a long time when she went back into the breach. She would never have been able to feel all those things if Holly hadn't been here, to be an anchor and a home base.

"You made all this possible," Tara told her, trying to sound less choked up than she felt. It was ridiculous to cry over this. "Having you here, on my team, allowed me to be present for them in a way I could never have otherwise. I would have been in my head, worried about how I was coming across and what they were thinking of me."

Before Holly could respond, Tara pulled her vintage mint and gold brocade dress over her head and turned so Holly could zip her up. She did, but then she dropped a soft kiss on Tara's shoulder blade, left bare by the wide boat neck that dipped low in the back.

"I feel very grateful to have been here for this," Holly whispered against her skin.

They walked hand in hand down the hallway, Tara trailing her fingers over the parrots on the brand-new, vintage reproduction wallpaper that didn't smell at all like mold. Everything was beginning brand-new this week. Hannah and Levi were growing a new life, Noelle and Miriam were starting a new marriage, and Tara and Holly...well, they might be starting something real.

Tara believed that Holly was talented, smart, and hardworking enough that, if she tried, she could do anything in the world. It wouldn't be simple, but Tara would happily work to convince her family that a small business owner was the ideal partner, if it meant she got to be with Holly. She just had to convince Holly that being with Tara was worth it.

She was absolutely certain that Holly would be happier if she left waitressing to bake full-time, but she wasn't convinced that Holly would be happier with *her*.

Chapter 22

Holly

Holly found Cole dutifully getting dressed, adjusting the sleeves of his suit coat and fidgeting with his hair—fixing wave by individual wave with his very expensive curler/blow-dryer.

"Nicholas Fraser, are there lobsters embroidered on your suit? For a Jewish wedding?"

He grinned. "I asked Rabbi Ruth and they assured me it was hilarious."

Holly eyed him. "Is hilarious what you were going for?"

"Holly Siobhan Delaney, letting people think I'm hilarious is how I get away with everything. Also, it's *fun*."

How did he know her middle name? She suddenly realized he'd probably run a full background check on her, to protect Tara, without telling either of them.

She didn't ask. Instead, she told him, "You're a beautiful

blond, blue-eyed cis white man with millions of dollars, Cole. That's how you get away with everything."

"I mean, you're obviously not wrong, but—wait, we should definitely have a conversation about the ways in which the kyriarchy both enables and tightly restricts behavior, but not today! I have to go take pictures, and watch my BFF get married, and dance with my cute boyfriend." He picked up his blow-dryer again, and Holly took it out of his hands.

"Your hair looks perfect. As long as you were going for majestic surfer waves. If not, we need to start over."

He looked in the mirror. "Do you think there's time to start over?" he fretted.

"*No.* Put on your tie and let's get moving." She put the tie in question in his hands.

He snatched it up, twirled it around, and began to tie it around his neck with a deft hand. He had, apparently, done this a time or two. "*So,*" he said, "how are things going with you and Tara? Any inconvenient feelings developing?" He waggled his eyebrows at her.

"Look," she sighed, "it would be hard not to develop some romantic feelings for Tara. She's one of the most incredible people I've ever met."

Cole pumped his fist in the air. "Honestly, everyone who's not obsessed with her is wrong."

"It's not that simple, Nicholas. We're way too different for it to ever work."

He made a scoffing noise. "That's fake. Look at Sawyer and me. We're wildly different people. He's an upstanding local politician. I'm..." He trailed off, clearly trying to decide how much to say about what he actually did.

She smirked. "I hate to tell you this, but local politicians and criminals have been in bed together since time immemorial."

"But I love the ocean, and he loves the mountains! I'm an Episcopalian who almost went into the priesthood and he's an atheist! I want us to commit to forever, but he doesn't believe in marriage, and I would never invite the government into my sex life!"

Counting on her fingers, she countered, "You're very rich, so you have a sailboat on the coast and you go there whenever you want. You can have a nice Unitarian commitment ceremony with a humanist minister and never file a marriage license, everyone wins. You almost went into the *priesthood*?!"

"Tara's also very rich, which I'm sure can solve several of your problems. We don't talk about the priesthood. If I look too closely at the call to ministry, it gets louder, so we pretend it's not there."

"You're a really odd duck," Holly told him. "Good, but odd."

"It's because I'm a swan," he said seriously, as if this made everything about him make sense. And, honestly, maybe it did. "Look, I'm not saying there's nothing standing between you and Tara. I know Tara. She self-sabotages like it's a full-time job. I don't know you well enough to know your fatal character flaws yet, but I'm sure you have them."

Holly gasped in mock indignation. "I'm practically perfect in every way."

She straightened his bow tie, patted him on the arm, and pulled him out the door. Once he was safely deposited with the photographer, she watched him pose with the brides and goof around with Tara. He said something to her that made her fold in half with laughter. She hadn't even known Tara's spine bent that way. Or that she was capable of laughing that hard. Holly wondered how Tara thought she could ever be happy living half a country away from Cole. Maybe the long-term separation would make her start to realize that there was nothing in Charleston that made her happy.

"She seems to fit here, doesn't she?" Elijah Green asked, coming to stand next to her.

"I wish I could convince her that she could be professionally and personally fulfilled here," Holly said. "Her family is slowly poisoning her, and I really like her, but I know if we got involved, it would poison me, too." She looked over at Elijah, who was listening politely. "Sorry, that's so much info I just dumped on you."

He raised one shoulder elegantly. "I wouldn't hang out with this group if I didn't sort of enjoy people dumping their drama on me. It's a hobby. Come to Carrigan's, make some popcorn, hear the mess."

"Aren't you, like, a very busy lawyer and a parent to young twins and a competitive Scrabble player in your spare time? Do you have time for other hobbies?" she asked him.

"You make time for what you love." He smiled. "But speaking of my children, I think it's time for them to join the photos. I'm going to make sure neither of them has gotten cookie crumbs on their clothes."

Holly looked around. "There are cookies?"

"Where Mrs. Matthews is, cookies also are," Elijah informed her.

She went off in search of Mrs. Matthews, who gave her pfeffernuesse and left Holly alone with her thoughts so that she, too, could join the pictures. Everyone, it seemed, was being photographed as part of the wedding, except for Holly. She was pretty sure they hadn't asked her to be in the photos because, even if they believed she and Tara were dating, they didn't believe she'd be around long enough to have her in the pictures.

The buzz of an incoming call pulled her out of staring forlornly at the blue delft kitchen tiles, mouth full of cookie, feeling sorry for herself that she couldn't grow old with someone like Tara. Holly twisted on the kitchen stool to fish her phone out of her purse, which she'd dumped unceremoniously on the floor beneath her.

"Fucking dress," she mumbled, falling off the stool and landing, hard, on her ass as she managed to snag the phone, only to find an unknown number calling. Because she was still flustered from falling off a chair onto the Carrigan's kitchen floor in her most expensive outfit, she answered instead of sending it to voicemail.

"Holly Delaney speaking."

"Miss Delaney. This is Mrs. Chadwick." On the surface, Tara's mother sounded a great deal like her daughter. Polished old money accent, familiar cadence. People who didn't know Tara well would have trouble telling them apart. Holly didn't. Tara's voice had a million facets underneath the top layer of ice.

Her mother's voice was ice all the way down, and Holly was pretty sure Mrs. Chadwick was calling to try to freeze her out of Tara's life.

"I hear from my dear friend Cricket that you are attending an event with my daughter. Naturally, since Tara told me nothing about this, I found myself curious and looked you up.

Your Instagram seems to suggest that you may be more than friends. This is, of course, unacceptable. You will stop seeing her immediately, or I will make you unemployable anywhere in South Carolina."

The call ended before Holly could respond or fully process what Mrs. Chadwick had said. It was like waking up in the middle of an earthquake and wondering why the floor was shaking, only to put the pieces together once the rumbling had stopped. Which was, Holly thought, not a bad metaphor, since Tara's mom was the equivalent of a natural disaster. She pushed the phone across the floor, instinctively backing away like it was a coiled snake. God, her butt was going to bruise so bad.

Had she just been daydreaming about a world where she and Tara could be together? How had she let herself forget that Tara's world, the world she'd chosen, would poison Holly? Not slowly and accidentally, but swiftly, intentionally, with malice. Unless Tara agreed to become estranged from her family and leave her law practice, them being together would always be a daydream.

Holly rested her head back against the island and closed her eyes. Yep.

She'd met a girl who made her want to try for the real thing again, after all this time, but she couldn't have her. Fucking amazing.

Her phone buzzed again and she reached for it, finding a text from her own mother.

> **Mom:** OMG Caitlin showed me more pictures of your new
> lady! Why aren't you bringing her home for Christmas,
> again?

Leaving aside the important questions of whether she was going to kill her sister and who needed to pay for teaching her mom to say OMG (probably Caitlin, so yes, either murder or glitter through the mail), she didn't have the energy for this. She dropped her head onto her knees, trying not to mess up the makeup she'd spent an hour on. The door swung open, and she looked up to find Tara sitting down in front of her. In her beautiful, outrageously expensive vintage dress. On the kitchen floor.

"Hey. You okay?" Tara's voice, so often sharp as a knife, was so soft. Holly wanted to tell her the truth about the phone call from Tara's mom, and how torn up inside she was about it. About them.

But Tara was here to be part of an event that mattered to her, and she didn't need to go nuclear on her mom right beforehand. And maybe a small part of Holly was afraid that if Tara heard that her mother knew they were dating (fake as it was), she would freak out and cut off their dalliance early.

So Holly did what she'd been training at for a decade, and what she'd promised Tara she wouldn't do as long as they were together: she put on her mask.

Smiling, she put a hand in Tara's.

"It's so embarrassing! I tried to grab my phone and fell right over! And now I'm stuck, because I can't get up in this dress. Help?" She forced herself to make her voice light, to laugh, to make it a joke.

Tara must have been distracted because she bought it. She tugged on Holly's hand, hauling her up. They ended up pressed against each other, and their eyes caught. The ice blue in Tara's was so warm, Holly didn't want to look away. She flushed, heat pooling between her legs but also, worryingly, in her heart. Finally, Tara pressed their foreheads together, only for an instant, then pulled back.

"Ready to go watch these goofballs become wives?"

Chapter 23

Tara

In the barn, Sawyer was saving seats for them in a row with Ernie and Lawrence (who both gave Holly a thumbs-up), Collin from the diner and his wife Marisol, and the Greens. They slipped in, Holly's fingers loosely tangled with Tara's in a way that felt natural, as if they'd been holding hands for much longer than a long weekend. Once they were seated, Sawyer put an arm around her shoulder and squeezed, leaving it there in a casual gesture that said he assumed they were already friends and would only become closer as time went on.

Historically, Tara didn't love being touched by people she didn't know well, but this seemed right. She settled their still-laced-together hands on Holly's thigh and felt her shiver with pleasure.

When the barn doors opened, the assembled crowd turned as one to watch Noelle head to the front to stand under the chuppah, followed by Cole, then Levi and Hannah. Hannah stood on Noelle's side, with a woman Tara had been told was Noelle's AA sponsor. Cole and Levi stood on Miriam's side, their heads—one bright and one dark—bent together as Levi whispered to Cole and Cole grinned back.

They were such deeply unlikely friends, Tara thought, the two boys, yet they seemed to have come to love each other deeply in a short time.

Miriam came in then, everyone rising as she walked down the aisle. Tara watched Noelle watch Miriam and knew only joy. She'd never once looked at Miri with that light of love shining from her face, and Miri deserved that, and more. She was so grateful that, no matter how hard it had been, the universe (or Cass Carrigan) had brought Miriam here, to Noelle.

Their rabbi, Ruth, leaned on their cane with the wolf's head and gave a crooked smile to the brides in front of them. Noelle reached up to adjust her yarmulke while Miriam's hair pillowed out from her head in the most perfect cloud of almost-black curls. Time froze, this tableau of all these people connected in an interdependent web of love and faith and community, sharing a Jewish Christmas Eve wedding on a Christmas tree farm.

The ceremony was beautiful, made only more so by both of the boys crying buckets behind Miriam's back. Noelle was obviously trying very hard not to meet Levi's eye, because every time she did, her eyes got noticeably more moist. Miriam was oblivious to anyone but Noelle. After the traditional religious vows, the brides each recited their own.

Noelle quoted Andrea Gibson and bell hooks, because she was a queer literature nerd, a fact Miriam teased her about through tears.

"I was going to find you poetry," Miriam said, "but I knew I would never be able to do it better than you. So I didn't write anything! We're going to see how it goes."

Tara laughed with the crowd at Miri's chaos. "The first time I saw you, you smiled at me and I knew my life was never going to be the same. You were somehow the only color in a grayscale world, and everything you touched turned to Technicolor. Meeting you was like coming to Oz for the first time, and not even realizing I'd been in Kansas."

In theory, hearing that should have made Tara feel angry, or sad, since they'd been engaged when Miriam and Noelle had met, and she was the Kansas from which Miriam had escaped. And she was sad, but only because Miriam had left her alone, still stuck in the beginning of a movie. Trapped in the first act of her own story.

She was still stuck there, if she were honest with herself, but now she was acknowledging it. That had to count for something.

Miriam went on. "You weren't the first person who ever saw the best in me, but you were the first person I believed. When I saw myself through your eyes, I trusted that I could become the version of myself you saw. Maybe it's selfish, but even though you're handsome and funny, smart and hardworking, ethical and great in bed—"

Miriam's mom made a hilarious noise in the back of her throat.

"—the thing I love best about you is who you allow me to be."

Tara looked over at Holly, who was staring at her. They smiled a little conspiratorially, and Holly leaned her head on Tara's shoulder. A chunk of the iceberg around Tara's heart broke off and floated away, and she was afraid the melt might be permanent. That was exactly it, what she felt about Holly. She wasn't in love, not yet, but she could be. Easily.

And if she fell, she would be falling in love not just with Holly, but also with who she was when she was with Holly.

When the glass had been broken and the couple declared married in the eyes of God, their families, and the state of New York, they recessed down the aisle. As they passed, Cole caught Tara's hand and hauled her up next to him, kissing her soundly on the head before reaching past her to pull Sawyer along with him.

As they walked away, Tara whispered, "Do you think they're disappearing somewhere to make out before the reception starts?"

"Oh, they definitely are," Holly confirmed. "Should we do the same?"

"God, yes." Tara nodded and let Holly lead her past the milling guests, out of the barn, and into the back acreage, away from the inn where people were heading in anticipation of dinner.

They tried to sneak into Noelle's work shed, but she had padlocked it, probably to keep Cole and Sawyer out. Damn her brilliant foresight. Eventually, giggling and tripping over their heels in the snow, they made it all the way around the back of the building to the side door of the kitchen.

"There's a pantry in here that I *know* is big enough for fooling around, because Hannah tells me way too much about her sex life," Tara whispered.

Before they could get to the pantry door, Holly pushed Tara up against the kitchen island, trapping her hands on either side of her. "Hey," she said, waiting until Tara met her eyes. "Wait a second."

Tara stopped and tried to get her raging lust brain to focus. "What's up?"

Holly took a deep breath.

"Do you ever think…Did the wedding…"

She stopped and breathed again.

Then, all in a rush, she said, "Do you ever think about extending our agreement, and maybe being, uh, more-than-friends? For a little while? I know it would be bad for your career, and your mom might kill me. Actually, when she called me earlier, I thought she might actually kill—"

The maelstrom of feelings that had erupted at the beginning of Holly's sentence, a mix of joy and terror, fell silent when Tara's brain processed the rest of what she was saying.

"My mom called you." She tried to inhale past the rage flaming up inside her.

Holly shrugged. "Yeah, she told me I had to stop dating you or she would ruin me, but, like, ruin me how? I was already going to quit Emma's because Matt won't let me bake, and no one who would hire me would give a shit what Bunny Chadwick thinks."

Her mom's name wasn't Bunny, but that didn't seem like the critical point.

Tara freed a hand and grabbed Holly's chin. "I do want to

keep seeing you. I have no idea how it will work, it's guaranteed to explode in our faces, and I absolutely want to do it anyway."

Holly's eyes filled with hope and tears. "Really?"

She nodded. "So much. It's all I can think about. But first, I need to call my mom and tell her to go all the way to hell on a one-way ticket."

Chapter 24

Holly

This was happening. Tara wanted to be with her, and she was going to tell off her mother. Carrigan's really was magic at Christmas.

Tara fished her phone out of the basket on the kitchen island—where they'd all left their devices so they could focus on the wedding—and frowned.

"Hol, why do I have an email from the Innocence Project?"

Oh shit.

"Why are they offering me a job?"

Holly swallowed, hard. "So, funny story. I drafted an email to them about you, but I didn't realize I'd sent it."

She'd drafted it in a moment of panic, trying to figure out anything that would make Tara happier and allow them to be together. But she'd known even in the moment that she should never send it. "I'm so, so sorry."

Tara stared at her, frozen. "You did what?"

"I had this whole brainstorm, that it would be so great if you worked for them, because you would still be doing activism work, but you wouldn't be beholden to keeping ties with your family if you didn't want to, and you might even be able to have a broader reach, but I would never have sent it intentionally. I should have had a conversation with you about it. It was a huge overreach, even to draft something," Holly babbled, her heart in her throat as Tara's face only became icier.

"What I don't understand," Tara said slowly, her accent as thick as molasses in January, "is why you would have been brainstorming ways for me to leave the career I've painstakingly grown, that I excel at and care deeply about."

Holly blinked at her. She'd expected Tara to be angry that she'd stepped in without Tara's consent, but she wasn't sure how to process the idea that Tara didn't understand why anyone would think she should maybe leave her job.

"Well, I'm not saying leave your career," she said, equally slowly, "just your job. And perhaps because I see you constantly arranging your life to meet your parents' approval, which they use to hold you hostage."

Tara shook her head, her bob swinging from side to side like a pendulum. "That's a choice I've made. I decided a long time ago that I was willing to accept the whole package when I decided on this path."

"You made the choice, Tara, but you don't have to keep making the choice." Holly was exasperated.

"I don't deserve another choice."

Wow. She wanted to say, "You don't have to earn the right to a less desolate life," but realized it would be wasted breath.

Nothing Holly said would ever fix what was broken in

Tara, her bone-deep belief in her inherent worthlessness. She needed to walk away now and cut any connection between them, so she did what she was good at—she brought out her knives and threw them.

"You're the exact same selfish, self-destructive kid you were at seventeen, Tara, and you're still throwing yourself on a pyre. I hope it brings you some peace eventually. I hope it's worth it, 'cause it's devastating everyone who tries to love you."

"That's a fucked-up, hurtful thing to say," Tara whispered. She rubbed both hands over her heart and took several short, shallow breaths. "Why did we ever think we could make this work in the real world? You're going to leave Charleston, go on waitressing and refusing to take a chance on baking, and I'll be a funny story from your past. That time you pretended to date a bitchy ice queen because she was too pathetic to go to a wedding on her own."

Holly wanted to scream. "Oh, fuck you for thinking that of me. And for throwing baking in my face. You know how much I want to see us together. You want that, too! You just told me you did! But your mom *threatened to blacklist me* not two hours ago, and I've never seen you happier than you are a thousand miles away from them, so forgive me if I think maybe a break from your job and family would be good for both of us!"

Tara nodded, her face stony. "So you emailed an institution I respect to tell them about me, without asking me first, and making me look like I can't get my own job?"

"It was a *mistake*!" Holly cried. "I didn't mean to!"

"Was it a mistake that had you talking to my friends all

week about how I should totally live here? It's interesting that you want me to take you as you are, but you don't want to do the same for me."

That was rich. "Oh, so it's okay for you to try to Pygmalion me, talk about how great it would be if I got a job that was less embarrassing for you than being a waitress, convince everyone to offer me charity, but I can't say, 'Hey, I care about you and I see you're unhappy'?"

"I never convinced anyone to give you a job out of charity!" Tara argued. "Any offers you got were sincere. And you told me yourself you don't want to be a waitress forever, that you want to bake! What's wrong with me trying to encourage you to do that?"

Holly cocked her head disbelievingly. "What's wrong is, it's patronizing and hypocritical. You can keep a job you hate for complicated reasons, but I can't choose my job for equally complicated ones? Maybe you should fix your own life before you decide to rehab your lovers!"

"Right back at you," Tara drawled, drawing up to her full height. "You want me to leave my entire life so we can be together, but you knew I never would. You were looking for a reason to run. You can tell yourself you wanted to try with me, but you didn't. Because that might ask something of you, for you to compromise or change or grow. Which you won't because you had one failed marriage and made it your whole personality."

Holly took a page from Tara's book and wrapped herself in ice so she didn't cry.

"Thank you for showing me that when I eventually fall for

someone, it needs to be someone who actually likes me for me, instead of trying to make me into a project." Holly rubbed her hands on her pants. "I think I'm going to go."

Tara was right about one thing.

Running seemed like a hell of an idea right now, so that's what Holly did.

Chapter 25

Tara

Blood was rushing in Tara's ears, but from the other side of the swinging door she heard Miriam's voice cry out, "You can't talk to my friend that way. You need to get out of my house."

Holly volleyed back, "Oh, you can treat her like shit, and her family can destroy her every day, but I can't tell her the truth?"

Tara couldn't hear what Noelle said after, just the rumble of her voice. Then they all tumbled through the door, Hannah and Miriam and Cole all pushing each other out of the way to get to each other.

"What are you all doing here?" she said, looking between them, confused.

Noelle snuck to her side and snagged a pfeffernuss off the counter. "We heard there were cookies so we came to get some before the reception starts and everyone eats them all. The Rosensteins are serious about their desserts."

Of course they hadn't come looking for her. That had been a ridiculous hope. Why would they go looking for the bride's ex-girlfriend, all of them in a pack?

Levi snorted. "We came looking for you, you dork. Elijah said you were in here."

"Why, though?" she asked, her voice so much smaller than she was used to.

"Because you're Team Carrigan's? And we need the whole team at the party?" Miriam sounded confused.

Not as confused as Tara felt. "But you'll be late."

"I don't think they can start without us," Noelle said. "Here. Have a cookie."

The last thing Tara wanted was a cookie, but she dutifully took one, robotically eating it, and it did make her feel better, or at least more grounded.

"You didn't have to kick her out. I mean, I appreciate the gesture, but..." Tara trailed off at the look on Miriam's face. "What?"

"Of course we're going to kick someone out who's mean to you! Why don't you believe we love you enough to choose you?" Miriam said, her fists on her hips, looking even more than usual like Peter Pan.

To her abject, undying horror, Tara started to cry.

"Did you hear everything we said?" She hiccupped, trying to save her mascara.

They all nodded.

"So you know we were pretending to date?"

They all nodded, but then Hannah said, "We kind of

already knew. We were hoping you'd trust us enough to tell us the truth."

"And why you thought you needed a buffer for us," Levi added. "Although honestly I understand that one."

"What if she was right about everything?" Tara whispered. "I guess...I don't believe you love me because why would anyone?"

"Tara," Cole said, taking her face in his hands so she had no choice but to meet his eyes. They blazed the same blue as hers, and it was like looking in a mirror, except that she'd looked at Cole's face so much more than she had her own, so it was much more familiar and beloved. "I need you to hear something right now. Like, really hear it. Because I've been trying to tell you all our lives and apparently you still don't believe it."

She nodded, to tell him she was listening, though she certainly wasn't ready for whatever he was about to say.

"You are the other half of me. Miriam might be my kindred spirit, but you *are* me. I can't exist without you. I *can't*, Tara. We are the other sides of each other's coins, and if I don't know you're on the other end of the phone or a plane ride away, if I don't believe that I can be hugging you or hearing your voice as soon as I need to, I wither. When you left me to go to school, and I didn't hear from you for almost a year, I went feral. And when you came back a ghost of yourself, I thought we were both going to die."

Tara tried to tear her eyes away, to wrench her body out of his hands, but he held her steady.

She couldn't believe that what he was saying was true. If it was, the reckless way she'd been treating her life was the same as playing with his life, and she would never do that. The only comfort she'd had, all this time, was that no one truly loved her so if she finally burned all the way out, no one would miss her.

"Please listen to me. You need to hear this. You can be brave enough to hear this. You're the bravest person I know," he said, and she breathed in, deep.

She wasn't, but she could pretend for him.

She wouldn't do it for her, but for Cole? She would do anything.

"Maybe you don't want to let Holly love you. Maybe you don't want to let yourself be turned inside out by falling in love with her, although I think it might be too late. But, Tara, you need to hear what she said about you working yourself to nothing. It doesn't help the cause if you abandon the work because you burned your soul to a crisp. *Our* soul. Your half of our soul. Because even if you don't want to belong to Holly, you belong to *me*, and me to you, and I need you to stop being so damn flippant about that. I need you. For my survival. On this earth."

It was unfair of him, and hypocritical, to accuse her of being careless with his life, when he lived a life that could, if he were caught, have him in prison for life. It was unfair of him to ask her to be careful for him, because he knew she couldn't say no.

"You don't need me," she whispered, her own eyes pleading. "You have Miriam, and Sawyer, and Carrigan's. I'm an old friend you used to get into trouble with."

He shook his head. "Hannah," he said, "who do you need most in the world? To survive?"

"Noelle," she said without pausing.

"Levi, you?" Cole asked, his eyes still on Tara's.

"Miriam," Levi said. "No question."

"Mimi?"

"You and Blue," Miriam said.

He raised his eyebrows, as if to say, *See?* But she didn't see.

"Exactly," she said. "You all have this spiderweb of connections and emotional commitments. I'm not part of that. I was invited for politeness and nostalgia. No one needs me." Her voice broke on this last word.

"I need you," Hannah said. "You're the person I call when I need a perspective outside of this tiny bubble we live in."

"I need you," Miriam told her. "Other than Cole, you're the only friend I had from before who still loves me. You're one of two people in the world who knew me through my worst time, and now. You always know the thing to say that gets at the hard truth."

"My wife needs you, so I do," Levi told her.

"I don't need you," Noelle said, "but I like you a hell of a lot. You're pretty extraordinary, and anyway, we don't have to need you to make space for you here. We do it because we love you, not because we need you."

Kringle yowled.

"I need you. Most of all the things. Ever on this planet. I need you more than oxygen or water. Do you hear me?" Cole asked.

She nodded.

"Do you believe me?" he asked.

She shrugged. "I don't know how to."

He shook his head. "When have I ever lied to you, Tara Sloane?"

"You lie to everyone, Cole. Yourself, us. It's who you are."
She didn't want to keep arguing with him, because she could
see the pain written across his face and she didn't want to
keep causing it, but she didn't know how to accept this. He
hadn't even known he was gay until he was thirty-five. What
if he suddenly woke up one day and decided he'd been wrong
about her, too, when she'd already turned herself inside out,
let herself believe in him?

His eyes filled up with tears, and her heart crumbled to dust.
He never cried. "Ask me anything. I'll tell you every detail of
my job. I'll tell you every bank I've ever illegally accessed. I'll
tell you any damn thing I've ever thought, or felt, or hoped, or
dreamed."

He was completely serious. Maybe the most serious he'd
ever been, about anything.

"I love you more than I love my own secrets. I don't need
privacy from you. We aren't separate. You can have anything I
have, know anything I know."

Nothing had ever mattered more to Cole than his secrets,
but when he said that he would give her all of them, she knew
he meant it. This, more than anything that had happened
today, broke her.

And she did break. Finally, she broke open and fell into
Cole's arms, weeping.

"Okay," he whispered gently. "I didn't think this would
result in you becoming a melted puddle."

"You love me," she sobbed, and he rocked her.

"I want you to have this cry," he told her through her hair,
because he had gathered her completely into his lap like a
baby, which would have mortified her at any other time but

right now felt safe and perfect, "and we're going to have a much longer conversation about what you thought was happening the past twenty years and also why you're trying to work yourself to death, but I do think we should get to the reception. And if you cry during it, people are going to think you're absolutely devastated about your breakup."

"I am devastated about my breakup," Tara blubbered.

"I meant your breakup with Miriam," he clarified.

This sobered her. She did need to cry, a great deal, but she was neither willing to miss the reception nor make a scene for the gossips. Not on account of her pride, but because she didn't want people to remember Miriam and Noelle's wedding as "the one where the ex cried the whole time."

Levi pulled a makeup wipe out of his pocket. He held Tara's face gently and wiped the mascara off her cheeks. "I cry a lot and I wear a lot of eyeliner," he said in answer to the unasked question of why he was carrying around makeup wipes in his pocket.

Once he was done, he and Hannah stood on either side of her, their arms around her waist. Cole walked in front of her, effectively blocking her from prying eyes. She felt like a celebrity being hidden from the press, and it was ridiculous.

"We're putting you at the Matthewses' table so people don't keep asking you all night where Holly is," Noelle told her.

"Oh my God, y'all. Everyone go be in the wedding party. I'll hang out with Esther."

"It's true." Esther nodded. "Mom and Dad and I will protect her. Go. Do whatever you have to."

Dinner was served, and the food was delicious, of course— it was Levi's menu, and the man was a force of nature in the kitchen. Because Noelle's parents were gone and Miriam hadn't trusted Ziva with a microphone, the couple had opted to forgo the traditional speeches. Instead, Hannah had made a video with well-wishes from loved ones around the country. For several minutes at a time, Tara was able to focus on celebrating. Every time she started to slide back into misery, somehow, Mr. and Mrs. Matthews knew and put an arm around her or squeezed her hand or drew her into conversation.

"I'm sorry I ruined your wedding day," she said to Miriam and Noelle when they came by the table to do their rounds.

Noelle waved her off. "Please. What's a Carrigan's event without us getting overly involved with each other's drama? You basically saved our wedding day, when you think about it."

Behind them, Ziva appeared in a cloud of perfume and jangles. "What on earth could you do to ruin this day, Tara? You didn't even object!" She tittered at her own joke, not noticing that no one else was joining her.

Panic rose in Tara's throat, and she flipped through lies she could tell Ziva.

Levi, who'd been sitting at the other side of the table talking to his dad and wife, caught her eye, put one finger up to his lips, and winked.

He elbowed Hannah, and she whispered, "What, right now?" with the sort of long-suffering exasperation that Tara was learning people often used when talking to, or about, Levi Blue Matthews.

Levi grinned the most cat-among-the-pigeons, self-satisfied smile she'd ever seen. She wondered, idly, how the man didn't get punched more often.

Hannah turned in Ziva's direction and loudly announced, "I'm pregnant!"

The entire room exploded in noise.

Mr. Matthews started to cry, Mrs. Matthews started to dance, Miriam did a cartwheel in the jumpsuit she'd claimed she couldn't bend over in. Cole jumped so high in the air, she was grateful the room had such high ceilings.

Mrs. Matthews and Hannah's mom, Rachel, immediately started arguing about Ashkenazi versus Sephardic baby naming traditions. No one paid any attention at all to Tara or asked her what she was going to do next about Holly.

Levi leaned across the table toward her and smirked. "You're welcome."

That sweet little weasel had planned this whole thing.

THE AFTERMATH

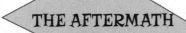

December 24–Early March

Chapter 26

Holly

When she left (okay, was kicked out of) Carrigan's, Holly had no spare clothes or car keys or toothbrush. She didn't even have her phone.

The front lawn was deserted, with everyone inside for the wedding. It felt eerie, snow blanketing the still-blinking reindeer noses and sliding off the tall pointy hats of statuary of Santa's elves. The trees were dark sentinels, whispering in the wind about what an asshole she was.

She shivered against the cold and wished that, if she was going to storm out, she'd thought to do so with a coat. She felt very much like Edmund Pevensie, out in an unknown wilderness and likely to sell out her loved ones for a little Turkish Delight.

As a kid, she'd always assumed that if she ever got sucked into a portal universe, she would be the hero. Lucy or Peter, hopefully, because Susan got shafted. Here she was, though, the villain of the story.

How was she going to get out of here? She didn't exactly know how to hot-wire a car. Not that she would steal a car from these people. Maybe Cole, he could afford it. Possibly this wasn't the time to be considering a career of Robin Hooding.

It was a moot point, anyway, because her misspent youth had been spent in the library, not learning how to steal cars, even from millionaires. She definitely couldn't walk into Advent. It would be a hike in daylight, in summer, in good boots. She was in heels, in winter, in the dark.

She couldn't call an Uber, because she didn't have her phone and there weren't any up here. She was weighing the benefits of trying to sneak back into the house to sleep in the library for the night, when Gavi Rosenstein stepped up beside her.

"I heard you fucked up *big*," Gavi said.

Holly nodded decisively. "Oh boy."

"Catch." Gavi tossed her a set of keys. "Take my Outback. It should make it down the road safely. Ernie's should be open with a skeleton staff, for people who don't have anywhere to go on Christmas Eve. I'll let her know what's going on, and she'll let you stay for a while."

"Are you sure?" Holly asked. If she were Ernie, she'd probably kick herself out.

Gavi smiled, as if they could hear Holly's thoughts. "If Ernie kicked out everyone who made terrible life choices, she'd have a hell of a time running a dive bar. Anyway, I have to get back inside, but I'll make sure your stuff goes with Ernie."

Wow, they were a master at predicting guest needs, even if Holly was no longer a guest.

"Go back inside before you miss the reception," Holly said, suddenly tearing up. Now that her anger had frozen in the snow, she wished she were inside eating her own cake. She'd been excited about it.

Instead, Holly inched the SUV down the hill from the farm into town, hunched over the steering wheel, her nose nearly touching the windshield. She was used to driving in snow, in Iowa, but snowy mountains were a different creature entirely.

They felt like that, a creature, alive and breathing around her. She was grateful that it took all her effort to drive without crashing, so she couldn't replay the fight with Tara in her head.

She pulled up in front of Ernie's bar, shaking, and pried her fingers from the steering wheel. She sat back against the driver's seat and closed her eyes. *Get out of the car, Siobhan. Go into the bar. Get a drink. Get warm.*

All of her internal monologue was directed toward Siobhan, but no one in her life ever called her that. That was probably something she should unpack at some point. That for the past several years, no one in her life called her by her real name, just by a part she'd been playing. That the only person in her life she'd stopped acting for, in almost a decade, was never going to talk to her again.

Tonight, however, she wasn't going to unpack anything.

Everyone she knew was at the wedding, so she was able to slink into Ernie's and get a table against the wall without anyone greeting her. The last thing she wanted to do right now was be in a crowd of people. What she really wanted was a room she could lock herself in, so she could—what? Freak out? Scream? Cry? How did a person exist in their skin after they fucked up as badly as she just had?

For the second time in an hour, she realized that the one person whose advice she needed was Tara. That thought, the feeling of desperately wanting only Tara, in front of her, immediately, and knowing she couldn't have that, probably ever again, because of her own actions, was almost too much to breathe through.

When the waitress came to ask if she needed anything, she ordered a Fried Everything platter, because getting plastered seemed irresponsible but she sure as hell needed something to dull her feelings. As she dipped fried pickles in ranch dressing and ate them, mechanically, one by one, tears streaming down her face and onto the mozzarella sticks, the last week flashed in front of her.

Tara's absolute inability to say no to her family or to listen to music made by straight people unless it was nineties country by women. Her deep-seated belief, trained into her by her family, that none of her friends loved her or wanted her around. The way she funded Miriam's art career, and forgave her for the breakup, and saved her wedding, in a desperate attempt to make herself indispensable to people who already thought she was indispensable for no reason but that she was herself.

Herself, the woman who sang like she'd been trained in a choir, who had an encyclopedic knowledge of lesbian history, who used to steal cars and set fires but now got her Draper James tailored into pencil skirts. The woman who put on bedazzled pink cowboy hats in truck stops and looked like a babe in them.

Holly had never met anyone as contradictory or as fascinating as Tara, anyone as committed down to their bones to making amends for a mistake.

When the shit hit the fan and Holly felt cornered, she got mean. She lashed out like a snake and bit whoever had the poor fortune to be walking by. Ivy's nickname for her had been Cobra. When Tara's shit hit the fan, her first impulse—her absolute in her bones gut reaction—was kindness. Sure, she could be a little petty, or cold, but when it came down to the wire, she instinctively gave people the benefit of the doubt, and she never walked away from things because they were hard.

Since her divorce, Holly had assumed that she would never want to get involved with someone for life, because she couldn't imagine another person she'd ever want to fall in love with. She'd never even been close, since Ivy. And then, out of nowhere, the last person she'd ever expected had blown into her life like a storm off the coast.

"Are you Holly?" the waitress asked. When she nodded, the woman told her, "Ernie texted to say you'd be in and that your meal was on the house? She says you'll be sleeping in the apartment above the bar for a while? It used to be Sawyer's place but I guess he rented something bigger to fit all of Cole's clothes?"

Her name tag said *Kinzi*, and she looked like she couldn't possibly be old enough to be serving alcohol legally. Holly blinked at her, trying to figure out when she'd gotten old enough to think the serving staff all looked like babies.

Kinzi smiled at her, a little flirtatiously. "I'm off in thirty if you want me to show you up?"

Holly put her head in her hands. How could she have a hangover when she hadn't had anything to drink? "How old are you, Kinzi?"

"Um, twenty-two?"

Holy shit, she'd been in elementary school when Holly had been getting married.

Before she met Tara, Holly had a habit of hooking up with the hottest waitress in any bar, but the very idea of hooking up with anyone made her tired.

"I'm flattered but unavailable, kid," she said, and winced. She sounded like a jaded old man in a noir movie.

"Oh." Kinzi looked down at her apron. "Well, I can still show you up? The lock has kind of a trick, and if you don't do it right, the door sticks?"

Holly did not ask if Kinzi was sure, since she obviously didn't know she phrased every sentence as a question.

Half an hour later, she let herself get led up the back stairs to a little apartment that had clearly been recently stripped of all its extra stuff by someone moving out. There was a neatly made double bed, faded blue paisley curtains that would do nothing to keep out the sun, and a beat-up old wooden dresser, plus a rickety metal bedside table with a lamp. It looked like someone had furnished it from their grandmother's garage sale.

It also felt like home and comforting as hell after a week of feeling like a fish out of water with millionaires and celebrities.

"Um, do you have, like, a bag?" Kinzi asked, hovering in the doorway as Holly sat down on the bed and felt the old springs bounce.

"It's coming with Ernie," Holly said.

Kinzi was silent for a moment, obviously waiting for an explanation that wasn't coming. "Okay, well, the bathroom should be stocked? Brady, the guy who took over for me? He can get you anything if you need it before Ernie gets back? I'm going to go wrap some presents for tomorrow?"

God, tomorrow was Christmas.

"Thanks, Kinzi, this is perfect," she said, trying to channel Tara and be polite, since this girl had done nothing but be kind and helpful (she'd even hit on her respectfully) and also because she thought Ernie would frown on Holly snapping at the waitstaff. Holly was, she was certain, already on thin ice.

Kinzi nodded and went to leave, turning back at the door. "The TV works but only on channel three?"

"Who needs more than one channel?" Holly joked to put Kinzi at ease. "Merry Christmas, Kinzi."

That got a genuine smile. "You too, Holly."

Sometime after midnight, she was propped up against the lumpy pillows on the bed, watching an informercial on channel 3, when Ernie knocked on the door.

"I wasn't sure you'd still be up, but I wanted to check that you were okay," she said, pulling Holly's duffel inside with her. "And give you your clothes, since you're still stuck in the dress you wore to the wedding."

Holly smiled a little wryly. "It's really kind of you, especially considering..."

Ernie waved her words away. "I don't have any loyalty to Tara, and she's got a whole battalion to ride for her. You helped me out when you didn't have to, so I'm returning the favor. So. What do you need? You obviously can't drive back to Charleston with Tara, but after Christmas, we could get you on a plane? Or you can stay here as long as you'd like. The offer stands—I could use a waitress like you."

"You don't think the Carrigan's crew would avoid the bar like the plague if I was there?"

This earned her an eye roll. "Please, what is this, high school? They can come in, or they can miss pub quiz, and Miriam *never* misses pub quiz."

It was a tempting offer. She liked Advent, and she'd already been thinking about moving on from Charleston. She couldn't imagine going back to Emma's, having to serve Tara coffee and cake and pretend everything was fine. But she would have to go back to pack up her apartment and get her car. And before that...

"I think," she said, taking a deep breath, "that what I'd like to do next is go home for Christmas."

Ernie blinked at her, then looked at her watch. "Okay, well, it's already Christmas, and I don't know where home is, but you might need to pull off some kind of magic trick to get there. Do you know what travel is going to be like today?"

"Know anywhere I can rent a car? It's a fifteen-hour drive, or twelve the way I drive. If I leave now, I can be there before they eat lunch."

"Oh, you're not leaving now. You're sleeping." Ernie shook her head. "If you want to leave after you sleep, I'll start look-ing at flights or find you a car. Or a Greyhound. But you might want to think about planning to do New Year's with your family."

Holly didn't want to wait. Now that she'd decided, after all these years of avoiding Christmas at home, she wanted to go immediately. She admitted to herself, though, that maybe she didn't want to keep sitting alone in her feelings. No matter how poorly she'd treated Tara, her parents would be thrilled to see her and would bandage over all her wounded emotions.

"I'll sleep," she conceded, and Ernie left her to do that.

Before she put on her pajamas, she finally texted her sister back. After the unanswered "Where are you?" text, there had been several more, increasingly worried, "What the hell is going on?" texts.

> **Holly:** Hey, I'm still in Upstate New York . . . but I'm looking to head home. Help?

By the time she woke up the next morning, there was a plane ticket in her email. She didn't know how her sister had done it—or how she'd afforded it—but she didn't question it. She just got her ass in gear to make her flight on time.

She left Ernie a note, taped to the old TV:

I can't thank you enough. Maybe I'll see you again, someday, when you really need a waitress.

She left the keys to Gavi's Subaru on the bedside table and ordered the town's one Lyft to the airport.

And then she headed away from Advent, and Carrigan's, without a backward glance. She'd finally found something bigger and badder to run away from than home.

Chapter 27

Tara

The Carrigan's crew had insisted that Tara stay through the end of the year.

Elijah and Jason threw a hell of a New Queers Party at Ernie's, they argued. Somehow, despite all the things she was supposed to be doing, she'd ended up agreeing. This place, once it had you, liked to keep you. She began to understand how people kept coming up for a visit and staying for a decade.

New Year's came and went, and she didn't leave. She had been thinking about Charleston every day for three weeks, but she kept freezing up and unpacking her bags again.

What was she doing with her life? If she burned herself out dealing with her family—which was inevitable, she had to admit, and she'd been doing it on purpose—would she be able to keep showing up for clients? What good would that be for anyone? It still wouldn't prove that she'd been enough all along.

She was obsessing about this at every moment that she

wasn't obsessing about Holly, although she was good at multi-tasking, so she was often obsessing about both at once. After all these years of building a life brick by brick on the idea that she didn't need romantic love—that falling in love would make her vulnerable and put any woman she loved in a terrible position—it had never occurred to her that maybe she should choose a less terrible position to put herself in.

Miriam had broken off their engagement because she'd realized she wanted love, not a marriage of convenience. Tara hadn't understood what she meant. Why would anyone want a love story? She'd spent all her life putting up walls against everyone she could possibly imagine falling for, but she could never have imagined Holly, so she hadn't guarded against her.

She hadn't tried to call Holly. Some days, she wanted to demand an apology for all the horrible things Holly had said, and the next day she wanted to apologize herself for devaluing Holly so much that she'd actually tried to get her a "respectable" job so that she would be acceptable to the Chadwicks. She also hadn't put on hard pants, or straightened her hair, for weeks. Noelle had told her, lovingly, that if she didn't stop listening to Miranda Lambert's "Mama's Broken Heart" on repeat, Noelle was going to lock her in the attic like Bertha Rochester.

"I should call her," she said to Cole, a month after the wedding.

"Oh no." He took her phone out of her hands. "You're not ready."

She snatched it back. "How do you know? And who put you in charge of making my decisions for me?"

"Well, you put me in charge, Tara Sloane, when you made me your best friend," he said calmly, as if this were the most obvious thing in the world.

She breathed deeply. "I did not appoint you to that position. You were just there. Can you answer my first question, please?"

"You asked two. I answered the latter. That's how conversations work. Anyway, I'm you, so I know you're not ready."

"What do you mean, you're me?"

"I have a theory."

Tara sighed. Cole always had a theory. "Tell me."

"You know how in *Hedwig and the Angry Inch*, the souls are split in two and then they try to find each other?" He pantomimed this.

"And also in Plato, the source of that story?" she reminded him.

He scoffed. "Whatever. I think our souls are actually the same soul and we didn't have to look for each other because we were already together."

Blinking, Tara said, "That's a *wild* theory, Nicholas."

"Mmm-hmm. So's COINTELPRO, but here we are. Because we're the same person, I know you're not ready, because you're falling in love, but you haven't decided yet whether or not you're going to let yourself fall all the way."

"I can't be," she argued, though she knew he was right. "It's ridiculous. We were together for a week. People don't actually fall in love on the first date."

Cole laughed. "Of course they do. People do it every day. There's not a correct way to fall in love. Some people never do, some people do with multiple people at once, and some people fall in love once in their lives, in the blink of an eye, and all those things are equally valid. It's not, like, logical. Also it happened to me, so I guarantee it's possible."

Maybe she only thought she was falling in love because he was.

The idea that she could, truly, have fallen halfway in love basically instantaneously was taking some adjusting of her worldview but, surprisingly, less than the idea that Cole Fraser actually loved her as much as she loved him. Maybe it was because she'd always known she was capable of deep love and had never known she was capable of *being* loved.

She sighed. "Okay, know-it-all. When will I be ready?"

He shrugged. "When you know what you want. With your life. With your job, your family, your heart."

"How the hell am I supposed to know that?" She couldn't even be trusted to know when to call a girl. She didn't even know who she was.

"You could always stay in Advent!" Cole singsonged. "We would love to keep you!"

How quickly he had become part of the "we" of this community.

"What would I do here?"

He shrugged, seemingly unconcerned. "Work with Elijah?"

"He practices estate law, and I don't," Tara pointed out. "I'm pretty sure they don't have a lot of need for a criminal defense attorney in the wilderness."

"So take a year off. Learn to knit. Take cooking classes. Volunteer at the library."

Had he met her? There was no way she could be happy doing nothing. Holly might have made her rethink how much of her identity she derived from her profession, but she wasn't ready to become a lady of leisure.

"I hate snow, and I love the South," she reminded him. "I love living and working in, and fighting for, the South, Cole."

Cole sighed. "Tara Sloane, as much as both of us hate to talk about the ramifications of this reality, we are rich. You know that, right?"

Tara nodded in resignation.

"So you have, like, so many options that only rich people have," he continued. "You can live in Advent in the summer, and Atlanta or Birmingham or Savannah or, hell, Asheville, with all the other white Southern gays, in the winter, for instance. It's actually a very short flight."

"I'm not becoming a snowbird," Tara scoffed.

He waved this off. He never let her have any of her excuses. "So split your weeks or something. You can decide that some options don't work for you, for a variety of reasons, but you can't say you don't have any options, Tar."

"How will I know which one is right?" she cried, pulling on her hair.

Cole cocked an eyebrow at her, stealing her own move. "Why do you need to?"

What did he mean, why did she need to? "All my life, I've tried to do the next right thing. You know this."

He stared pointedly.

"What?!" she demanded.

"I mean, babe, how has that worked out for you so far?" A mean but fair point. "Maybe you should try doing the next wrong thing. Or even, the next thing."

February brought one answer about the next right—or maybe the next wrong—thing.

Lucy, her assistant, called her right before Valentine's Day in a panic. "Boss, you gotta get back here pronto."

What kind of twenty-four-year-old said "pronto"? Lucy was a treasure.

"What's up, kid?"

"Randolph is taking the case to trial."

Again, Tara didn't ask what case. The huge one. The one she'd fought to be allowed to take, because the partners at her firm thought it was social justice warrior bullshit that wouldn't make them any money, and that her client wasn't worth defending. The one she'd pushed her ethics to the line trying to keep on track.

"He's fucking what?" Randolph was the senior partner at her firm.

Lucy drew in a sharp breath. "Some of the true crime podcasts have started talking about the case, and HBO called about doing a special. You've been off the grid, and Randolph…"

"Wants the glory. And now he can take my work and spin it to make the firm look altruistic and progressive." Tara nodded to herself. Fuck. She couldn't even argue, even if her boss would listen to her, because as good as she was in front of a jury, Randolph was the best, and at the end of the day, Tara wanted her client to get the best defense.

The case had been the only thing pushing her to get back home, the only real responsibility she had left there. She had a moment's hot anger at having so much work stolen from her, and then an overwhelming wave of relief. She didn't have to go back yet. Oh, she was going to eventually. The South was in her bones and her blood, and she loved it deeply. But right now, she could stay at Carrigan's, wrapped up with her friends in this little magical pocket universe for a little while longer while she figured out who the hell she was. Because if she went back to Charleston now, she'd never know.

Carrigan's had shown her a mirror version of her life, and a version of herself that she'd never imagined, but she didn't know how to take that version of herself out into the world yet.

"Lucy, my dear girl, I am quitting the firm. I highly recommend you do the same. I have absolutely no idea what I'm doing next, but when I figure it out, I'll call you to see if you're available."

"Oh, I will be," Lucy assured her. "Where you lead, I will follow."

Tara only knew this was a *Gilmore Girls* reference because she'd been letting Cole catch her up on TV she'd missed, and they'd been systematically making their way through the WB catalog. She now had a lot of opinions on Piper vs. Prue Halliwell, and teenage aliens who loved hot sauce.

Then, rather than having Galentine's Tea or a Valentine's special for couples, the Carrigan's team leaned hard into supporting Tara's broken heart by hosting an Anti-Love Party.

They played angry breakup music, decorated broken heart cookies, and wore their best black outfits.

It was...fun? It was a lot of fun. She hadn't played, for the fun of it, since she'd burned down her life. Until she came to Carrigan's.

While she was gleefully writing *Luv Sux* on a cookie in pink icing, Elijah Green sat down next to her. "Needs glitter," he observed.

"You're not wrong." She picked up some edible glitter and sprinkled it on.

Jason and Elijah were constantly planning fun outings with what seemed like every queer person in Upstate New York. Noelle and Miriam often went and always invited her along. Getting to know them and their friends had put into stark contrast what she had waiting for her at home—polo matches and brunches where drunk straight women complained about dating.

"Not to add salt to the Valentine's wound," Elijah said, gesturing at the broken heart in Tara's hand, "but any thoughts about what you're doing next?"

She made a face. "Lots of thoughts, but none of them great. You got any ideas, most brilliant lawyer friend?"

"Have you thought about consulting?" he asked, popping some cookie into his mouth. "Working with people around the country defending tough cases? It would give you a lot of outside-Charleston options. Hell, you could do it from here."

She almost said no, reflexively. She almost said, "I can't settle anywhere but Charleston." But she stopped herself. Even if that were true, eventually, for the rest of her life, what was true right now? That she had no job to go back to and no real connections to do the kind of work she wanted to do going forward.

Consulting was smart. Really smart. It would let her collaborate with amazing people, on her own schedule, anywhere. And she could still take on her own cases. No wonder the Carrigan's crew spent so much money keeping this man on as their lawyer.

"I'll think about it," she said. "Consulting, not staying here permanently. I'm not the kind of gay who wants to start a commune in the woods with her ex."

"I can't wait to hear what you decide," Elijah told her warmly. Then, looking over her shoulder, his eyes widened. "I think your friends are descending."

He fled in the face of Cole and Hannah. They flanked her, Cole on her right and Hannah on her left. Cole stole what was left of her cookie.

"Isn't Elijah a great friend?" Hannah asked. "Wouldn't it be great if you lived here and could hang out with him all the time?"

They were relentless. "I can't just live in your hotel. You need to rent out the rooms."

"We are renting them!" Hannah reminded her. "To you."

Noelle appeared and sat across from them. "You could stay here in the back cabin. Unlimited Rosenstein's pastries and Kringle snuggles, zero parrot wallpaper."

"If I stayed, I would have to earn my keep. I can't stay here and do nothing," Tara argued, breaking a cookie on the table into crumbs.

"You're not 'doing nothing,'" Hannah asserted. "You're self-actualizing."

"I try to avoid self-actualizing at all costs," Tara deadpanned, although she wasn't kidding. "Why won't you let me help?"

Hannah glared at her. "I'm already letting you pay to stay here, against my wishes."

Tara glared back. This wasn't the first time they'd had this argument. "I'm paying you because I have a lot of money and you're a new business. But you keep saying I'm part of the Carrigan's team, so let me help."

Hannah threw up her hands. "You're not here to help us. You're here for *us* to help *you*."

That thought made Tara want to vomit. "People don't help me. I help people."

The whole table stared at her for a long beat.

"If I'm not helping, why would people keep me around?" Tara whispered, the words tumbling out of her mouth.

Cole gathered her in his arms. "I hate that your family made you feel like you had to earn love. But we're your family, and we love you because we fucking want to. Because we can. You never have to prove you're good enough for us."

"That's true," Noelle said. "We hang out with Levi and he's the worst person we know."

Goddamn it, she was sobbing again. It was so embarrassing.

"Why is Tara crying?" Miriam asked as she walked up, sounding appalled.

Taking several shuddering gasps, Tara got enough air in her lungs to say, "I'm self-actualizing."

"Oh no." Miriam shoved Cole out of the way. "I know how much you hate that." She crouched down next to Tara's chair and said, "C'mere."

Taking Tara's hand, Miriam dragged her out the back of the inn and toward the carriage house where she and Noelle lived.

Everyone trailed behind her.

"What are we doing, Mir?"

Miriam didn't answer, a tiny elf intent on mischief. She stopped in front of the windows to the carriage house, which were painted with the name of her business.

"What does it say?" She gestured at the windows.

Tara looked at Miriam, and then the window. "It says Blum Again Vintage and Curios."

"No no no. What does it say *under* that?" Miriam huffed.

Oh.

" 'What you never knew you always needed.' "

Nodding and shaking her mass of dark curls frantically, Miriam said, "Yes. That's what you find here. So what did you never know you always needed?"

"Are you going to say romantic love?" Tara asked. "Please don't."

"That's what *I* never knew I always needed. I don't think it's what you needed, though. It just helped you get what you needed."

All right, she was curious. "And what, my dear, is it that I always needed?"

"To stop being afraid of your power, Tara! You burn down *one* country club, and you put away the wild child forever, but she's still in there! You think she's a terrible person because you've been railing on her for so long. But she's you! You have to embrace who you truly are. Messy, wild, radical Tara Sloane. That's the only way you'll ever figure out what you most want."

"You want me to heal my inner child," Tara said flatly.

Miriam nodded. "More like your inner punk-ass teenager. And I have a perfect way for us to heal her."

Ushering Tara into the workshop and store space, Miriam

kept chatting, but Tara wasn't listening. All around her were Miriam Blum upcycled art pieces, and Mimi Roz paintings. All the funky, strange, thought-provoking art that Tara hadn't wanted in her home. Probably because she hadn't wanted her thoughts provoked, and she was afraid letting in any chaos would open the floodgates.

"Ah, here we go!" Miriam exclaimed from the back. She emerged holding something unwieldy and emitting a mildly unpleasant smell. Looking more closely, Tara recognized that it must have, once upon a time, been a carved wooden pineapple. "I got this in a shipment but it's rotting, and I can't use it."

Tara eyed it suspiciously. "And you want me to, what, go *Office Space* on it? Let out my inner feral kid?"

"Oh no, love." Miriam grinned maniacally. "We're going to burn it."

Nope. Oh no. No way in hell.

"I can see your brain working, but we're doing it! We're going to build a very safe bonfire, with Noelle's assistance because she's weird about fire near her trees—"

"I would call that prudent," Tara interrupted.

"Sure, sure." Miriam brushed this off. "We're going to build a bonfire, and you're going to write everything you're letting go of on this ugly, rotting decorative symbol of Carolinian colonial oppression, and then we're going to burn it."

Tara wanted nothing more, on this earth, than to not participate in this, but she knew once Miriam got her mind around something, she wouldn't let it go. And maybe her inner wild child was whispering, just a little, that it would be fun. "Fine. Give me a Sharpie."

Miriam pulled out a giant box with every color of marker ever made.

What the hell was she going to write? It felt overwhelming.

She couldn't write *my whole personality* and burn it. She needed specifics.

The door to the carriage house burst open, and Noelle and Hannah pushed through arm in arm. "What's happening in here?" Noelle asked, giggling. "We're missing you both! The anti-Valentine's party needs you!"

Miriam explained her idea, complete with gestures and waving of Sharpies. When she finished, Tara was still staring at the half-rotted pineapple, unsure what to put on it.

"Help?" She looked up at Hannah, beseeching.

"Aw." Hannah gave her a quick, fierce hug. "Let's look at some things that aren't working for your happiness."

"Okay...maybe the marriage of convenience thing," Tara admitted. "Let's start with that. It's definitely not working." That was an easy one. Every situation she'd gotten herself into, the idea that she needed a society wife had blown up in her face.

That earned her a high five. She wrote on the wood:

Marrying for anything other than love

"It turns out," she admitted, "I was never doing it to further my career, it just felt safer."

Miriam snorted a laugh. "I know." Then, she volunteered, "Aunt Cricket?"

"I think I gotta go bigger," Tara acknowledged, both to her friends and herself. On the wood, she added:

Talking to my family

"Go big or go home, I guess," Noelle said, sounding impressed.

Tara nodded. "And I can't go home. At least not right now."

She needed one more thing. Marriage and her family, those were external challenges. She could change her relationships with them, but in the end what she most needed was to change her relationship with herself.

Trying to earn my right to exist

There. That was it.

Outside, they stood around a beautiful, very well-managed bonfire that Noelle was nervously tending.

Everyone who had been inside for the anti-Valentine's party spilled out and gathered around. Ernie was overseeing (kosher) marshmallow roasting, and Levi was making too-fancy s'mores. Cole and Sawyer were canoodling. Elijah was watching his kids, while Jason made sure none of the teenage drama students he'd brought lit themselves or the woods on fire. Tara shouldn't be surprised that somehow this private emotional catharsis had become a whole Carrigan's crew event.

It was the kind of thing that used to annoy her about Carrigan's, but she admitted to herself (if not to anyone else) that she loved it now.

Hannah spoke because she had the biggest voice. "Friends, we are here today because it's time for our beloved favorite, Tara Sloane Chadwick, the phoenix of Charleston, to once again consign her old self to the flames and be reborn! Tara!"

She turned to Tara and held out the weird wooden pineapple. "Are you ready?"

"I am." Tara solemnly took the object. She ran her hands over the words she'd written, saying goodbye to an outdated identity that had served her well, grieving the years she'd been telling herself not to be who she was.

For a moment, she thought about lobbing the thing overhand into the fire, but she was afraid Noelle would kill her. Instead, she walked up to the fire and carefully placed the wooden object in. She looked deeply into the flames, watching until the pineapple collapsed in on itself.

Turning around, she walked into Cole's arms. Where had he come from? He kissed her hair, and she was fairly sure she felt some tears drop onto her head.

"Are you proud of me?" she whispered.

"Baby girl," he whispered back, "you're my hero."

Looking around at everyone she loved, she said, "You know, I should probably at least stay until the baby comes."

Chapter 28

Holly

All the Delaneys met Holly at the airport in matching Christmas sweaters.

Her dad's hair, burnished copper with age, stood a head taller than most of the crowd, and Dustin's, equally tall, was almost radioactive in its orange. Holly snickered to herself that his hair had never chilled out, no matter how much he'd prayed as a kid. Hers was exactly the same shade, but unlike Dustin, she owned it.

Mostly. Except for when people talked about it incessantly and touched it.

Caitlin had inherited their mom's black hair, and both mom and daughter had tears in their blue eyes.

While she was struggling with her duffel (the strap of which was held on with duct tape), her dad grabbed the handle and handed her a sweater that matched the family's. It occurred to her that, to have ordered one for her, her mom must have been holding out hope she'd come home.

On the car ride home, she was stuffed between Caitlin and Dustin into the back seat of the Saturn her parents had owned for twenty years. She and Dustin immediately got into a pinching contest, trying to see who could hurt each other the most without making any noise to alert their parents.

The trailer her parents lived in could probably be seen from space, it was so lit up with decorations. Her mom fussed that the neighbor three lots down had driven one town over to the Walmart with the better inflatable Santas, but her dad assured them all they'd win next year.

Win what? It wasn't clear.

Under the tree were presents with Holly's name, and a stocking for her hung on the mantel of the faux fireplace. It didn't have the polished kitschyness of Carrigan's, but after a week with millionaires, being home was a breath of fresh, seasonal-Glade-PlugIn-scented air. She felt her shoulders relax as she followed her dad back to the room she'd grown up sharing with Caitlin, only to tense again when her mom came after them and sat on Caitlin's old bed.

She said, "So, we can't help but notice you needed an emergency plane ticket to come home, and Tara's not with you."

"Yeah, Hol, where's your rich girlfriend?" Dustin asked, leaning against the door frame. Behind him, Caitlin grabbed him by the collar and hauled him out of her way. She came through the door, then shut and locked it behind her.

He banged on it. "I can still hear you, you know! These walls are paper thin!"

Looking at them, Holly was too tired to keep lying. These

people, who loved her so much they hung up her stocking even though she never came home for Christmas.

She took a deep breath, steeling herself. "She's not my girl-friend. We were pretending, because Tara needed a date to the wedding, and I needed to convince you to stop trying to play matchmaker."

"You lied to us?" her dad whispered, sounding heartbroken.

"I knew something was fishy!" Caitlin exclaimed.

"I can't believe you!" Dustin yelled through the door. "Miss Self-Righteous made up a girlfriend!"

Her mom, who had been sitting silently wringing her hands, said, "Why didn't you just tell me you didn't want to get back together with Ivy?"

"She did," Holly's dad, Caitlin, and Dustin all said in unison.

Wow, even Dustin was taking her side on that one. The same thought must have occurred to her mother, because she looked toward the locked door in surprise.

"I'm sorry, you guys. I shouldn't have lied to you. I just..."

She couldn't figure out what to say that would be a reason-able excuse.

Caitlin filled in for her. "Was afraid of getting steamrolled by Mom?"

Holly smiled a little, for the first time all day. Caitlin might give her shit, but she also understood Holly like no one else.

"Hey!" their mom objected. "I only steamroll because I love you all."

Turning to Holly, Caitlin said, "I thought you liked her."

"I do like her." Holly sniffled. "I like her so much. But she wants to change me, and she won't change."

Through tears, the whole story (minus the sex pact) poured

out. By the time she finished, everyone except Dustin was somehow piled onto her bed, and she was buried in a pile of hugs.

"You should apologize," her dad said simply.

Holly shook her head. "She needs more time. If she wants to talk to me, she'll reach out."

"What I don't understand," her mom said thoughtfully, resting her chin on Holly's head, "is where you got this idea that you're inevitably going to be unkind to anyone you settle down with."

"Because she's really mean!" Dustin yelled.

Her mom threw a balled sock at the door.

"Because I was really mean *to Ivy*," Holly corrected.

Caitlin scoffed. "You were a baby. You're ten years older now. Your frontal lobe is done baking."

"Cait, lots of people in their thirties are mean as snakes," Holly reminded her.

"Sure, but those people don't spend a decade arranging their whole lives so they won't be mean anymore," her sister argued. "Don't you think it's worth trying to see if you've grown?"

From outside the door, Dustin said, "It sounds like she was already a total bitch to Tara. Why would Tara want to give her another chance?"

Holly hung her head. "Dustin's right." Those were the worst words she could ever utter, and saying them made her feel like she'd actually, genuinely hit rock bottom.

Her dad waved this away. "Dustin's never right. You should talk to her."

"If she calls me first," Holly said.

All the eyes in the room looked at her with disapproval.

As Valentine's came, she started to feel comfortable in a way that made her itchy. And she realized it wasn't the fault of her parents, or Davenport, or even Dustin. It was something inside her that was built for constant change. She'd thought she'd accepted that about herself long ago, but she'd kept trying to find someone or something to blame for it. No blame was needed, though, because it wasn't a flaw.

What she did need to work on was keeping friendships as her life changed. Because she'd been using her restlessness as an excuse to not get close to people, and she couldn't keep doing it.

She also realized that the idea of spending years getting comfortable with Tara didn't make her feel itchy at all, which was a truly depressing realization to have at this point in the situation. Or just in time for Valentine's Day. Especially when Tara hadn't called. And she was still too chicken to call Tara.

Her mom, God bless her, had decorated the trailer in red and pink heart bunting and hung a seasonal wreath on the door. When she was younger, she'd thought it was pathetic that her parents lived in a double-wide, but now she was proud of them. They'd looked at their options and done the best they could by their kids. They'd bought the trailer, the nicest one they could with their income, and rented a lot in a safe, quiet neighborhood park. Everyone there had known each other for decades; everyone watched out for each other.

When the kids she'd grown up running around with heard she was back, they'd brought their kids around to meet her. It was nice, and it felt like home—more than Charleston ever had. No one looked askance at the black ink covering her legs, or let their gaze linger on the holes where her dimple piercings used to be.

In fact, she went back to the kid who'd pierced them in high school, who had his own shop now, and got them put back in. Tara had said Holly wasn't afraid to be herself, but she'd been putting on a show for too long. She'd told herself that the act was to make herself safer at work, to get her more tips, to keep part of her to herself. And any of those would have been good reasons, if they were true. But, like the face Miriam put on for the Bloomers or the Perfect Debutante facade Tara wore for her parents, it was there to stop anyone from being close to her, to keep anyone at all from the real her. Including maybe herself.

She was ready to take her walls down and learn how to be close to people, but she still needed to do it somewhere that wasn't Iowa, and that wasn't going to change.

At first, when she left her parents and retrieved her car and all her shit, she thought about going to stay with Barb and offering to cook for her. But that would always be a temporary gig, and Tara's words were ringing in her ears. She was still waitressing because she was afraid to take a chance on what she wanted, in case she failed. Like she was refusing to take a chance on love because she'd failed at marriage, once, when she was twenty-two.

She was holed up in a motel outside Madison at the end of February, because she'd run out of gas while driving aimlessly around the Midwest, when she realized she needed to talk to someone who would tell her the absolute, unvarnished, ugly truth about herself.

So she called her ex-wife.

The heavy, cigarette smoke–laden curtains that maybe used to be baby-puke green gave the room an oppressive gloom, so Holly went out to sit in the pale midmorning sunlight on a crumbling lounge chair by the pool. Maybe she would buy and renovate a vintage motel, she thought idly while the phone rang, like Stevie Budd. Hannah would probably help her with a business plan, if the Carrigan's crew ever talked to her again.

"Sio? Is someone dead?" was how Ivy answered the phone, which was fair. They hadn't spoken on the phone in…probably five years, since Holly had called to say that her grandfather had died and to invite Ivy to the funeral.

"Everything's fine. Well. Everything's not fine, but no one's dead. I have to ask you a favor."

There was silence on the other end of the line. One of the things they'd fought about most, in their marriage, was that Holly never asked for help. It felt like a sort of dull cruelty to now, so many years later, be asking for help when their marriage was not only dead but also long buried, and no longer even mourned.

Ivy cleared her throat. "Who is she?"

Against her will, Holly's eyes welled up. "You will never believe this, but she's a debutante lawyer…"

She poured all of it out, the whole story, warts, wounds, terrible behavior and all. To her immense credit, Ivy gasped in horror at Aunt Cricket, got indignant about Tara trying to make Holly into someone else, and defended Holly's reaction even though it was kind of indefensible.

Even though Ernie had been incredibly generous to her, pretty much everyone in Advent (and certainly at Carrigan's) had been Team Tara. Hell, even Holly was Team Tara. And she wanted that for Tara. Tara needed a team. She'd never had one, all her life, just Cole, and she deserved it. But it was nice to have someone be fully, irrationally on Team Holly, even if it was perhaps the least likely person on earth.

"So, what do you need from me?" Ivy asked. "Do you need help with a plan to win her back? You know I'm good with a diabolical scheme."

Holly smiled. She'd forgotten that about Ivy, but it was true. In high school, she'd had the same wild child streak that Tara must have had. She would have gone right along with burning down a golf course. "I think I should probably step away from schemes, after the whole fake dating fiasco. I'm obviously not skilled at them."

"Shoulda stayed friends with me, like every other lesbian with their starter wife," Ivy told her, munching on something in the background. She was like Danny Ocean, always snacking. And she was right. Holly probably should have.

"I feel like I can't...I can't remember how to be in love. All I remember is how bad I was at it, at the end, and I'm terrified I'm not built for it," Holly said, all in a rush.

She shifted, trying to unstick her legs from the plastic of the chair, not sure if her emotions or the sagging seat were more uncomfortable. "Will you, like...I know this is such a shitty thing to ask, but will you post-game our marriage with me? Can we just talk about what the fuck happened, so I can actually figure out what to do this time? You're the only person who really knew me during that time. The only person who's known me all along."

Ivy laughed. "I actually think it's a pretty normal thing to ask, at least for us. We were each other's Day Ones, and even though we needed some space, who is going to unpack that time with us, if not each other?"

They talked for hours, through most of a day and into the night, like Max sailing to where the wild things are. Or, maybe back home, because at the end of the journey, Holly found her best friendship, like Max's supper, waiting for her, and it was still warm. Somewhere in the middle, Holly moved back into the motel room to avoid getting sunburned and lay on her back, sideways on the bed, her eyes closed, listening to the sound of Ivy's voice over the speaker.

Ivy's version of why they'd broken up was kinder than Holly's and had more room for nuance. The story she told— that they were two kids who married the first person they ever found themselves in, and then found themselves both totally incompatible and way too young to handle it well— left so much space for them both to grow, to make new and better choices. It wasn't that Ivy was unaffected by their divorce—she'd been dating the same wonderful person for several years and wanted to propose to them, but hadn't, and she couldn't quite explain why.

"You should maybe call more often," Ivy said as they were hanging up.

"Eh," Holly said, "maybe we can start by texting some GIFs? You know, ease back into it? I'm out of the habit of having friends."

The next time Shoshana Rosenstein called to offer her a job, as she'd been doing every week, Holly didn't politely put her off.

"Are you ready to come back to Davenport?!" Shoshana asked, pitching her voice like a movie announcer. "Beautiful scenery, Quad City–style pizza, and we were once voted the ninth queerest city in America!"

"That was almost ten years ago, Shoshana," Holly reminded her.

Shoshana laughed. "And it's only gotten gayer!"

"Well," Holly said, "as much as I…appreciate…the lure of my hometown, I'm not ready to move home. It turns out I like to visit but staying for more than a few weeks makes me kind of volatile. However, I have an idea. You all have been expanding into new territories, but that's a big monetary commitment, even with market data, right?"

Shoshana hmmed, sounding surprised that Holly had a brain for business as well as baking. It was the red hair, Holly thought. People were always expecting Anne Shirley, or Ariel, and were surprised when they got, well, a foul-mouthed blue-collar socialist with both feet firmly on the ground.

"What if you had a traveling storefront, with an accomplished baker, who could take Rosenstein's into places that had only ever experienced it pre-packaged and shipped?"

"So, a food truck?" Shoshana asked. "I don't hate it, but I gotta ask, how is cooking for our food truck going to help you build your own business?"

"Why would I want to?" Holly asked. "I don't want to be a business owner. There's so many taxes."

This brought more laughter. "There are. But I still would

like your work, as a baker, to be recognized. Not for churning out Rosenstein recipes—that's not what I want to bring you on board for. I want your imagination."

"So, you want me to work for you, and I want to work for you, but in different positions?" Holly clarified.

"I feel like we should absolutely be able to come up with a solution that makes sense for all of us," Shoshana said. "Why don't I put my head to it, and you, too, and we'll talk next week?"

Something about that willingness to live in the gray area spoke to Holly, on more than just a career level. She'd been so sure, with Tara, that there was no gray area. And there wasn't one when it came to Tara's racist, elitist, homophobic family. But maybe there was when it came to Tara's career, which she loved.

She'd wanted Tara to open up, let down her walls, and become a softer, more vulnerable version of herself, but then she'd proven herself someone who couldn't be trusted with that kind of vulnerability. Even if Tara never gave her another chance, she wanted to show that she'd been wrong. Tara deserved that. But even if Holly didn't have a right to ask, she did hope Tara gave her another chance.

She wanted to be able to go to Tara and show her that she'd listened. She understood that Tara loved the South, and being a part of the fight for its soul. That the place Tara'd grown in could still nourish her roots, even if Holly didn't fully understand that concept. She also wanted to apologize in a way that was meaningful. Not an empty gesture, but something that showed she was committed to learning to fight kindly, to sit in discomfort and nuance, and to take a risk again.

"Holly? You still there?" Shoshana asked, and Holly came back to the present.

"Yeah, I'm in. Let's find a compromise."

They did find a compromise: Holly would get the food truck she'd dreamed of, and Shoshana (or, more accurately, Shoshana's accountant and lawyer) would take care of the taxes and business licenses. Holly would go into new markets to introduce people to the genius of Rosenstein's Bread and Pastries baked fresh, but she would also offer a new product line, under their umbrella. A line of reimagined, updated versions of the most classic vintage Rosenstein's recipes.

They roped Miriam in to design the logo, only after Holly assured her, at length, that she was going to make real amends with Tara, to make things right. And even then, Miriam was skeptical of her.

"I'm doing this under duress," Miriam said, "because my friend is sad. But if you make her sadder, I won't come after you. Cole will."

Once they had a mock-up of everything, the first product off the line went not to Rosenstein's home office, but to New York.

A pink and green box with a starburst sticker reading *Siobhan & Sloane* that opened to a pineapple upside-down bar featuring handmade maraschino cherries, a gooey butter cake base, and a bourbon caramel was supposed to arrive at Tara's apartment in Lake Placid, by courier. The morning it was set to be delivered, Holly watched the app on her phone, the little dot getting closer and closer to Tara's address, and she waited for her phone to ring.

If it did.

When it did, she almost dropped it in her haste to answer it.

"Tara?" *Brilliant opening, Delaney.*

"You named your business Siobhan and Sloane?"

She inhaled, trying to breathe in the deep Southern cadence of Tara's voice. She'd missed it, and missed, also, Tara's unwillingness to say hello at the beginning of a conversation. If she'd expected anything, it was that Tara would be back to treating her with the same icy polite reserve she used on everyone she thought might hurt her.

Holly hadn't realized it when they'd first met, but it must be something Tara only did with her inner circle. After all, she had impeccable Southern manners and must have to start most conversations, with most people, with ten to twenty extra minutes of empty pleasantries before she could get around to what she actually wanted to say. It was a sign of real trust when Tara just started talking; it meant she wasn't wearing any of her armor. There was no reason for Tara to be showing her that vulnerability now, but she wasn't going to argue.

"It's not a business! Exactly," Holly protested. On the other end of the line, Tara was silent. "Yes. I named it Siobhan and Sloane. I thought, even if you didn't ever talk to me again, I wanted to honor that you pushed me out of my comfort zone and inspired me to do all this."

"You thought I would never talk to you again?" Tara asked, her voice squeaking in a way Holly had never heard. "I thought *you* would never talk to *me* again."

"Tara, I was so mean to you I got kicked out of Carrigan's.

Carrigan's! The Jewish Hotel California!" Holly cried. "The place no one else ever leaves! I said horrifying things to you, things that keep me up all night, hearing them in my head, over and over."

Tara laughed, and it was the most beautiful sound Holly had ever heard. "You were mean. So was I, for that matter, and I'm so sorry. And people had been trying to shake me out of my misery the nice way for a lot of years, and nothing worked."

"Oh no. Just because it worked out in the end does not mean we're going to push my behavior under the rug. I care about you, and I don't tear down people I care about."

Well, she didn't want to anymore. It turned out that with the right motivation, a person could change a hell of a lot of their behavior. For Holly, the combination of Tara and feeling like a total asshole who didn't want to look herself in the mirror was enough motivation.

She still held on to a tiny seed of hope that maybe, someday, they would be able to start something new, and they couldn't do it with the shadow of Holly's unkindness between them.

"Thank you for the apology," Tara said soberly. "I was an asshole, and I'm sorry for making you feel like you weren't good enough exactly as you are. For not listening to you or trusting that you knew what was best for yourself."

"I mean, I don't know what's best for me," Holly said ruefully. "I thought I did. I was so sure that I had my life all figured out, and only you needed to change. It turns out I was as lost as you were. I could ignore that while I was focusing on you. But maybe I'm starting to get...unlost? Found. I think I'm starting to be found."

"The magic of Carrigan's?" Tara guessed.

Holly scoffed. "The magic of Tara Sloane Chadwick."

"Holly, tell me you didn't get a corporate job just to somehow apologize to me," Tara said. "You hate capitalism. You could have called and said, 'Can we talk?'"

It sounded so simple when Tara put it that way.

"I was hoping the job would be a gesture to show you I was serious, so you would take my call for me to tell you I was sorry. Which I am. Incredibly, immensely sorry. I'm figuring myself out, so I don't keep repeating this pattern." All of this came out in a rush, and Tara was quiet again, so Holly kept going, trying to fill the silence.

"Okay, yes, I hate capitalism, but I also hate being on my feet for eight hours a day and getting my ass slapped by customers, and my tips shorted by asshole rich bros. Besides, Rosenstein's is a legacy family business. It's not like I'm answering phones at Haliburton."

Biting her lip, Holly continued. "I wanted to show you that I was serious about us, and I felt like I needed to prove that I was willing to compromise…"

"Oh, Holly." Tara sighed. "I would never want you to give up something that matters so much to you. That's not a responsible way for us to start something."

"You quit your job!" Holly protested. She knew this from Ernie, who kept her updated on the comings and goings of the Carrigan's crew, even though she said Holly should "probably talk to them herself." "Was that some kind of 'Gift of the Magi' thing? I can't decide you were right, but you can decide I was?"

"I didn't quit my job so we could be together someday," Tara argued. "Honestly, I didn't think we ever could be together someday. I quit my job because I really, really needed to, and because I decided if I ever let myself fall all the way in love, I wanted to be ready."

"Well, I didn't quit my job for us, either. I did it for me." Then, what Tara had said sunk in. "All the way?" Holly asked, holding her breath. "Did you fall...part of the way in love with me?"

"I know, it doesn't make any sense," Tara said, sounding embarrassed.

Holly shook her head and laughed a sad little laugh. "No, no, I mean, yes, it doesn't make sense, but I started to fall, too. I'm glad I wasn't alone. But what do we do now? Did we screw it up forever?"

This time, when there was silence, she let it stretch. Somehow she knew it was a different kind of a quiet, and she needed to give Tara time to say whatever she was going to say. Even if Holly held her breath the whole time.

"I want to jump in," Tara said. "I want to say it's all okay. You apologized. You named a line of pastry after me! And I owe you so much for showing me that I wanted more out of life. I want you in my life. Hell, I might need you in my life."

Holly scoffed. "Sloane, you have Cole and the Carrigan's crew. You have everyone you've ever needed."

"I don't think that's true," Tara argued. "Do you know the story of the Snow Queen? Not the Elsa version, but the Hans Christian Andersen one?"

"Sure, trolls make a mirror that distorts peoples' perceptions, it shatters, gets in a kid's eye, he becomes a grumpy little snot," Holly said. "The library has a lot of fairy-tale audiobooks available on their app. I spend a lot of time in the car."

She almost made a self-deprecating comment about being poorly educated but well-read, but she bit her tongue. Tara knew she hadn't gone to college, and Holly was going to believe her when she said it didn't bother her.

"Well, I think I sort of had a shard in my eye. Some ice inside me made it impossible for me to see love when it was given to me. No one managed to melt that in me. Not Cole or Miriam. You showed up, and in a week all my walls fell, when Cole had been laying siege to them for years. I want to see what that means, because I'm pretty sure it's something extraordinary. *You're* extraordinary."

"But?" Holly asked, her heart in her throat. After a speech like that, why did it still sound like there was a "but" at the end?

"Well, first, it's going to take time for me to learn how to let myself be happy, again. To learn to stop punishing myself and calling it restitution. Also, I feel like...maybe we should get to know each other? No fake dating, no Shenanigans—"

"*No* Shenanigans?!" Holly interrupted, a little appalled.

"Minimal Shenanigans," Tara amended.

Thank God.

Holly thought about this. "What would that look like?"

"Texts? Video calls? Emails? I don't know, some kind of slow dating that's not just jumping all in and hoping everything works out?" Tara said.

It seemed kind of like shutting the barn door after the horses got out, but Holly didn't say that. It was more than she'd hoped Tara would be willing to give her, and she was more than happy to take it slow if it meant she got to take it anywhere at all.

"I'm not moving to the South," Holly said. "Or to Carrigan's, for that matter. I don't have some deep-seated trauma to unpack, and it's weird that the magic cat keeps collecting people."

"I know," Tara agreed. "Right at this instant, I'm also not moving back to the South. I'm taking an enforced hiatus above the Mason-Dixon while I find myself or whatever. Someday I'll go back. But in the meantime, your job is mobile and I'd like to see more of the country, so I figure we can see each other in all kinds of cool places. After all, no self-respecting lesbians would let a little thing like distance get in the way of being together. I'd like to try, if you would."

"I'd like that," Holly said.

Chapter 29

Tara

Tara knocked on Holly's apartment door in South Bend, Indiana, where she'd settled at least temporarily, needing a home base. She remembered the first time she'd shown up at Holly's door, on the morning they left for Carrigan's. That morning, she'd been so in her head she'd barely noticed anything around her.

Now she noticed everything. The little border of flowers someone had planted optimistically, despite the fact that spring was having a hard time breaking winter's grip. The flaking paint around the door, the door number hanging slightly loose.

She bounced a little on her feet, waiting for the door to open. Worried that it wouldn't.

Behind the door, she heard a cat yowl. Holly had a cat?

"Shoo, Carol," Holly's voice said. "You cannot go outside, ma'am. You moved in here, and now you live here."

She must have looked through the peephole, because the next thing she said was "Oh!" and then she was out the door, shutting it quickly behind her.

"Sorry, if I keep the door open, my cat gets out," she said, brushing hair out of her face.

Tara looked her over, looking beautiful in an old Black Flag shirt with the sleeves cut off and a pair of ratty, too big joggers that she'd rolled at the waist. The death moth tattoo on her stomach peeked out.

"Carol, huh? Keeping with the holiday naming traditions of Carrigan's?" Tara smiled. "Or is it Carol, like, they're lesbians, Harold?"

"Oh, well…she jumped into my car somewhere around Des Moines. I figured any cat who shows up and won't leave is a gift from Kringle, so I named her accordingly. Although the lesbians were a deciding factor. She's a good buddy on the road."

They stood looking at each other for a long moment, Carol yelling from inside.

"Hey," Tara finally said.

When she'd gotten in the car to drive out here, it had seemed obvious that she needed to come. That having apologized and said everything they should have said months ago, the only thing standing between them was distance. Now she didn't know what to say. She didn't know how to get over this barrier, to go forward into whatever future they were heading toward.

"What are you doing here?" Holly asked, shoving her hands into her pockets and pulling her pants down another half inch. Tara tried not to watch the movement. This probably wasn't the time to think lustful thoughts. "I thought we were, like, texting and taking it slow?"

"Um," Tara said, "I wanted to ask you a question."

"That you couldn't ask over the phone?"

Tara grinned. "Yeah, this seemed like an in-person one."

"Okay."

"Okay?"

"Ask your question."

She shook her head to clear it. "I was wondering if you'd like to go on a real date with me."

Holly's face lit up. "I thought you'd never ask." She stepped forward, slipping her hand around the back of Tara's neck and pulling her in for a kiss. They smiled against each other's mouths; then Holly brought her body flush up against Tara's and dragged them both back through the door.

Carol, a small, loud orange creature with no tail and hair sticking up in every direction around her body, squawked at them.

"I thought maybe we could go out on a date now," Tara said as Holly kissed down her collarbone.

"We will," Holly said. "But we have to work up an appetite first."

Tara smiled. "How does this count as taking it slow?"

Holly looked up at her from where she was kissing downward. "You're the one who showed up at my door."

Who was Tara to argue with that kind of logic? She reached down and pulled Holly's shirt up over her head. Tangling her hand in Holly's curls, she thought about stopping her and taking back control, but she was committed to turning over a new leaf. And she was going to start with letting Holly give her as many orgasms as she wanted, without bossing her around even a little.

After, as they lay in a giggling, naked heap on Holly's bed, Tara ran a hand over Holly's tattoos.

"I'm sorry my mattress isn't as comfortable as the one at Carrigan's. It's shitty, and secondhand, but it doesn't have bed-bugs," Holly apologized.

Tara reached down to kiss the snake on her knee. "I would be thrilled to be naked with you anywhere, although if we're going to keep having dates that end in sex, maybe some of them can be in New York? I have a very expensive new mattress that feels like sleeping on a cloud with great lumbar support."

"Damn, as much as I believe in complete wealth redistribution, there are going to be benefits to having a rich girlfriend."

"You can help Cole and me do some serious wealth redistribution, but maybe we can keep the swanky mattress?" Tara offered.

Holly shivered in pleasure. "That's the sexiest thing anyone's ever said to me. If you're trying to get into my pants, it's working. But you do still owe me a date. A first one, in fact, so you'd better make it good."

"Are you up for a road trip?" Tara asked, loath to put clothes back on and leave this (admittedly uncomfortable) bed, with this beautiful woman and funny tailless cat, but excited to take the girl she thought she probably wanted to marry on a date.

"Um, only always." Holly rolled onto her side to look at Tara, and Tara tried valiantly to keep her eyes on Holly's rather than wandering lower.

"I hear there's a lesbian bar in Bloomington. I'll let you drive and pick the music." She pushed off the bed and held out a hand. "Are you ready? Are you ready?"

Holly grabbed her hand and followed her up. "Let's roll."

Epilogue

June came, and with it, Hannah and Levi's daughter—and the end of Tara's paper-thin reasons for sticking around Carrigan's, a place she'd sworn she hated and never wanted to stay longer than a long weekend. When the baby-naming ceremony was over, she was planning to join Holly on the road while studying to take the bar exam in New York and California. From there, she would work part-time with Elijah with the plan to eventually start her own practice (with Lucy) offering pro bono consulting and taking on cases she felt passionate about.

Cole had taken on a new project, helping fund families of trans kids who needed to move to safe states, and Tara and Elijah had their heads together getting him the legal support required. Plus, she and the Advent librarian were fighting book bans all over the county. She was busier than she'd ever been at home, and a hell of a lot happier. She was singing in a cover band that played a standing gig at Ernie's on Friday nights. They weren't very good, and that itself felt like freedom.

Tara had been talking a lot to a new therapist, not only about the fire but also about feeling like she deserved to be free of her family. She'd had a therapist for years, but it was amazing how little you could get out of therapy, if you deliberately chose a therapist who never pushed you to tell the truth.

Now she was waiting for Holly to get here. They'd been apart for three weeks, and it turned out long distance was not Tara's preferred way to have a girlfriend. She was checking her phone for the thousandth time in an hour when the door to the great room opened and the woman in question strolled in. Only a lifetime of debutante training, and the presence of the baby, kept her from leaping into Holly's arms. Her best friend did not, however, have debutante training.

Watching Cole try to be Cole without waking up the sleeping newborn on Levi's chest was hilarious. He was currently pantomiming with his entire giant wingspan, his extreme joy at seeing Holly. There was no good reason he couldn't greet her at a semi-normal volume outside the front door of the inn, but of course, he insisted on doing the most ridiculous thing possible.

The newborn and dad in question were on a chaise longue to which someone (presumably Miriam) had affixed glitter-covered moose antlers. Miriam had her head on Levi's shoulder and was gazing adoringly at her niece. In keeping with Jewish tradition, the child did not have a name yet, would not until the naming ceremony tomorrow. (Tara had received two separate invitations to this ceremony, one from Rachel Rosenstein and one from Felicia Matthews, which called the ceremony two entirely different things, but when she'd asked Miriam the difference, Miriam had just laughed at her.) The baby might not have a name, but she did have lungs that worked, which Tara'd heard for herself. It was to everyone's benefit that she stay asleep.

In obvious opposition to Cole's energy, Levi lifted three fingers from his child's back and wiggled them in a tiny wave.

She texted Holly, who looked down at her phone when it buzzed. She'd sent Hannah would say hi, but every time she gets close enough for the baby to smell milk, she wakes up.

Tara looked over at the very wrinkly potato being gazed at adoringly on her father's chest and felt deeply grateful that she'd chosen not to have children.

Also, her next text said, I'm glad you're here. So is Cole.

She slipped silently off her chair and grabbed Holly's hand, slipping past the entrance to the great room. She waved at Mrs. Matthews in the kitchen, who grinned at her so big, Tara was afraid her face might split. She suspected the Matthewses might be excited about their first granddaughter. Upstairs, they found Hannah huddled in the library with her parents and Noelle.

Hannah hugged Holly hard and said, "I'm so glad you made it! And not just because this one is whiny when she needs to get laid."

Tara gasped in mock indignation, and Holly glowed under the regard of people she'd once thought would never forgive her.

"I wouldn't miss it for the world," Holly said truthfully.

"Okay, I gotta go pump so someone else can feed little girl while I have dinner with you all later," Hannah said. "Hang out with my parents. Or, since Tara said you were staying here for a few days instead of in Lake Placid, I put you in the room you were in last time. Feel free to go break in the new mattress."

"Oh no," Holly said seriously, "we would wake up the baby."

At dinner, Levi raised a glass. "I'm so grateful that you're all here to celebrate our beautiful baby girl. But my siblings and I"—he stopped and gestured for Esther and Joshua to stand up—"would also like to take this opportunity to celebrate our parents, Ben and Felicia Matthews, who are officially retiring at the end of the summer."

Everyone broke into applause. After almost losing the business to bankruptcy when Cass died, it was amazing how the entire team had rallied to make it one of the most sought-after tourist destinations in the Adirondacks. Miriam was painting as much as she was upcycling these days, as she'd always wanted. Noelle's trees were healthy. Levi's show had been renewed for another season.

So now the Matthewses could take a step back and truly leave the Christmasland to the next generation.

"None of us can imagine a Carrigan's without them, and thankfully, they're not going very far, because there's a grand-baby here now," Levi continued, and everyone laughed. "But we're ready to steer this ship of Cass's into the future, and they are ready to sail into a future of quiet Shabbat dinners and no dinner rushes."

Everyone toasted the Matthewses, and then Miriam and

Noelle's six months of happy marriage, and then Cole and Sawyer buying a house, and then Tara's new job plans, and then Holly's. Eventually, they'd gotten down to toasting Grant Matthews's most recent lost tooth, and the Green twins finishing first grade, and it was time to go to bed. Holly and Tara did break in the new mattress, as quietly as they could, and the next morning, they all took the baby to synagogue so Rabbi Ruth could bless the sweet, wrinkly potato with a name.

Actually, once Tara got to hold her, she had to admit that she was less weird-looking than Tara's own nieces had been at that age. She already, at a week old, had a head of hair like Miriam's, and Tara thought she might look an awful lot like her aunt Mimi, who in turn was the spitting image of her great-aunt Cass. Though she did, perhaps, have her father's judgmental eyebrows.

Tara knew from Hannah that there'd been some drama between Rachel and Felicia over the baby's name. Levi and Hannah had, initially, considered naming her after Cass's Hebrew name, Rivka, as the first baby born into the family after Cass's death. But Rachel's Sephardic upbringing and Felicia's Ashkenazi one differed on naming traditions, and there had been intense back-and-forth.

As a result, once Levi and Hannah had settled on what they thought her name might be, they hadn't breathed even a word of a hint to anyone. All inquiries as to whether or not she would be called an English name that coincided with her Hebrew name, or given something totally different, were passed off with a smile on Hannah's part or a growling and hissing on Levi's.

At the ceremony, Hannah read from the "Song of Songs" and the baby was given the name Kezia, who was, Cole whispered, a daughter of Job. (Cole knew a weird amount about the Bible for a dude who insisted he definitely for sure never wanted to go to divinity school.)

Because Kezia was also a word for cassia, or cinnamon, and the child's father was, after all, a chef, they gave her another spice for her English name—Clove.

"You've named her after eggnog," Mrs. Matthews pointed out, laughing.

Hannah smiled. "Well, she may have been born in June, but she is a Christmasland baby."

Her cousin, Grant, asked to hold her. Jayla and Jeremiah Green sat on either side of him, like bookends. Tara snapped a picture on an old Polaroid they'd found in Cass's things. On the bottom, she wrote:

The heirs of Cassiopeia

She didn't notice, until Holly pointed it out, that Kringle was peeking over the back of the chair, carefully guarding the next Carrigan's generation.

Acknowledgments

There is something extraordinary, thrilling, and bittersweet about reaching the planned end of a series (although, if I've learned anything from Hannah and Levi Blue, it's to never say never). The fact that Carrigan's Christmasland exists at all is a miracle to me, and when I began drafting *Season of Love* in 2018 I could never have guessed that it would, someday, feel as much home to me as any real place I'd ever been.

This particular book has been a very different process than the first two—written in months rather than years, and shared with a very small bubble of people rather than a widespread community. Tara Sloane is not only my favorite Carrigan's character (except for Kringle) but also the closest to my soul, so it was probably inevitable that I kept her story the closest to my chest for the longest.

Thank you to my editor, Sam Brody, who trusted me to write a romance that was as much about the main character's platonic love as her romantic one, and that is filled with both wacky hijinks and melancholy loneliness. To my agent, Becca Podos, who once again (always) understood the heart of the story I was trying to tell and saw Tara for her true, perfect self. My beloved Jake Arlow, who read this book, loved it, and offered insightful criticism when I most needed all of those things. Huge thanks to Estelle and Dana, Anjuli Johnson, and the whole team at Grand Central/Forever that makes book magic happen, and to Daniela Medina and Leni Kauffman for possibly the most perfect cover of all time.

Heather Manning, thank you for quoting Audre Lorde to me at the exact right moment. Saniya Walawalker, eternal and unending thanks for your sensitivity-reading genius (and hilarious DMs about Levi). Chencia C. Higgins, my favorite three-hour brunch friend, thank you for talking to me over pancakes until I finally unlocked the piece that was missing inside my brain.

Thank you to my kid, who tells everyone he meets that his mom writes books. This is the best possible cure for imposter syndrome and I highly recommend it.

I am supported by a wide, deeply rooted network of love that stretches across time and space in a truly dizzying way that I continue to be astonished by. Family, friends, authors, Discord buds, fandom friends of thirty years—all of you showed up for me, and for Carrigan's, and made all of this possible.

To all of you who have fallen for this queer, Jewish little Narnia—if I were Cass Carrigan, I would write you an airplane napkin that said, "Au Revoir, beloveds. The gates will always be open the next time you need Carrigan's." If I were Blue Matthews, I would say, "Keep up the Shenanigans." Because I'm me instead, I'll quote the first piece of storytelling that rewrote my wiring, *My So-Called Life*: "We had a time. Didn't we? Didn't we have a time? We did. We had a time."

About the Author

Helena Greer writes contemporary romance novels that answer the question: What if this beloved trope were gay? She was born in Tucson, and her heart still lives there, although she no longer does. After earning a BA in writing and mythology, and a master's in library science, she spent several years blogging about librarianship before returning to writing creatively.

Helena loves cheesy pop culture, cats without tails, and ancient Greek murderesses.

You can learn more at:
HelenaGreer.com
Instagram @BlumAgainCurios